The Pool of Mnemosyne

FROM THE SAME AUTHOR

The Pool of Mnemosyne

by

Brian Stableford

A Black Coat Press Book

Visit our website at www.blackcoatpress.com

ISBN 978-1-61227-731-8. First Printing. April 2018. Published by Black Coat Press, an imprint of Hollywood Comics.com, LLC, P.O. Box 17270, Encino, CA 91416. All rights reserved. Except for review purposes, no part of this book may be reproduced or transmitted in any form or by any means, electronic or mechanical, including photocopying, recording, or by any information storage and retrieval system, without permission in writing from the publisher. The stories and characters depicted in this novel are entirely fictional. Printed in the United States of America.

Introductory Note

This is the fourth volume featuring the autobiographical narrations of Axel Rathenius; the first of the four, *The Wayward Muse*, consists of three separate stories, whereas the present volume completes a trilogy containing a single coherent narrative, begun with *Eurydice's Lament* and continued in *The Mirror of Dionysus*; it will complete the project definitively. Attentive readers will undoubtedly notice several discrepancies between the four volumes. Rathenius' memory is not always reliable, and his accounts of what he thought and did at particular moments, written some time after the events in question, are often embroidered, not always consistently. It must also be remembered that the language Rathenius speaks is only distantly related to the French of our world by virtue of its Latin descent, causing problems in translation. Those problems are compounded by the fact that the translator knows nothing about the history of the alternative world and its geographical variations from our own world except what is actually written in Rathenius' pages, inevitably inviting occasional false improvisations, for which he can only apologize.

Brian Stableford

THE POOL OF MNEMOSYNE

I. The Artist's Eye

Elise, fatigued by her slightly artificial pose and, perhaps more remarkably, weary of playing her instrument, lowered her arms with a decisive gesture of defeat and dropped the lyre she was holding. For form's sake, she said: "May I rest, Master Rathenius?" but I had no choice in the matter.

It was a moment that I had been anticipating for some time, with a certain amount of dread, but it was inevitable, and I was resigned to it. I looked at her during the few seconds that she maintained the stance of her head and the expression on her face, more by virtue of inertia than determination.

"Yes, of course," I said. "I shouldn't have kept you so long—I'm sorry." I didn't comment on the fact that she had not called me Axel; it was probably a sign of slight criticism or annoyance.

My eyes returned to the painting then, making the fatal comparison.

I couldn't work out work out what I was doing wrong. I could still see all of Elise's beauty, which had ripened somewhat in the months that I'd known her. Her black hair was more lustrous now than when I'd first seen her in the Sprite on the first night of the black snow, and her complexion, which had had no opportunity to lose its Lutecian winter pallor during the weeks she'd spent on Mnemosyne during the bizarre season that had followed the volcanic eruption, had taken on a delicate amber sheen under the subtropical sun of the Island of Dionysus. I could still see all her beauty, but I couldn't capture it. What was worse, I had suspected for weeks that I wouldn't be able to capture it. I had put off the acid test for as long as I could, but in the end, I had simply had to grasp the nettle—and I had been badly stung

We now knew, thanks to research carried out by Madame' agents in Gaul, that Elise was older than she had first seemed when I had first seen her on Mnemosyne, and guessed that she was twelve. She was presently a few weeks past her fourteenth birthday, and that knowledge seemed to have helped her to appear more mature; always robust, her figure now seemed more luxurious in its feminine roundness. Perhaps she was not quite a young woman yet—although I was certain that she would disagree—but while she maintained the ardent concentration that she brought to playing any instrument, her features had an intense seriousness, and a hint of deep melancholy, that had absolutely nothing child-like about it. I didn't think of it as a symptom of adulthood, but as a sign of true artistry, essentially ageless.

I could see all of that, and not with any common eye. When I looked at her, I could see her with my artist's eye. Only fools think that beauty is in the eye of the beholder, but a beholder requires an artist's eye to appreciate beauty fully, and to read the soul within the appearance. So what was wrong with my normally-reliable hand? Why hadn't it begun to transfer that beauty to the canvas with its customary surety?

Had it been a mistake, I wondered, to ask her to pose with the lyre, which she'd only recently begun to play, instead of the viola da gamba, to which she was far more accustomed, in the interest of having her hold her head a little higher? She had certainly not been playing with her usual fluency or verve, and that had inevitably had a slight influence on her expression, which had occasionally taken on a perceptible frustration and disappointment, but she had made an effort every time, and had succeeded in restoring the composure I needed.

No, the problem was elsewhere, in me and not in her. Somehow, a kind of fracture had taken place in me, between the eye and the hand—and very recently, because no such fracture had been evident only six or seven weeks earlier, while I had been putting the finishing touches to my portrait of Mariette—a trifle belatedly, by my normally rapid standards, but with complete efficiency. Since then, I had only done sketches, although six weeks was an unusually long interval for me not to apply paint to canvas; the simple truth was that I had been direly anxious about making the attempt, and today's fiasco had proved that I was right

My heart sank as Elise came across the room, saying: "May I see it?"

I have never been one of those temperamental artists who refuses to allow his sitters to see portraits in progress, and have rarely regretted the fact, even when the work was going poorly, but I had never before felt such sharp premonition of a sitter's likely disappointment, or my own disappointment in having generated it. Elise had assumed a peculiar importance in my life, ever since the moment when she had instantly identified a crucial flaw in the then-incomplete Orpheus triptych, and had provided one of the crucial hints that had enabled me to complete the work—more successfully, it now appeared, than I had ever thought possible. I knew that she would not be able to provide the insight that would help me rescue her own portrait from the ignominy into which a dismal lack of inspiration was casting it, and I was fearful of any interpretation she might put on that failure, however temporary it might prove to be.

She looked at the incomplete portrait for a long minute, which seemed even longer, before finally saying: "Is that really how you want to see me?"

Obviously, she had no intention of putting up any pretence in order to spare my feelings. I supposed that I ought to be grateful for that, since it testified to a lack of any awkwardness in our relationship, which could easily have become manifest when I began sleeping with her adoptive mother, but it was difficult.

"I've hardly started," I said, my quiver of apologies fully loaded. "I know it seems that it's been a long sitting, and it has, but sometimes it takes time to get a grip on a subject. Sometimes, even after years of experience, it takes time and effort to develop a sketch into a painting..."

"That's not what I asked," she said bluntly, staring at me.

I couldn't meet her eye, and felt desperately ashamed of the fact. I. Axel Rathenius, couldn't meet the eye of an adolescent!—an exceptional adolescent, admittedly, but still an adolescent, barely out of childhood. To what had I been reduced, and how?

"I don't know how to answer the question that you asked," I admitted. "I'm not even sure what you mean by it."

Her stare hardened. "You promised to tell me the truth, Axel," she said. "I need that from you. You know exactly what I mean."

What I had actually promised, a trifle recklessly, when she had asked for my advice on Mnemosyne, in circumstances very different from the ones in which we now found ourselves, was that I wouldn't lie to her. I knew that she knew the difference, but I also knew that she probably had every intention of stretching the point as far as she could, and I wasn't unsympathetic to her feeling that she needed the truth from me, for want of any other ready source.

"The simple truth is," I told her, truthfully, "that I'm having a bad day. It happens sometimes. You know that. You first saw me when I was part way through the Orpheus triptych, when it wasn't working...but in the end, it did. This is a work in progress; please don't judge it until I've had a chance to put it right."

She could have repeated her demand that I answer the question she had actually asked, and I think she hesitated over doing that, but it seemed that she became slightly alarmed by her own aggression, and the ill humor of which it was evidence. She really did feel that she needed me, as a source of advice, and she certainly didn't want to risk alienating me. In a way, though, her sympathy would have been even worse than her disappointment. She had every right to be upset.

"It's my fault, isn't it?" she said, dolefully. "If I weren't playing so poorly...in any case, how can I possibly criticize you, when I seem to have lost my own artistry?"

That surprised me slightly. I had certainly noticed that she wasn't playing well, but, concentrating on my brushwork, I hadn't attributed any importance to it, given that the changes of facial expression it induced were so fleeting. While I was painting her, the music she was playing was simply an element of the pose, rather than a performance, so far as I was concerned. It hadn't occurred to me that she wouldn't—couldn't—think of it in the same way.

On the other hand, I honestly couldn't imagine that my own failure could be any kind of reflection of her music. Living on Mnemosyne, I had had occasion to paint a great many musicians, ranging from the brilliant to the utterly incompetent, and I didn't think, looking back, that I had ever been distracted from the focus of my own gaze simply because they were not playing well.

There had been times when music had been inspiring, perhaps magically, but usually with regard to works of art alternative or supplementary to portraiture.

"No, Elise," I said, positively, "it certainly isn't your fault. The flaw is definitely in me. I don't know why, but for the moment, I've lost my touch. To tell the truth, I've been out of sorts for weeks, and that's why I've been putting this off for so long. It's happened before...I suspect it happens to all artists. Young as you are, you must have experienced something similar more than once. Sometimes, the inspiration simply isn't there. It always comes back. It's not something you can lose forever."

I couldn't be absolutely sure of that, of course, but I wasn't lying. If I had faith anything, it was the resilience and durability of my own genius.

"Young as I am...," she repeated, pensively. "Is that the problem? You still want to think of me as young, as a child, even though you know now...?" She stopped.

I remembered the odd way in which she's framed her initial question, and realized that it might have been more significant that I had thought. Belatedly, I suspected that it might also be significant that she had assumed that I knew exactly what she had meant.

"I try to see all my subjects as they are," I said, still drawing arrows of cliché from my quiver. "That's the essence of the art. I aim for accuracy, for an essential truth. In this instance, I admit, I'm falling short for the moment, but..."

She didn't let me go on. "You painted Mariette exactly as you wanted to see her," she said, sharply. "What's more, you painted her as she wanted to see herself—but that's because you wanted to screw her, isn't it?"

"That's not...," I began.

Again, she didn't let me finish. "No," she said, with a sigh. "I know it's not."

I was still at a loss, though, I didn't know what it was that she thought it wasn't.

She looked sideways at the portrait on the wall behind me: the portrait of Mariette, her adopted mother, and, at least for the moment, my mistress. Then she went to sit down on the sofa that was positioned beneath it, perhaps in order to turn her back on it. She didn't have to take her eyes off me, and she didn't.

"Sit down, Axel," she said. "You've been on your feet for a long time. It can't be good for you...at your age."

That was pure malice, but I managed to smile at it. I had to admit that I felt older on the island of Dionysus than I ever had on Mnemosyne, and not simply because I had confessed my true age to Elise and Mariette. At that moment, I could almost have believed that, after more than seventy years of apparent existential stasis, I was beginning to age physically again. But that had feeling had come over me before, too, and the moments had always passed.

I didn't sit down immediately, though, feeling that there was a point to prove. I had already set down the brush and the palette, but I folded my arms and stared at the portrait, as if staring might somehow cause the reason for its woeful imperfection to become manifest.

Her expression softened. "Please, Axel," she said. "I need to talk to you. I need your advice..."

That sounded ominous, especially as I still considered myself bound by the promise I'd given her, but it was a tone of voice to which I couldn't help responding. She was by no means the only female who had ever been able to soften me to that extent with a mere inflection, but she was the only one on the Island of Dionysus. I gave in promptly, and sat down beside her. "About what?" I asked.

She laughed, briefly. "Everything, alas," she said. "First of all, though, I think I owe you an apology."

"For what?"

"For making a stupid mistake. I practically told you to screw Mariette, while you were still hesitating. I did that because I thought it would make her happy. It was so obviously what she wanted."

"Ah," I said. "It's a common mistake, I suppose, to assume that getting what we want will make us happy, but you don't have anything for which to apologize. I had every intention of seducing Mariette if I could, having made the decision on the steamer, almost as soon as I discovered that she was aboard. I appreciated your blessing, obviously, but it didn't change the course of events."

"And you never had any intention of seducing me," she said. It wasn't a question. She glanced at the portrait

14

as if she were putting two and two together. It was the wrong sum, even if it had produced the right answer.

"No," I said, simply. "I never had. But that's not why..."

Yet again, she didn't let me finish.

"Where I grew up," she observed, in a tone that was pretending to be clinical and distant, "girls my age are rarely virgins. As often as not, they're already professionals. Mariette's determination to save me from that by bringing me to Mnemosyne was...exceptional."

"That's not the point," I said.

"Isn't it?" she said, sounding more curious than challenging. She was frowning slightly, apparently not following the same train of thought as I was. I wondered whether she had been talking to Helen, and, if so, whether Helen had given her an excessively elaborate account of the reputation that I had cultivated on Mnemosyne—but I knew that she was far from stupid. She had had an opportunity to weigh me up now, and she knew that reputations acquired by gossip are highly unreliable measures, especially of artists.

"You don't find me attractive—or don't want to," she said, looking at the portrait again.

"On the contrary," I said. "I found you enormously attractive the first time I saw you, in the Sprite, and my appreciation has only grown since then—but one of the things I find enormously attractive about you is your innocence, and I wouldn't want to spoil that for the world. In any case, I know perfectly well that you couldn't find me attractive, even if I were only the age that I appear to be."

I thought that was true—or, at last, that it ought to be.

The frown deepened. "You *do* want to see me as a child," she affirmed.

There was no point in denying it. "In a way, I do," I said. "I can see quite clearly that you're in the process of becoming a young woman, but looking back from my antiquity, yes, I do still want to think of you as someone very young, very new. And I don't believe that you ought to want anything different, as yet. I think Mariette is entirely right in trying to protect you in that way, just as her own mother was right to try to protect her."

There was a slight flash of anger in her eyes, which I thought unjustified. "She's not my mother," she said.

"She didn't give birth to you," I agreed, "but circumstances have dictated that she's been the only mother you've known, and it seems to me that she's exercised that function as well as anyone could reasonably have hoped, given the circumstances in which she found you."

"Given that my grandfather had had my parents murdered, you mean?"

In fact, I had meant that fact that Mariette had been a very reluctant whore, trying to survive on Martyr's Mount, and that Elise had just been dumped, as a helpless infant, on a struggling artist who hadn't a clue how to look after her. Both Charles and Mariette, I thought, had executed the function of improvised and unlooked-for pseudoparenthood as well as could possibly have been expected. I didn't bother to correct Elise, though; it seemed more politic to follow her agenda, wherever it might lead,

"I've told you before that I don't believe that's true," I told her. "I had no reason at all to like Lord Dellacrusca, and I honestly feared at one point that he might have me murdered, but I'm perfectly certain that he didn't have your mother murdered. She was his daughter. He would never have done that."

She knew perfectly well what I wasn't saying, but we were only talking about mothers, for the moment.

"She didn't really love Charles," she said, meaning Mariette. "She just wanted somewhere safe to live. I was just a ticket to that safety."

I shrugged my shoulders. "Perhaps, to begin with," I said, "but she certainly came to love both of you, deeply and sincerely. I could see that clearly, on Mnemosyne. You mustn't think that because she's with me now..."

"That it's just a matter of convenience? Or wayward lust?"

Now there was challenge in her tone. I couldn't help remembering that the last time I had seen Hecate Rain, she had not only predicted that I would seduce Mariette, but that it would be like spearing fish in a barrel—except that she was uncertain as to whether I would be the spear-wielder or the fish. Since then, Madame had suggested to me that the passions that sometimes sprang from my painting might be regarded as supernatural impositions over which I had no control—but that was not an excuse I could have offered to Elise, on my own behalf or Mariette's, even if I had believed it.

"Even if it were as simple as the convenience of the situation or a whim of lust," I said, softly, "it would be no reason to judge her harshly."

"And innocent as I am," she retorted, "I already know that it's more complicated than that. I'm not judging anyone...but perhaps it's as well that you're...not at your best." She looked at the painting again, which was looking worse by the minute.

"What do you mean?" I asked, guardedly.

17

"That if you make me as beautiful as you made her, she'll be biting her knuckles over me as well as Helen and Madame."

I grimaced. I didn't know what to say. When I had started the affair with Mariette it had been clearly understood between us that it couldn't be permanent and might not be exclusive, but understanding a contract isn't the same thing as liking its terms. In the decades I'd spent on Mnemosyne I'd grown used to summer visitors who never wanted anything more than a temporary fling, and artists who often thought it a essential part of their vocation to feel the same way, but Mariette, for various reasons, was an exception to the latter rule, no matter how much she strove to pay lip service to it. She had apparently monopolized Charles Parenot's fidelity effortlessly, with an iron grip, perhaps not for the reasons she would have preferred—and perhaps, too, it had diminished him in her eyes and helped paved the way for her desertion—but there had been a security in that monopoly whose value she might only now be beginning to realize.

"But you can hardly stop painting, can you" Elise said, in a softer and more thoughtful voice. "And you can't stop looking for the beauty in the people you paint, can you?"

"I hope not," I muttered, almost reflexively.

That surprised her. "You're really worried?" she queried, glancing at the painting again. Her initial disappointment had worn off, and she seemed to have accepted my judgment that it was just a temporary hitch.

I shrugged. "I can't help it," I said. "No matter how many times I've recovered from bad spells, I can never entirely convince myself that the next might not be the last, any more than I can convince myself that the morning will never come when I look in the mirror and see my hair beginning to turn white. This time…well, as I say, I've been out of sorts for weeks."

"But that…," she began, and then stopped, in a fashion that was most unlike her. I took the inference that the advice she had said she wanted wasn't just a matter of her adoptive mother's seemingly-uncontrollable jealousy. A nasty suspicion that must have been lurking in the back of my mind for some time, deliberately suppressed, began to make itself manifest—and became ominous.

I had to make an effort to collect myself. I looked out of the large bay window at the long hill that climbed up from the headland on which the house stood, all the way to the wooded slopes of the upper mountain, displaying cultivated fields, orchards and meadows of every sort.

Normally, it was a relaxing sight, especially now that I was completely used to the sight of patient Sileni working in the fields. This time, I took no comfort from it. That, too, intensified the lurking feeling that something was wrong—that somewhere in this improvised Eden, or in the depths of my own being, there was a dangerous presence lurking.

"I've been…out of sorts myself," she murmured. "I've been trying as hard as I can to fight it with the music, but…well, this time, I know it can't be the house that's haunted, and since the viola da gamba played that strange chord just before my grandfather was stabbed, it no longer seems to have a life of its own. So it must be me, mustn't it?"

Suddenly, I had a flashback to the night I had taken Sister Ursule back to the Convent of Shalimar. *That child is a visionary*, she had said, after seeing Elise for a mere matter of minutes. And I had believed her. But since the night Dellacrusca had been killed, that impression had faded. In the months we'd been on the Island of Dionysus, and her true age had been revealed, she had seemed less precocious, less uncanny...but perhaps the shocks she had received had simply made her more cautious and more prudent.

When Sister Ursule had made her observation she had made it sadly, as if being a visionary was more of a curse than a blessing—and I had believed that too.

II. The Costs of Magic

"I need some air," I said to Elise, because I needed time to process the thought that had just occurred to me, and to find some sort of helpful reaction to it, if I could. "The light's beginning to go, so there wouldn't be any possibility of my doing any more work today, even if I weren't disgusted with myself. Would you like to take a walk along the cliffs, when I've cleaned my palette and brushes?"

"Yes," she said.

She didn't say anything more while I tidied my apparatus away, but it was obvious from the way her gaze followed me that she too was mulling over what she's said, perhaps deciding what else she could say to me about it—and how honest she ought to be. I gathered that it was something that she must have been holding back, not merely during the long sitting, which had built up pressure in the interim, but for days, perhaps weeks.

I felt guilty about that. Why hadn't I seen it? *How* had I not seen it? What had happened to my artist's eye? Had I really been so preoccupied with my own malaise that I had become blind to hers, when she obviously needed attention, and her mother's attention had been deflected even more manifestly than mine?

I felt that I had let her down—and there was no one in the world, including Mariette, that I didn't want to let down as much as I didn't want to let Elise down. If ever I had needed magical power, I thought, it was now, and not merely to restore my ability to paint…which seemed ironic, given that I had only just begun to believe, in recent weeks, after a century of denial, that I really did have something magical about me, as well as my strange longevity.

I was still exceedingly reluctant to believe that I was the sorcerer that many people believed me to be. I had always repeated to myself endlessly that I didn't believe in magic, only in art, but that had always been quibbling—mere wordplay, as poor Tybalt Sphendon used to put it, in the days when he took it upon himself to disapprove of my flippancy. The mantra had usually worked before, even when I'd been confronted with blatantly supernatural events, but since my initiation into the cult of Dionysus, and the seeming magical intervention in which I had participated, across half the width of the Great Ocean, via the Orpheus triptych, my trust in its efficacy had been worn to wafer-thinness. I knew that my involvement in that magic operation had been that of an instrument, not an instigator, but that wasn't a distinction in which I could take any comfort. Quite the reverse, in fact: I had never felt more in need of the elusive ability to take control of the wayward thrusts of the inexplicable.

When I had first begun writing the series of documents that this one will conclude, I had only been recording interest incidents, which had seemed intriguing and worth recording simply because they had something of the incomprehensible about them. Their supernatural aspects had seemed more intriguing than threatening, even on the fatal night when Eirene Magdelana had involved me—much as Madame had—in one of her own magical exploits. I had certainly been in danger earlier that night, and those surrounding me even more so, but Eirene's magic, the only purposefully directed magic in which I had consciously participated prior to Madame's evocation of Orpheus and Dionysus, had been a benign act of healing. In telling that story, and others, I had merely been relating marvels, in a detached and slightly cynical fashion

The events in which I had become entangled involving the fates of Claudius Jaseph, Conrad Othman and Lucien Sombre had all seemed separate, unconnected and carrying no particular implication with regard to myself or the nature of the world beyond the eternal conviction that I was a true artist, and that the world was mysterious. Even when I had begun to write the story of the Orpheus triptych, mere days after its completion, I had thought it another accident of happenstance of the same kind, and a closed incident. Writing the subsequent account of the aftermath of the triptych's delivery and my abduction to the Island of Dionysus, however, had been a very different matter, as had the consequence of writing the story down and accommodating it to my consciousness.

That experience had altered my perspective. However skeptical I might remain regarding the nature and value of my initiation into the cult of Dionysus, there was nevertheless a sense in which I was now an initiate into mysteries. I could no longer regard the affair of the triptych, or the preceding events, as something isolated, a mere transient event in the ever-unfolding pattern of life.

I had certainly hoped, immediately thereafter, that it was a closed incident, that the completion of Madame's Dionysiac rite would put an end to a distinct phase in my life that had necessarily be about to end anyway, and signal a new beginning, with a clean slate. That had been foolish optimism; the slate was far from clean, and there had been far too many loose ends dangling—so many, that I was beginning to fear that I might never be able to get free of them, no matter how long my extended Macrobian existence might last.

And in the weeks that had elapsed since the initiation, while I had written it down—and, to some extent, *because* I had written it down—I had become increasingly aware of the fact that my old pretences, the mental fortifications that had served me so well during their painstaking construction, had lost their resilience.

I had changed.

And Elise, I had to admit while I was conscious of her watching me tidy my apparatus away, in the shadow of the incompetent sketch that I already suspected would never become a true portrait, was one loose end that might turn out to be particularly entangling. I loved Mariette, but in the way that I had loved dozens of other women, in a fashion that would not make it unduly difficult for me to part with her when the time came. I had told the truth; I had no intention whatsoever of trying to seduce Elise...but that made matters between us more complicated, not less, just as my relationship with Hecate Rain had become more complicated rather than less once we were no longer sleeping together, inextricably bound by ties much subtler than brute passion.

When I had taken off my smock and washed my hands, Elise was still sitting patiently on the sofa, waiting for me...or waiting for something.

While we walked through the garden and out on to the headland she seemed to be gathering her thoughts. I glanced along the road to the port. Mariette had gone shopping in the town, and would be coming back very soon, but there was no sign of her yet. I couldn't help feeling a slight unease because of her absence...and not only hers. I hadn't seen Helen all day, and I hadn't seen Madame for more than a week, in spite of her promises to continue my education in the true history of the empire and the authentic secret of magic. I had not been short of things to occupy my time but I was beginning to wonder whether, having served my immediate purpose, I had now became a matter of indifference to the island's enigmatic monarch.

When we were two hundred paces away from the house, I began to feel a modest invigoration in the evening breeze. The headland along which we were walking bore very little resemblance to the headland on which my house on Mnemosyne was situated, in its topography or its vegetation, and the subtropical sea that extended away from it was very different in color and texture from the channel that separated Gaul from the Cassiterides, but there was something about the breeze, in spite of its comparative warmth and mildness, that seemed familiar, reminiscent of my island, of the idea of home.

Perhaps my stance or gait changed in consequence, because Elise suddenly rallied her own vivacity, and began to broach the subject that was really preying on her mind.

"I don't want you to think I'm foolish," she said, "but I hadn't quite realized, even when I saw the work you'd done today, that you might be feeling something akin to what I'm feeling. You'd done such an expert job on Mariette's portrait that…well, to get to the point, you must have noticed that my playing has been seriously deficient in the last few days, no matter what instrument I use."

Subconsciously, perhaps I had. Consciously…I had had other things on my mind. "It's not surprising," I said, judiciously. "We're in a strange place, far from anything we've known before. We both had an initial burst of enthusiasm simply because of getting off that damned steamer, where we'd been so horribly ill, and a further surge of elation after that bizarre rite of initiation. Since then, there's inevitably been a let-down effect. It's natural that we should be…a little out of sorts."

"Perhaps," she said, dubiously. "But…as I say, I don't want to seem foolish, but I've been having bad dreams…"

I didn't stop dead, but I certainly lost my stride for a moment, and she looked at me with a strange expression, which seemed to be hovering uncertainly between relief and ominous confirmation.

"You too," she murmured. "I thought…I hardly dared say…but you can't be haunted…."

"Neither can you," I was quick to say.

She weighed the matter up, and then said: "Mariette must have told you, probably before we even left Mnemosyne, why we left Lutèce? And now I come to think about it, that blabbermouth agent of yours probably told you even before we set foot on the island."

"Yes," I admitted. "And Charles told me himself about not being able to shake off his absurd superstition about the viola being one of the devil's instruments. But none of it was true, in any literal sense. Charles's studio wasn't really haunted; nor was the viola. Now we know that you're older than you seemed, it's possible that the first stirrings of puberty had something to do with your feelings, but I know that Mariette felt something too. I suspect that it had a good deal to do with developing tensions in the relationship between Charles and Mariette, which made all of you uneasy."

She looked at me in rank disbelief. "The truth, Axel!" she demanded. "You know it was more than that."

"I don't *know* anything," I said, feeling that it was cheating, even though it was the truth. "And the factors I

26

cited probably did have something to do with it—perhaps a lot."

"But we really were haunted," she insisted, "and it was...well, not my fault, but I was the center of it, the...focal point. And now it's back. And don't tell me, please, that they're just bad dreams, Axel, because I'm not stupid, and although I have no idea what's going on, I know it's *something*, and that's why I've finally plucked up the courage to tell you about it, and *ask for your advice*."

The pitch of her voice had risen somewhat, but it was far from hysterical, Elise didn't suffer from hysteria.

She didn't bother to spell out the nature of her dreams, because she thought she didn't have to. The moment that I had reacted to her confession, she had leapt to the conclusion that I already knew. I had the same conviction myself, although I knew that there was no rational basis for the assumption.

"All dreams are just dreams," I prevaricated. "It's unwise to take them too seriously, or to allow them to disturb us unduly." I wasn't lying, just stretching the truth...too far.

She had no trouble guessing that. I hadn't spent a great deal of time with her recently, and almost all of it in Mariette's presence, but both of them had been curious about my life on Mnemosyne, and I had told them the story of Phelim and Candida Kracy, and the mysterious Lucien Sombre, because it was the most exciting sequence of events that had happened on Mnemosyne for years, and in order to do that, I had had to explain the art and dubious science of morpheomorphism, the shaping of dreams. In so doing, I had eliminated any possibility of persuading Elise now that her recent nightmares were mere accidents of circumstance that could simply be dismissed as irrelevancies and forgotten

"Please don't treat me as a child, Axel," she said, in a tone that cut straight to my heart, "no matter how much you want me to be one. Mariette can't help it, and I understand why she's denying that it's happening, but she's sharing your bed, so she can hardly conceal it from you..."

As soon as she said it, its truth became obvious, as well as the fact that my own attempts to conceal the fact from Mariette must have been equally futile. None of us had wanted to seem foolish to the others, and because of that, all three of us had been trying to fool ourselves. Perhaps it had always been inevitable that it would be Elise who would break through the web of deceit.

I licked my lips, and resumed walking again.

"How much do you... remember?" I asked her

Elise matched strides with me. "That is frustrating," she said. "They seem to slip away when I wake up, dissolving in a matter of minutes...but they leave a kind of aftermath, a sticky residue of...not fear, exactly, but an aftertaste of fear...and not demonic, exactly, not...well, not like the sensation nightmares often have of being oppressed...violated...although that might be just a girl thing, or even a virgin thing that Marianne and you don't have...but anyway, not a simple sensation of being held down or hurt.. more insidious than that, more penetrating, *burrowing deeper*...infecting, polluting, corrupting...you don't know what I mean do you?" Her voice was suddenly plaintive.

"Actually" I said, "I do...only too well. And it's my fault, not yours, for not having brought this out into the open, for not having admitted it. Being habituated to secrecy is no excuse. You're right, I did know that Mariette was suffering, although she wouldn't confess either, and it was idiotic of me not to guess that you were too. I'm sorry."

"It's not nothing, then, is it?" she asked.

"No," I admitted. "It's not."

"It's what you told us about, isn't it? About the woman who used to live on Snowspur, who could shape people's dreams? Our nightmares are being shaped, aren't they? And that's why I can't play and you can't paint? We're being *attacked*?"

"We don't know that," I told her, "and it might be premature to jump to that conclusion. There are other possibilities."

"Such as?"

I had promised not to lie to her, so I had to be very careful. "We have to weigh up the probabilities, Elise. I suppose there might be people who would try to hurt us if they had the opportunity, by magical means, the Marquise de Mesmay probably being the most obvious candidate, but we ought to be careful of believing too readily that she or anyone else has the ability, because entertaining that belief can be dangerous in itself. Magic thrives on that kind of credulity; when supposed sorcerers put curses on people, those curses work almost entirely through their victims' belief. Skepticism is a sound defense, in ninety-nine cases out of a hundred. Even in the hundredth, skepticism can weaken the effect."

"*What* other possibilities?" she persisted, justifiably—but I had a reason for taking the matter slowly. Skepticism isn't easy; it needs foundations and reinforcement. You can't just ask people not to believe something; not only do you have to give them an alternative, you have to give them a reason for preferring the alternative. It isn't just curses that work through the victims' belief. Protective spells obtain much of their armor by virtue of the same psychological process.

"Think about it," I said. "If there's an occult influence in our present debilitation—and I can't deny that it seems that way—it's surely more likely to be an after-effect of the spell that Madame cast during the rite. Successful magic is said to carry costs. The fact that all three of us are having nightmares, especially nightmares that seems saturated with the impressions of residues and after-effects that you've just described, suggests strongly to me that they really are residues and after-effects of a common experience, a psychological reaction to the intensity of what was, in essence, a kind of induced shared hallucination."

"You think we're doing it to ourselves?" she said, incredulously.

"I think there's a sense in which we have to be," I told her. "I can't rule out the possibility of an attempted morpheomorphism, even over half the breadth of an Ocean, but what we have to remember is that it can only be an attempt, a kind of provocation. For morpheomorphism to work on us, we have to collaborate with it. It can't hurt us unless we're willing to let it…willing to hurt ourselves, in a way. If we can succeed in thinking of the nightmares simply as nightmares, and resist the temptation to try to remember them more clearly, and in more detail…to collaborate in forgetting them, in fact…then that's all that they'll be."

She thought about that. I could see that she was wavering.

"Madame undoubtedly knows far more about morpheomorphism than I do," I added, calling up the available reinforcements. "I'm sure she'll tell you much the same thing, and give you the same advice—and I suspect that she probably has methods at her disposal that will help you do it, ranging from simple mantras and supportive amulets to more complex collaborative operations. Helen can ask for an audience, if you like—for all of us, not just for you. I doubt that she'd refuse, no matter how busy she is trying to track the progress of the Orpheans' internecine conflict from the end of her precious telegraph cable, or whatever else she's doing that requires her to seclude herself at present."

She thought about that, too. "No," she said, after a brief pause. "I just wanted to know what you thought— seeking reassurance, obviously. I trust your reassurance…more than hers, at any rate. I decided to trust you back on Mnemosyne; I ought to stick to that. And after all, you haven't just told me that it's nothing, and that I ought to forget it. That's all I wanted, really…not to be fobbed off. Thank you for that."

If she had sounded more convinced, I would have congratulated myself on my wise handling of the problem, but it was obvious that she was still trying to convince herself. On the other hand, that was exactly what it was necessary to do.

As we passed the opening of one of the flights of steps that led down to the sea shore, still aiming for the tip of the promontory, a group of Sileni women went past us, carrying enormous baskets full of mollusks that they'd been collecting from the rocks. They saluted us with an exaggerated reverence. Their expressions were difficult to read, by virtue of not being completely human, but they seemed genuinely fearful of us, even though we were manifestly physically weaker than they were. They were much shorter and slimmer than the average male Silenus, let alone the colossi that provided Madame's guard of honor, but they were very muscular, and I knew that I wouldn't stand any chance against any one of them in a wrestling match, even though they were showing the effects of age much more obviously than I was.

They had all been present at the rite, however, and they knew that something extraordinary had happened there, even if they had little idea of exactly what it was. I had no idea whether they thought of me as a magician, or merely someone who enjoyed Madame's favor, but either way, they were in awe of me, and of Elise too. I assumed that they knew that I was a Macrobian, and that that probably added to my prestige. Elise, of course, fully deserved their reverence; simply because they had heard her play.

We both returned the women's greetings with the aid of the few words in their language that we knew, as politely as we could. They weren't beautiful, even by the standards of their own race—none of them was young, and they must have had laborious lives—but there was something in the slow grace of their movements that was almost majestic; their intimidation in our presence seemed rather bizarre.

They couldn't understand a word we were saying, of course, but Elise still left a respectful pause for them to draw out of earshot before she resumed her interrogation, changing the subject, as if that might help her to forget the nasty aftertaste of her nightmares, and probably with that intention.

"Do you think we'll ever be able to go back to the Empire, Axel? To Lutèce, or Mnemosyne?" she asked.

"I don't know," I said. "Would you like to?"

"Yes, I think so. It's pleasant here, paradisal even, but I've lived all my life in a city...*the metropolis*, and I can't help feeling unsettled here. Mariette missed Lutèce even on Mnemosyne...but she certainly won't go back without you, and she thinks you intend to stay here forever...or as close to forever as you can get...so she's trying to come to terms with the idea of living here permanently."

"The prospect has its attractions, for me," I said, warily, feeling the effect once again of her inquisitive gaze.

"But?" she prompted.

"I can't deny that I'm feel unsettled here too, because rather than in spite of its paradisal pretentions. Mnemosyne wasn't Lutèce, but in the summer, at least, it became an extension of Lutecian high society, a branch of its civilization, its art...in every sense of the word. I'd already made up my mind that I had to leave Mnemosyne, but not in the way that it happened, and I'd have gone very regretfully, even so. I had a good life there, perhaps as perfect as I could ever hope to attain, and the way we were taken away forced me to leave unfinished business there, some of which I feel quite badly about. I'm not sure I could live there again, now...not in the easy and pleasant way I did before. On the other hand, I'm uncomfortable about the fact that no one there—or hardly anyone—knows what has happened to us. So, while I'm trying to come to terms with the idea of settling here, I'm finding it even more difficult than Mariette, for the moment."

"Helen says that a message has been delivered to Charles assuring him that Mariette and I are safe and well," Elise observed, "but whether he can believe it is another matter. You've written a letter to your servants, haven't you?"

"I've written several letters," I told her, "but whether any of them have been delivered, or when...Helen's evasive, but I gather that Madame thinks there's some advantage in maintaining the mystery of what has become of us on Mnemosyne, at least for the moment. Helen took some pleasure in telling me, a few days ago, that a quarter of the islanders think I've run away with her."

"What do the other three-quarters think?"

"Mostly that I've run away with Mariette, although there's a substantial fraction that thinks that I've been murdered, either by the Marquise or the Dellacruscas."

"But nobody thinks you've run away with me?"

"I suppose they might, if they didn't prefer the hypothesis that you've either been kidnapped by the Dellacruscas or by their enemies."

"But some people must know the truth?"

"Of course—but the truth can only just one more rumor, except for a handful of people who know what really happened before and after your grandfather's death. The Marquise probably knows where we are by now, and the Dellacruscas, but the people who might actually care...I don't know."

"Hecate Rain, you mean?"

I looked at her sharply. "I was thinking more about Jean-Jacques and Luzon. Hecate will know that I didn't leave voluntarily, because she knows that I wouldn't have broken the promise I made to her in order to run away with a woman, And I got a very strong impression that she was the only person in Mesmay's house on the night of the near-bloodbath who sensed my presence in the Dionysian visitation. It might have just been an illusion, but...well, I'm sure that Hecate knows, even if my letter didn't reach her. She might have been able to reassure Luzon, if Jean-Jacques couldn't...perhaps Charles too, if he's still on the island."

"Is Hecate the only woman you've ever really loved?" Elise asked, seemingly genuinely curious.

"No," I said. "Nor am I the only man she's ever loved, by any means."

"But you have something special, different from…all the others?"

"We have—or at least had—something special. Don't make it more than it is, though. Lots of people have enduring friendships, which all have something special about them. It was different from all the others, but it wasn't the only special relationship I've had, by any means…it isn't even the only one I have now."

She laughed. "You can't mean me," she said.

"Why not?" I said.

"Because you've only known me for the blink of an eye, in your terms, even though it seems like almost forever to me, so much more has happened in the last few months than happened in my entire life before."

"Importance," I told her, "is not a matter of duration."

"You shouldn't humor me or flatter me," she said. "I can get that from anyone. You're the one who's supposed to tell me the truth."

"Which already makes our relationship special," I countered.

She didn't say: "Touché." She had probably never held a fencing foil, but she probably wouldn't have conceded the hit if she had. It would have seemed like a joke, and she wasn't in a joking mood.

"I liked Hecate a lot," she said, pensively. "She treated me like an adult."

"She treated you like an artist," I said. "It's not quite the same thing—but yes, I think you could have had a special relationship with Hecate too, if things had worked out differently. She never let anyone else accompany her, even musicians of great talent, one or two of whom worshiped the ground she walked on and begged for the favor."

"She mentioned that," Elise agreed, "but she added that she was much younger then. She said that the days when young men wanted to kiss her feet were long gone."

"She was exaggerating," I said, a trifle weakly. "She still has young men lusting after her." It wasn't a lie, but it was a much weaker truth that it had been twenty years before.

Elise changed the subject again. Perhaps she was ticking off a mental list, or perhaps her mind was simply restless. "What does Madame want of me, Axel?" she asked, abruptly.

"I'm not entirely sure what she wants with either of us, now that her initial project has been completed," I told her, "and for the moment, she seems to be neglecting us completely. If and when she returns her attention to us, I strongly suspect that it will be more of the same. She'll want to use us in further magical practices, when the time for the next Bacchanal comes round. Of what nature they'll be, or what effect, or after-effects, they might have on us, I have no idea, as yet—and she certainly doesn't seem to be in any hurry to inform me."

She undoubtedly noticed the resentment in the speech. "You really ought to paint her," she said. She didn't add anything else, but it was obvious enough what she was implying. I felt that she was being a trifle unkind to her mother—who really was, in every sense that mattered, her mother.

"Perhaps I will, one day," I said, "but I suspect that it will be nothing more than painting. Contrary to what you might have heard about my reputation, I've painted hundreds of women, including beauties after whom I've yearned, that I never succeeded in seducing. It didn't prevent me from doing them justice on the canvas."

"And do you yearn after Madame?" she asked, bluntly.

"No," I told her, equally bluntly. "I suppose there might come a time, when I know her better, or if she decides to use her magic for seductive purposes, but at present, no. You're welcome to tell Mariette that—but I'd leave out the qualification about magical seduction, if I were you."

She laughed, dryly. "It wouldn't do any good," she said. "And I didn't ask for Mariette's sake. I asked because I was curious. I'm entitled to be curious, aren't I. even though you consider my innocence precious and necessary of protection?"

"Of course," I said. "I must confess to finding this line of questioning a trifle uncomfortable, though."

"Good. That probably means you're making an effort to answer honestly." She paused, and then said: "I *am* right to be frightened, though, aren't I? There really are things to be frightened of? All sorts of things?"

I had to admire the way she'd set the trap. "I don't know," I said, truthfully, "whether it's ever a good idea to be frightened. It doesn't help clarity of thought. But yes, I think that we both have grounds for anxiety, and that it might be a good idea for us to find a mean of fighting back, of strengthening ourselves against corrosion, no matter what its source. The people who might mean us harm probably can't hurt us here...but that doesn't mean we're not vulnerable, as our present unease proves. We're fully entitled to hope that it's something that will pass, but..."

I stopped, not because she seemed to be about to interrupt me, but because something had just caught my eye. We had almost reached the tip of the headland, and from the height of the cliff, which was some way above sea level, the horizon was distant. Two of the other islands in the archipelago were visible as green lines interrupting the blue horizon. At least, they should have been simply slightly hunchbacked green lines. Above one of them, however—the nearer one—a faint smudge of smoke was visible.

In itself, that would not have been particularly surprising. Although the island wasn't permanently inhabited, human boatmen often went out there, to fish, or to collect birds' eggs. They sometimes lit cooking fires.

But the smudge that had caught my eye seemed to be moving.

Elise followed the direction of my gaze. "Is that the steamer coming back again?" she asked. The prospect seemed to please her, presumably because she was thinking that it might have brought something more substantial from the Empire than the unreliable telegraph messages that came along the cable it had laid with so much care and effort, not so very long ago.

"Perhaps," I said. *But if it is*, I thought, *why is it lurking behind the island?*

Clearly the captain of the ship, assuming that it was a ship, must know that the island was too low-lying to conceal the smoke from his funnel; but that didn't mean that he wasn't seeking to hide the identity of his ship.

I wouldn't have been able to recognize the steamship that had brought us to the island, because careful precautions had been taken to make sure that we didn't see enough of it to be able to identify it, even on the one occasion that it had returned to the island since delivering us, but that had seemed absurd to me at the time, and still did. I was thinking in more general terms.

In my youth, there had been no such things as steamships, or steam locomotives, or telegraphs. Those were all innovations that had happened in what seemed to me to be the recent past—but it wasn't just my age that caused me to think of them as world-changing inventions. The existence of the trans-Oceanic continent had been known before I was born, but reaching it, in old-fashioned sailing ships, had been a difficult and perilous business, given that the prevailing wind blew the other way and so much of the Ocean was cluttered with huge expanses of floating weed. Steamships had changed that. Communication between the so-called Everlasting Empire and the much more precarious Iroquois Federation and Mayan Empire was now routine, a matter of political diplomacy as well as commerce.

Given the geographical situation of the Island of Dionysus, whose very existence must have seemed legendary for most of Madame's centuries-long lifetime, its position must be on every mariner's charts by now, and the archipelago must be reckoned a convenient place for renewing supplies of fresh water and fruits capable of warding off scurvy. Few ship-masters, as yet, could know anything at all about the population of the Island of Dionysus, but the fact that it was inhabited must be becoming common knowledge. It was no longer a secure hiding place, if it could be reckoned a hiding place at all…and the number of Imperial steamships was increasing as rapidly and railways and telegraph lines were spreading.

Given all that, the possibility that an unknown steamship was lurking out of a direct line of sight from where I was standing, marginally visible but unidentifiable, seemed a trifle ominous…or, at least, it did nothing to assuage the nightmare-induced feeling I already had that dire events were in the offing.

"What's the matter?" Elise asked. She had grown up in the capital of the Empire, in a world in which steamships were already unsurprising. She had little conception if how much they had already changed the world, and how much more profoundly they might, and surely would, change it in the course of her lifetime.

"Probably nothing," I said.

The faint smudge of smoke was no longer moving. If there was a ship beyond the green streak, it must have dropped anchor.

I looked at Elise. Her expression had clouded over. My momentary unease had infected her, and renewed her own, just as she might have on the brink of dispelling it.

"Perhaps we ought to go back now," she said. "Mariette will worry if she finds us gone."

"We're visible from the house," I told her. "She won't even need a telescope to be able to see and recognize us."

She knew that. I suspected that it was precisely the fact that Mariette would be able to see and recognize us that was adding to her unease. I wondered exactly how far Mariette's unreasonable jealousy had developed, and how it was affecting her conduct with Elise—but that certainly wasn't something I wanted to talk to Elise about, and I wasn't sure that it was a topic I could investigate, however obliquely, with Mariette.

I was about to agree that we ought to go back having already turned round, when I saw someone coming toward us along the cliff edge at a pace that, although not exactly a run, seemed urgent. It was Helen.

Elise had turned round too, and her gaze followed mine.

"Perhaps we're about to find out what Madame requires of us next," she said, dully.

I had a strong suspicion that she might be right.

III. Helen in Quest of Protection

Elise was, indeed, right.

When Helen arrived, while still somewhat out of breath, she gasped: "Madame would like to see you, Master Rathenius. It's urgent."

"About what?" I asked.

"I don't know." After the long and scrupulously honest conversation I'd been having with Elise, the lie seemed blatant, but there didn't seem to be any point in challenging it. If she had been instructed not to tell me, as she presumably had, she would obey the instruction. I noticed, however, that she seemed more than a trifle anxious about something—perhaps more things than one.

"Does she want to see me too?" Elise asked.

"No," said Helen, rather curtly. "You'll be quite safe in the house. Your mother will be back soon."

"I'm not frightened of being on my own," Elise told her, contemptuously. "It's not a good idea to be frightened. It doesn't help clarity of thought." She made it sound like an accusation. I tried to take a little flattery from the imitation, but my unease had grown to proportions that made such facile indulgences seem puerile.

"That's always been my experience," Helen replied, seemingly unflustered. "I didn't mean to insult you, Mademoiselle Dellacrusca. But I need Master Rathenius to come with me right away."

I'd never heard her, or anyone, call Elise "Mademoiselle Dellacrusca" before, but I didn't think it worth challenging either the accuracy of the nomenclature or her motive for employing it. Elise presumably felt the same way; at any rate, she raised no objection and made no comment.

"Is there bad news from Mnemosyne?" I asked, partly to override the awkwardness of the observation, and partly because, automatically connecting the summons and the distant smudge of smoke, I suddenly felt a twinge of alarm.

"No," Helen replied, swiftly, but was equally quick to add: "Not that I know of. Please—I've already lost time looking for you at the house. Madame was very insistent."

"You'd think that living for two thousand years would have taught her patience," I observed, sarcastically. She made no verbal response to that, but indicated by her manner that she would appreciate it if I would stop procrastinating.

"Go," said Elise, seemingly relishing the idea that I might be waiting for her permission—or, at least, the idea that Helen might think that I needed it.

I set off immediately. Elise lingered behind, deliberately, even though we would be taking the same route for a full half-mile. She was deliberately emphasizing the fact that she wasn't with us.

The journey was all uphill, once we had left the headland, and Helen was already a trifle weary, so I had no difficulty in keeping up with her, in spite of her urgency. My stride was leisurely, and I was able to look around, trying once again to savor the Edenic qualities of the island...or, given the presence of fauns and nymphs, the Arcadian qualities. It was easy, as an artist, to appreciate the beauty of the verdure, the orderly disorder of the fields and the orchards, the flowers in the hedgerows, and the smooth slope of the mountain. It was a place, I knew, that ought to be entirely suited to my liking for a quiet, serene life. But it wasn't.

I felt slightly guilty about that as I watched the patient Sileni working in the orchards and tending their flocks, seemingly perfectly adapted to their pastoral way of life, devoid of any desire for change, but what I'd said to Elise earlier was true. I needed the branch of Lutecian society that was the lifeblood of the artist's colony of Mnemosyne. The colony needed its isolation from city life, but it also needed its contact with the civilization and artistic appreciation that only city life produces. As a portraitist, I was the perfect summation of that dual need. I not only needed people to paint, but I needed a particular kind of people to paint, and a particular environment in which to paint them. And it was when they took their ritual vacations that they wanted to sit for portraits, that being part and parcel of the whole social ceremony. On Mnemosyne, I had belonged; on the Island of Dionysus, I didn't—and I was far from certain that I ever would, in spite of all its manifest attractions. I simply couldn't see myself as a painter of landscapes, or imaginary mythological scenes, even though the Orpheus had demonstrated that I could adapt my technique if necessary. I was, and feared that I always would be, a portraitist, a reader and drinker of souls.

After three or four minutes, Helen broke into my contemplation and said: "I saw your painting at the house."

"Oh," I said, unenthusiastically. She didn't offer any criticism, though; it had just been something to say. Even though she didn't want to tell me anything, she seemed to want to talk. I waited for her next gambit, in no hurry to help her out, given that she was obviously no in hurry to give me a hint as to why Madame wanted to see me so urgently, after seemingly ignoring me for so long.

Eventually, she said: "The little girl doesn't like me, does she?"

"Well," I observed, reasonably, "you did have her kidnapped, and locked up in a tiny cell on a steamer, being sick all over the floor for days on end. Not everyone's as forgiving as I am. Anyway, I thought you'd been getting along quite well recently. She seems to have been spending time with you lately."

"She's stopped giving me the cold shoulder, but not because she's trying to make friends. She just wanted to ask me a lot of questions."

"Oh? About what?" The idea that Elise might have sought Helen's advice before asking for mine was wounding.

"About you, mostly."

"Should I be flattered, or alarmed?" I asked—actually slightly relieved by the thought that Elise had been in search of information, not advice.

"How should I know? She asked me point blank whether I'd slept with you."

"She's at a curious age. You said no, obviously."

"Obviously. Then she asked me whether you were still going to paint me—but I don't think she was just thinking about painting."

"I suspect not. What did you say?"

"I said I didn't know. What else could I say?"

"Nothing. I'm sure she was grateful for your honesty."

"Then she asked me if I still wanted you to."

"She can be a little disconcerting, and she likes setting traps." I was beginning to see why Helen had wanted to provoke Elise slightly by addressing her as *Made-*

moiselle Dellacrusca, although she was now fully aware that her legal name was Mademoiselle Almiras, given that her father had acknowledged her when registering the birth. "What did you tell her?"

Helen sighed. "I said that I had no intention of begging. It was only afterwards that I thought that I might perhaps have phrased it better. I'm sorry if you think I might have I given her...an impression you'd rather she didn't have."

"Don't worry about it," I told her. "As I said, she's at a curious age, and there are questions she'd be embarrassed to put to her mother...especially now. She probably was trying to make friends with you, albeit in an awkward fashion"

"No, it wasn't just curiosity. I felt under attack. As you say, perhaps there's no reason why she should like me, even though I was trying to save her from a possible threat to her life, but there's no reason for her to think that I pose any threat to her mother...or to her. You might take the trouble to tell her that."

"I might," I agreed. Mischievously, I added: "Do I take it, then, that you no longer want me to paint you?"

She hesitated for a moment, and then said: "You could have had me that night in the Sprite when I drugged your wine, or again on the ship," she said, "but you didn't. I can take a hint. As I told the girl, I've no intention of begging."

There was evidently something she was not saying, although I couldn't deduce what it was.

"But?" I prompted.

She didn't blush. "But I would like some reassurance that you're not bearing a grudge against me, the way the girl and her mother are."

46

I was slightly surprised that that was the particular *but* that she had had in mind.

"I'm not," I said, honestly. "I can't say that I'm not annoyed that you drugged me and spirited me out of the Sprite without warning, and without giving me a chance to let my friends know that I hadn't been assassinated and wasn't running away, but I understand your reasons. You were doing what you thought best, for the best of motives. Anyway, you were spying on me for years, before you left the island—you must know that I don't hold grudges against pretty women."

She didn't seem to feel that that was as much reassurance as I might have given her, and reacted with a slightly sulky silence. There had to be a reason why she wanted more, but I couldn't work out what it was. It seemed to be a good opportunity to hazard some guesses, though.

"Are you being sent back to Mnemosyne?" I asked her.

"That would be dangerous," she said. "Too many people there will have connected your disappearance with mine."

I took note of the fact that the observation fell some way short of a denial, but shrugged my shoulders slightly. "Well, you have nothing to fear from me," I said. "And don't read too much into my hesitation that night in the Sprite, or what didn't happen on the steamer. If it actually matters to you, I did think about it, both times, but…well, it hardly matters now. I certainly don't think of you as an enemy."

"That's not the same thing as offering me your protection," she pointed out.

The persistence seemed bizarre. "Why would you need my protection?" I asked. "From whom?"

This time, she did blush. I wondered whether she could possibly be afraid of Mariette, or even Elise, but it seemed absurd.

"It doesn't matter," I said, when she didn't answer. "Yes, for what it might be worth to you, if you ever need protection, and I can offer it, you'll certainly have it. And some day, I would still like to paint you, if you're still agreeable…but it might be a while."

She seemed strangely relieved. "Thank you," she said. I didn't think that she was talking about the painting.

"What else did Elise ask you?" I asked her, curiously, thinking that it must have been something the girl had said that had alarmed Helen.

"She wanted a complete account of your personal history. I told her that I'd never observed you at close range and didn't know anything at all about your intimate personal life. I said that I thought your reputation as a callous exploiter of women was probably exaggerated, and that, although there's no such animal as a trustworthy man, you're probably more decent than most."

"There is such a thing as damning with faint praise," I observed.

"That wasn't my intention. She asked me a lot of questions about Madame too, but I had to avoid most of those. Madame dislikes indiscretion. She also asked me point blank whether I was a prostitute, I said no, but I don't think she believed me. She knows that I worked in the Sprite, so that's not surprising…but I wasn't lying."

"I know," I said.

She raised an eyebrow. "How?"

"I've spent a lot of time in the Spite over the years. I know you thought you were effectively invisible there, but I have a painter's eye. I never guessed that you were a Dionysian spy, let alone that you might be spying on me, but I never thought you were a whore."

The eyebrow remained raised. "She also asked me about Hecate Rain. I told her that I didn't know much about her beyond her drinking habits, but that you and she seemed to enjoy one another's company. Was that all right?"

"Perfectly."

"She's a strange child. I wish she liked me. Madame thinks very highly of her—because of her music, not because of…who she is."

"She has a great talent," I agreed. "But there is a slight hint of Dellacrusca about her. I'm not sure you ought to go out of your way to remind her of it, but she didn't seem to take offence just now. Perhaps she was even pleased—she barely caught a glimpse of the man, after all, and the only time she saw one of her uncles he was perfectly charming, to her and to everyone else present. Perhaps heredity is having an effect too. I'd have been very interested to meet her mother."

"Well, you were said on the island to be the only person there who actually liked the dreadful twins, except for the old madwoman, so I expect there's no one better qualified to be her guardian."

There were two elements in that remark that nearly threw me off my stride, the first one being that I was now reckoned to be Elise's guardian. Perhaps oddly, it was the other one that caught my more immediate attention.

"What madwoman?" I asked.

"*The* madwoman. You must have known about it. Apart from the twins and a couple of the Sisters of Shalimar, you were the only other person who ever bothered to climb the mountain to see her, as far as I know."

"Eirene Magdelana?" I queried. I had never known that the Dellacrusca twins even knew that Eirene existed. I hadn't hated them with the same righteous wrath as the rest of the island's population, but I certainly hadn't made a habit of hanging out with them.

"That's right. I think they first climbed Snowspur just because they wanted to get to the top, but they must have stumbled across her, and for some reason, they took to her. They made a point of going to see her every summer. At one time I wondered whether they might be relaying messages back to her father. She had a reputation as a seer—but Dellacrusca wasn't the kind of man to consult oracles, was he?"

"He wasn't suspected of it," I said. "And you think Eirene actually liked the twins?"

"She seemed to. She had a son of her own once, so rumor had it, who was a bad lot…but you know something about that, don't you? I was away when she died, but I heard something in the few days I was there before I left with you. Something to do with Ramon Barling being a murderer, Nicodemus Rham's replacement as the keeper of Lucifer's Light, and an old shipwreck on the Devil's Rocks?"

"Yes," I said. "It was a big scandal, by Mnemosyne's standards." It was all in the past now, though, so I returned to the other point. "Am I really supposed to be Elise's guardian."

"You're screwing her mother and living in the same house," Helen point out. "Parenot's still on Mnemosyne. She's your responsibility now. You don't mind, do you? It might dent your image a little, I suppose, but Parenot coped…not that he had the same reputation, from what

I've heard. Totally obsessed with little Mariette. You're not, I presume?"

I ignored the indelicate question, still thinking about my new title. I had lived for a very long time, and slept with a good many mothers along the way, but I had never been estimated to be the guardian of any of their offspring. I didn't know how I felt about the idea.

"It could be worse," Helen suggested, provocatively. "At least the twins are old enough to look after themselves now. If Dellacrusca had been assassinated on Mnemosyne ten years ago, Constable Clovis might have come knocking on your door asking you to take them in until someone could come from Lutèce to collect them. He could hardly entrust them to the old madwoman up on Snowspur, could he?"

"Probably not," I agreed. The scenario didn't seem that unlikely, in retrospect, except that Lord Dellacrusca had always seemed invincible and immortal...until Antoine de Mesmay had caught him off guard while he was waiting, like a spider on the edge of a web, to hear his long-lost grand-daughter play her duet with Hecate Rain.

A thought occurred to me. "Did Madame know in advance that Antoine de Mesmay was planning to assassinate Dellacrusca?" I asked her.

"I don't think so. The Mesmays played their cards very close to their chest. The word from the island now is that old Ursule, the Marquise's aunt, is in a holy rage about her convent being used as a cover for the plot. If the Sister of Shalimar weren't pacifists, she'd probably have brought the wrath of heaven down on her niece, or at least launched the most powerful curse she knows. The Marquise is rumored to be so frightened that she's had a brace of hex-doctors shipped in from Nubia to offer extra magical protection."

"I've met Sister Ursule," I said. "She didn't seem to me to be the curse-launching type. She's a scholar, not a would-be magician, like her niece."

"Family feuds brings out the worst in folk," Helen opined. "The Dellacrusca twins seem to be moving in perfect harmony, though, more's the pity."

"Why more's the pity?"

"I'd like it better if they'd turned on one another to fight over the inheritance. As things are, it seems that they might actually stand a change of rallying all the opposition to the Marquise and Duc d'Alectryon. If they can do that, they might well launch a violent vendetta that will drown Lutèce and Rome alike in blood…and perhaps Mnemosyne too. Personally I'd prefer a balanced tension and a contest of cunning. Especially…"

She stopped, having evidently let her tongue run away with her.

"Especially what?" I prompted.

"Especially now that things are so complicated," she said, lamely.

"When were they ever simple?" I said—ruefully, because, from my viewpoint, things had been very simple indeed, until the last few months. Not for the first time, I cursed my bad judgment in ever having agreed to paint the Orpheus triptych. While she was off balance and out of breath, I hazarded: "This has something to do with the steamer that's dropped anchor behind the nearest offshore island, doesn't it?"

As it was, the fact that she was out of breath gave her a chance to think before answering, although she would probably have been able to come up with the countermove she used by reflex alone.

"What ship?" she parried.

I seized her by the arm and turned her around. We were half way to Madame's palace already, and a good deal higher up that I'd been on the headland. I pointed to the island, but the smudge of smoke was no longer visible. The captain of the steamer had doubtless killed the engine after dropping anchor,

"The ship that dropped anchor less than half an hour ago, behind that island," I said, and risked adding: "The steamer that isn't the one you used to bring me here."

She could just have said that she had no idea what I was talking about, but she didn't. She looked down at my right hand, which was still gripping her left arm. She didn't pull away. Then she looked me in the eyes. It was true, so far as I knew, that she wasn't a whore, but she had worked in the Sprite for a strong time. She was no stranger to being grabbed and having to repel unwanted advances. Her expression was challenging. I released my grip immediately.

"There you are," she said. "As I said, probably more decent than most." She was changing the subject, to what she judged to be safer ground.

There was no point in putting pressure on her. Madame would tell me soon enough why she had summoned me.

I resumed walking uphill. "I'm sorry if…my ward has been giving you a hard time," I said. "I can have a word with her, if you like."

"Don't," she said. "You might make it worse. I'll just have to try to win her over. Not much chance with her mother, though." She shot me a sharp glance, to make sure that I understood her implication.

"No," I admitted. "You shouldn't hold it against her, though. She's not malevolent, just anxious."

"I know."

"Of course you do," I said. "After all, you're still spying on me, aren't you, for Madame? Your recent reports must be quite graphic."

There was evident fear in her eyes, and I realized that I had just ruined the reassurance I'd offered her of my protection by suggesting that I was, in fact, still nurturing resentments against her.

"It's all right," I hastened to assure her. "I understand. It's not as if I have any secrets—not any more. We're both in an awkward situation."

She sighed. "You don't know the half of it," she said, "and I can't tell you."

An idea occurred to me. "When you asked me for my protection," I said, "was it in case you need it against Madame?"

"No," she said. "Madame won't hurt me, even if I fail her again. She'll just be…disappointed."

"Again?" I queried. "My impression is that you carried out your last mission with complete success, in difficult circumstances."

She didn't say anything. The silence was effective; I wasn't at all sure that I could fill in the gap by guesswork, but it did occur to me to wonder whether the fact that she'd been so blatant in offering herself aboard the steamer, when I must have been as far from seductive as I had been in at last fifty years, had had less to do with my sexual charisma than the fact that she'd been given orders to seduce me…orders that she had had difficulty carrying out, because she wasn't, in fact, a whore, or the kind of woman who would beg.

I didn't pursue the point.

"You saw the painting in the house," I said. Although it wasn't something I wanted to talk about, it seemed the safest topic available.

"Yes," she said. "I wasn't spying, though. I was looking for you to give you the message."

"I know," I said. "What I mean is that you saw how terrible it is."

"You've hardly started," she said. "It's far too early to judge."

"I hope you're right," I said, "But Elise didn't think so, and she's anxious about her playing. She's been having nightmares. So have I—and Mariette too. She asked me whether it's possible that we're under some kind of magical attack."

Helen seemed genuinely surprised. I deduced that she hadn't been having nightmares herself—no more than usual, at least. "And what did you tell her?" she asked, with a certain intensity.

"I told her that I thought it was very unlikely that anyone could be influencing our dreams from the far side of the Ocean, and that it was more probably a delayed reaction to our involvement in Madame's...experiment. I was thinking about a simple psychological reaction, but people sometimes talk about the costs of magic. You must have been involved in many such rituals before, as an important participant. Have you observed, or felt any such effects?"

She paused, as if for deep and serious thought; I didn't think she was faking.

Eventually, she said: "Yes, I have, but I can't be certain whether they were magical. Madame will be able to tell you much more than I can. You should certainly mention it to her, if you think that you and Elise are affected...and Mariette too?"

The idea that Mariette's recently-exaggerated jealousy might have an external cause, rather than being an innate aspect of her character, was by no means unappealing. Indeed, the idea that the unexpected disconnection of my hand and might not simply be a failure in my own art also offered a hint of relief. I would have been quite content with that meager reward, but Helen was still thinking.

"Aethne de Mesmay really has got it into her head that she's a powerful magician," she mused, pensively. "She seems convinced that magic is the key to following through with her husband's scheme. She's crazy, of course, but that can be more dangerous than sanity, and the African witches she's imported…it's a hundred to one that they're charlatans, but that doesn't mean they're not dangerous…not to you, but there are innocent bystanders involved in this, who might be vulnerable. Magic does have costs, even when it doesn't really work."

"You're thinking of Sister Ursule?" I queried.

"Among others. The Marquise is quiet, for the moment, but she's still a loose cannon. The problem is that she has support. Mesmay's co-conspirators are sticking together because they're afraid of what might happen if they don't, and she seems to have Alectryon in her pocket. Madame aborted a bloodbath during your initiation and bought everyone a respite, but the problem isn't solved…"

She left it there, tempting me to wonder whether the fact that I hadn't seen Madame for a couple of weeks, and the fact that she wanted to see me so urgently now. might indicate that she was serious anxious, perhaps even becoming desperate, and perhaps planning another attempted magical intervention..

"Which others might be in danger?" I asked coldly.

She shook her head. "It's not my place."

"Jean-Jacques and Luzon?" I asked, although I couldn't believe that a woman as proud and arrogant as the Marquise de Mesmay would stoop to attacking a man's servants.

"They're fine," she assured me. "Your letter to them got through."

"Hecate Rain?" I queried.

No such similar reassurance was forthcoming. That was a bad omen.

"Charles Parenot?" I hazarded.

A flicker of expression crossed her face. It was unreadable, but the mere fact that she'd reacted to that name but not to Hecate's seemed significant.

"Please, Master Rathenius," she said, demonstrating that she wasn't above all kinds of begging. "Don't put me under pressure. I can't tell you anything, and if I even drop accidental hints…"

"She'll be disappointed," I finished for her.

"Yes."

It seemed to be time to make good on my promise of protection. "I'll let up," I told her. "I don't want to cause trouble for you. If things are going to become difficult, it's probably best if we can all stick together, or at least remember that we're all on the same side."

"Thank you," she said—although it wasn't really necessary, because we'd almost arrived at the house, and she was off the hook in any case.

As always, there were two massive Sileni standing guard outside the grounds, but they didn't challenge us. In fact, they showed exactly the same reverence as the old women that Elise and I had encountered earlier.

Perhaps I ought to have been delighted by that, or at least have taken comfort in it, but it simply made me feel that the entire population of the island thought that I was something that I wasn't, and that there might eventually come a time when I was going to disappoint them all.

IV. The Seismograph

Madame came into one of her tastefully-decorated reception rooms in order to talk to me, but she didn't offer me any ritual beverage. She didn't beat around the bush at all. She really was afflicted by a sense of urgency.

"Something has happened," she said. "It might be a good thing, or it might be disastrous, but it's certainly unexpected and it changes things dramatically. There's a ship at anchor not far away. My boats went to investigate it while it a still some way out, and reported back a little while ago. Tommaso Dellacrusca is aboard. He wants to see you."

I was steeled for a bombshell, but hadn't anticipated its magnitude. Suddenly, it became abundantly clear why Helen thought she might need my protection, insofar as I could provide any.

"Me?" I queried.

"Not just you, obviously—but he wants who see you first, before his niece, and he wants to see her before he sees me. He's in no position to make peremptory demands, of course, but…well, you can understand that refusing to comply with his requests might have consequences. It's an important decision, from my point of view. Are you willing to do as he asks?"

"Yes, of course," I said, without hesitation. "Are you?"

"Yes, for now. It's a risk, obviously. I don't know what he wants yet, and I certainly can't trust him, but…well, it's such an unexpected move that it would be very foolish indeed not to allow him to make it. He must think that he's running a considerable risk himself, given that our organizations have been at odds for centuries, sometimes violently. What do you think he wants?"

"How should I know? I'm completely new to this strange game you've been playing against Dellacrusca for decades...centuries. This time last year I was only vaguely aware that there *was* such a game, and I was under the blissful illusion that Mnemosyne was a peaceful haven of culture, which the likes of Lord Dellacrusca visited in order to get as far away as possible from such wearisome cares for a month or two of relaxation."

"But you've known the Dellacrusca twins since they were children. You've painted them. You must have insights that I can't possibly have."

"I doubt that very much," I said. "I sympathized with them, to some extent, when they were young, and they amused me, but the Tommaso I've seen in the last few months is someone new and strange—someone who had grown up considerably even before his father was murdered. Any assumptions I made on the basis of what I knew about the boys before have been flagrantly invalidated."

"So you have no idea why he wants to see you first?"

"None. I can only assume that he wants to talk to me about Elise. I presume that he wants to take her to Lutèce, or at least to reassure himself that she's safe here."

Madame seemed startled by that suggestion. "But the child means nothing to him!" she protested. "I can understand, I think, why the Duc was so obsessed with finding her, but I can't imagine that he communicated that obsession to his sons—sons by a different marriage."

Surprised by her surprise, I countered: "Why do you think he's here, then?"

"To make a treaty, obviously," she said. "Or at least to make the offer, probably with the intention of breaking it as soon as it has served its immediate purpose."

"Ah," I said. "You think he wants your help in his squabble with Aethne de Mesmay?"

"I assume that he's hoping to use me to defeat her, or at least to deflect her attention away from the coalition that he and his brother are trying to form against her. And I suspect that the reason that he wants to see you before he sees me is because he wants to know everything you can tell him about me, about the island, and about what really happened on the night when the bloodbath the brothers almost launched against his father's murderers was aborted."

She was looking at me intently, and I felt a slight frisson as I realized that I might be in a rather awkward position, through no fault of my own.

"That's why you were in so much of a hurry to see me before granting his request to see me," I said, slowly, "after studiously neglecting me for some time, in violation of your promises, and deliberately keeping me in the dark about what's happening on Mnemosyne. You've initiated me into your bizarre cult, but you don't think I'm ready to be a docile pawn, like poor Helen. Well, I can't say that you're wrong—but if you wanted me for a worshipful pawn, it doesn't seem to me that you've gone about things the right way."

She sketched the merest ghost of a smile. "No," she said. "If that had been what I wanted, I would certainly have handled matters differently. But it's unjust to accuse me of neglecting you in violation of my promises.

I've been very busy tracking certain ominous indications."

"Not very efficiently," I opined, "if Tommaso's arrival has taken you completely by surprise."

"You're misunderstanding me," she said, equably. "There are worse things in the world, believe me, than the internecine squabbles of the fractured Cult of Orpheus. Come with me, and I'll explain."

She swept out of the room, and I followed her. She took me to her laboratory. I'd been there before several time, but not for long—certainly not long enough even to begin to understand all of the strange apparatus she had there. I knew that she was making heroic efforts to keep up with all the experiments that were being carried out with electricity in the Empire, and even trying strenuously to make discoveries of her own, but that was one of the many mysteries that she had not yet kept her promise to explain to me.

She took me to a corner where there was what seemed to be an extremely simple apparatus, of which the visible part simply consisted of a long, thin arm with a stick of charcoal suspended from the tip, which was tracing a line on a solely unwinding scroll of paper. The line was almost straight, but subject to slight deviations that seemed random to me. It was not the only one of its kind in the capacious room, and to judge by the accumulation of scrolls on a nearby table, along with stacks of mariners' charts and various items employed in geometrical drawing, there must be others in other locations.

"What is it?" I asked.

"It's a seismograph," she told me. "I wish I could claim to have invented it, but I didn't. This particular model is an improvement on devices that have been around for more than a thousand years—possibly before

I was even born—but it's a substantial advance. It was invented in Italy, and has been in productive use there for some time. It measures vibrations in the Earth's crust. Strategically deployed, the machines can measure direction as well as intensity. Such vibrations can travel over enormous distances—perhaps all the way around the world. The Empire scientists in Italy are using them to monitor volcanic activity, with the hope of being able to predict eruptions of Etna and Vesuvius."

"And you're trying to do the same?" I queried. I knew that the entire archipelago of which the island was a part was volcanic. More than one island had a visible cone, although none seemed to be active at present.

"Among other things. The recent eruption of Hekla is cause for concern, because the effects of such eruptions can extend a long way. Eruptions tend to occur in clusters, and a violent eruption like the one that caused Mnemosyne's falls of sooty snow can cause subtle effects of that sort all the way around the northern hemisphere. Sudden disruptions of the crust in one location can alter the balance of forces thousands of miles away—and that seems to be happening. There's been a marked increase in the disturbances detected by the seismographs since Hekla's eruption, particularly in the last three weeks. I've been examining the traces very carefully, trying to interpret them."

"You think that one of the volcanoes in the archipelago might become active again in the imminent future?"

"That's certainly a possibility, but it's not the only worry. I'm particularly worried, for the moment, in fact, about the possible effects of shifts in the crust on the far side of the Ocean."

"Could an eruption on Iroquois Federation or Mayan territory really have dangerous effects as far away as this?" I asked, surprised.

"It's not eruptions that I'm worried about. In fact, my suspicion is that volcanoes generally act like safety valves, releasing tensions beneath the crust. They can be locally devastating, obviously, and can play havoc with the weather for months, but in my experience—adding up the legacy of my two thousand years, with the benefit of hindsight—the most dangerous of all upheavals are earthquakes, and the most dangerous of all are earthquakes that rupture the sea bed. They can trigger enormous waves, which can travel thousands of miles—all the way from the Great Archipelago to my much smaller one. Much of the island, of course, is a long way above sea level, but the port is vulnerable and nine tenths of the population lives along the coast. A wave of that sort, even though they take hours to cross an Ocean and lodes some energy on the way, can cause utter devastation in low-lying areas.

"If they can be anticipated, or detected early, even by a matter of two or three hours, those areas can be evacuated, and a great many lives can be saved. Boats that head for open water can usually ride them out, provided that the captains know that they have to steer into them, and are skillful enough to avoid capsizing. If they're caught unexpectedly, though, and close to the shore, they're simply smashed. This is the first time since I've had the apparatus set up that I believe that I have a good chance of issuing the required warnings, if I do detect a major quake. I'm very anxious, as you'll understand, to test the apparatus, as well as to avert a possible disaster. If my judgments—visionary as well as scientific—can be trusted, there has been considerable activity in the vicinity of the Great Archipelago and the Weed Sea since Hekla exploded, so I'm keeping a very attentive eye on all my instruments and continually making calculations. Nothing might happen, of course, and I suppose I ought to hope that it doesn't...but if it does..."

"I see," I said, making a rapid mental calculation as to the height of the house where I was living above sea level. I couldn't imagine a wave that high—but Mariette, Elise and I all went into the port at regular intervals. Although it wasn't facing the Weed Sea, it obviously wouldn't be unaffected by a considerable mass of water heading in that direction. "Do you think that there's any truth in Plato's story of Atlantis, then?" I added, as an afterthought.

"It's unlikely," she said. "It seems to me that his invention was more likely inspired by a recent event closer to home, when an earthquake in the vicinity of the Greek town of Atalanti resulted in the sinking of a tract of land. Having said that, though, considerable areas of land in various parts of the Empire have sunk during my lifetime, and islands have been literally blasted apart. People forget very easily, and when living memory doesn't go back any longer than half a century, it's easy to believe things are more stable than they are. I've lived through enough disasters to know how costly they are, not just immediately but over decades and centuries."

"You mentioned visionary as well as scientific judgments," I said. "Does that mean you've been having nightmares about earthquakes in the Weed Sea?"

"I don't think of them as nightmares," she said. "Nor do they concern the Weed Sea, specifically. But I've been sensing some kind of disturbance for weeks."

"So have we," I said, bluntly.

"*We?*" she looked slightly surprised. "All three of you? I've asked Theano to keep an eye on Elise, but..."

"But Helen hasn't reported back anything relating to Mariette and me?"

"I didn't install her in the house to spy on you," Madame said, "but to act as an intermediary between you and the islanders and to make sure that you have everything you need or want...but no, she hasn't said anything to make me suspect that you were subject to any disturbance. Would you like me to talk to Elise about it?"

"Yes I would," I said. "I'd also appreciate it if you'd talk to me about it. If you'd explained why you were so preoccupied..."

"You're right, of course" Madame said, although her attention had already wandered slightly because the stick of charcoal on her machine had just begun describing a series of irregular curves.

"Can you really read the future in that?" I asked.

"Alas, no," she said. "At least, not yet—at present, I'd be content if I could read the past more accurately. If something bad does happen, it could be a matter of life and death for a small island like this one, which is so dependent on the port and the fishing fleet."

"At least your fields are mostly at high altitude," I observed. "Mnemosyne has even more low-lying land— but mercifully, we're in no danger from events in the Weed Sea."

""Don't be too sure of that," said Madame. "Tidal waves can travel across Oceans, sometimes growing as they go rather than dying away—and the Channel between Gaul and the Cassiterides can have a funneling affect on water flowing from the Ocean. Mnemosyne has seen devastating floods before, although not in your life-time, let alone those of the island's current inhabitants."

"I've seen bad storm surges," I said, I said. "The port and the coastal areas often have limited floods—but there, as here, my house is on a high headland, way above sea level. The islanders are used to it, but boats do get smashed up in the worst storms, and people do get killed."

"The worst storm surge you've ever seen would be trivial by comparison with a tidal wave," she assured me, "but if the island had an apparatus like this, and a user who knew how to draw the correct inferences from its agitation, a few hours' warning could save hundreds of lives."

"We have the telegraph. According to Helen, Dellacrusca's secret link has now been supplemented by an official one. You've been able to get messages to and from the island for years, haven't you?"

"After a fashion, but often with long delays, and the ciphers are often garbled. The wires conduct information rapidly, but every time a link has to be made there's a delay, minutes in the best cases, but hours, or even days, in the worst—and now that the traffic of information along the Empire's lines is becoming a flood it-self...obviously, if I detected something that might af-fect Mnemosyne, I'd try to get a warning to the island immediately, but it might take hours to get through, and might not get through at all if it sparked a panic on the mainland first. The official cable from Mnemosyne to the mainland has only been operative for a few weeks, and I doubt if its operators are very expert yet, even if the machines themselves can be trusted."

I glanced in the direction of the cabinet where Mad-ame's telegraph apparatus was. It was continually manned, by a half a dozen decoders working in shifts, including Helen, but the signals just seemed like random noise to me. It was easy to believe that many of the novice operators in the Empire's heartland, let alone the northern coast, might not be very reliable.

"It's a temporary problem," Madame was quick to add, "but it won't be solved overnight. It doesn't take that long to become skilled in manipulation of the key, and the basic code is quite simple, although I have to communicate with my agents with the aid of additional ciphers, which can be awkwardly disrupted by inaccurate transcription. But that's quite enough idle chatter—we really don't have time for long dissertations about the ineptitudes of earthquake detection and telegraph messaging...as long as you're satisfied that I really have been extremely busy, and haven't simply forgotten you?"

"I nodded. "I'm sorry," I said.

She didn't bother to take me back to the reception room, but simply waved me to one of the laboratory stools, and sat down herself next to an incomprehensible apparatus under construction, which was bristling with wires.

"You're an intelligent man, Master Rathenius," she said, "and even though you're new to the game, I'm sure you grasp it well enough to understand how it has been played for far longer than you can remember. So you can understand well enough what advantages I might be able to obtain from a formal alliance with the Dellacrusca brothers, as well as the dangers of making any kind of alliance with men who are, shall we say, instinctively treacherous?"

I appreciated the compliment to my intelligence, but I wasn't at all sure that I could measure up to the challenge. On the other hand, I thought that I might, in fact, have a better insight into the complexity of the Dellacrusca twins' motives than she had. She was an Italian herself, allegedly born in an exceptionally bloody phase of the peninsula's history, but that didn't mean that she understood the subtleties of vendetta in the same way that Tommaso and Lorenzo did, I had had lived in several locations within the Empire for more than a hundred years, always studying the workings of its societies with an artist's eye. I thought—in fact, I was convinced—that I knew how modern people's minds worked better than she did, as much because of, as in spite of, her alleged two thousand years of experience. And I was convinced, too, that whether Tommaso and Lorenzo were prepared to love their niece or not, they were in no doubt at all as to her symbolic importance as their father's granddaughter, and the object of one of his most enduring obsessions.

I knew now how deceptive Tommaso could be, because he'd taken me in completely in prompting me to discover the mysterious manuscript that Toustain had bequeathed to me without my being aware of it, but I had seen him speak to Elise in my house on the night of his father's murder, and to Mariette and Charles, and I was sure that what he had said at that moment was true: that he wanted his niece to be safe, and that he was leaving her in their custody because he believed, at that point in time, that it was the safest place for her to be, as well as the one most comfortable for her.

Perhaps he thought now that he she might be safer in Lutèce—safer, at least, than in the custody of his father's supposed arch-rival—but I was sure that if he wanted to talk to me, it must be because he wanted to be able to calculate her situation accurately. Doubtless he would also like to know whatever I could tell him about

Madame and the island, and to investigate the possibility of an alliance with her against the Mesmay cabal, but in my estimation, the family matter was probably his primary concern.

Madame gave me time to think, but she was still impatient. Eventually, she said: "You and I are on the same side, Master Rathenius. You're a Dionysian—not because you're an initiate, although that counts for more than you might realize, but because you want the same things as we do: to preserve peace and order within the Empire."

"*We?*" I snapped. "You and the god, that is? Well, you doubtless know him better than I do, and I'm well aware of the fact that reputations can be a trifle misleading, but nothing I ever heard about Dionysus suggests that he's a god of peace, and if you're now the leader of his Bacchantes…well, let's put all that aside and stick to simpler matters. I'm under your thumb here, I know that, and perhaps, like Helen, it would be better for me not to risk *disappointing you*…but if you want my active support in your negotiations with the Dellacrusca brothers, or with anything else, I'll need a better reason than that kind of empty rhetoric."

She sighed. "I seem to have disappointed you," she said. "I'm sorry about that. But I really do believe that we're on the same side, and I really would like your advice on how to handle the situation that has arisen."

"How can I advise you when you're deliberately keeping me in the dark?" I demanded.

"Am I?" she said. "I asked Helen not to tell you about Tommaso Dellacrusca's arrival, it's true, and not to pass on certain other items of information that may be nothing more than mere rumor, but that was because I wanted to tell you myself. Helen has my full confidence,

70

but she only has partial information, which might be misleading. Specifically, I confess, I forbade her to pass on certain rumors regarding Hecate Rain and Charles Parenot, because I wanted to have them investigated more carefully before passing them on."

"What rumors?" I demanded.

"Rumors to the effect that the Marquis de Mesmay has co-opted them both into her conspiracy, and is seeking to use them…with their active cooperation."

"Use them for what?" I queried. "And how? I can't see that a painter and a poet can be of any use in her attempt to gain control of Dellacrusca's intelligence network."

"She's a sorceress," said Madame. "A charlatan, certainly, but not without learning and not without a certain power, although she doubtless overestimates the extent to which she's in control of her power. She appears to believe, perhaps correctly, that Hecate Rain and Charles Parenot have latent power of that kind, just as you and Elise have—and that their relationships with the two of you might be uniquely useful to her in making use of that power."

Again, I felt a slight frisson. I had tried to dismiss Elise's suggestion that the Marquise de Mesmay might capable of acting against us by magical means, even though she undoubtedly had the motive to do so, no matter how little she understood what had happened during her ritual, but I had not succeeded completely. The news that the Marquise was recruiting African sorceresses to help her had only made that suggestion seem more absurd in my eyes—but the suggestion that she was recruiting Hecate and Charles Parenot seemed more ominous...at least for them. Hecate, I felt sure, would never cooperate in any venture aimed against me, but Charles might be a different matter.

"Is Parenot one of the people on Mnemosyne who thinks that I ran away with Mariette?" I asked

"If my information is reliable, he's convinced of it," Madame told me. She added, maliciously: "And as things have turned out, he's not wrong, is he?"

"Is that why you ordered Helen to seduce me on the ship?" I asked.

Again, she seemed startled—and annoyed.

"I did *not* order Helen to seduce you," she said. "I would never do that."

I was startled myself. Had I really read the situation so wrongly? "She seems to think that you did," I observed, warily. "And that she disappointed you by failing do so."

Madame frowned. "Then she misunderstood," she said. "But, on reflection, I can see...I did give her permission...but I really was just giving her permission. I thought..." She paused, and then added: "I had formed the impression, from the reports that she made on you, in the past, that she might...want to. Perhaps I was wrong."

My vanity told me that perhaps she wasn't—but my intellect told me that that wasn't the important issue. I knew that time was pressing, so I wanted to get back to the ones that were. "So Parenot thinks that I've stolen his mistress and adoptive daughter," I said. "And, as you say, I suppose I have. So the Marquise thinks she can use him against me...and he presumably imagines that he might be able to use her. What do they think they can do?"

"My agents are trying to find that out—but it's very difficult. The Marquise is being very careful. I have no one inside her cabal. All I have is a rumor that she has commissioned Parenot to produce a painting...what's the matter?"

I gathered from the question that I must have shown some outward sign of distress, although I was trying with all my might to keep a straight face. But a thought had just struck me that seemed, for the moment, at least, truly terrible.

I had never really believed in the powers of so-called magicians, and had held on to that conviction even when confronted with manifestly supernatural occurrences. Madame's account of her magical exploits, and what I'd seen of them, had only undermined that belief marginally. Now, though, I remembered one of supernatural the occurrences I had witnessed: Vashti Savage's séance at the Marquise de Mesmay's house; the séance at which the shade of Eurydice, or some force temporarily adopting that identity, had made itself manifest, via Charles Parenot's painting of Eurydice, and the painting's model, Mariette.

I had thought at the time that no one but me had realized that particular detail of what had happened—Mariette certainly hadn't, and nor had Lord Dellacrusca, who was also present—but I hadn't known then that Aethne de Mesmay thought of herself as a powerful sorceress. Now, it seemed perfectly understandable that she might think that there was a latent power in Charles Parenot's art, specifically connected with Mariette...and that perhaps it would be foolish of me to deny the possibility.

"What painting?" I asked, curtly.

"I don't know," she said. "All I know for sure is that Parenot has moved into the Mesmay manse, temporarily. Not unnaturally, many people are assuming that he's the Marquise's lover, even though Alectryon still seems to be dancing attendance on her, and Fion Commonal too. I'm not jumping to that conclusion myself, but..."

"What about Hecate?" I asked, in a hurry now myself to enlighten myself as much as possible.

"About that I know even less. She has been going to Mesmay's house frequently, usually with Vashti Savage. She has been initiated into the cult...but you know that already. Again, your guess is likely to be better than mine as to what her motivation might be...and how impressionable she might be."

"Not as impressionable as Vashti Savage," I muttered. I looked Madame straight in the face, trying to summon up as much force of command as I could, even though I knew that I was probably facing an immovable object. "You're the one who's been studying magic for a thousand years," I said. "Do you think that the Marquise really can strike back at us...at all us...for disrupting her great magical plan? Assuming, that is, that she knows that it was us?"

"She must know," said Madame. "If she were wise, she wouldn't hold it against us, and might even be grateful...but that doesn't seem to be the way that her mind works. As for striking back...I doubt that she can direct any force that she tries to use against us very precisely, and might well do far more damage to herself than to us, but I am certain that there are active forces that can be stirred, and which can affect us...but you know that already. And you say all three of you have been having nightmares, which might have the same source as my own anxious visions...but which might not."

She fell silent. Obviously, the situation was not only more complicated than I had thought, but also more complicated than she had thought.

V. Confusions

"It isn't just a matter of dreams," I told Madame, while she was mulling over the possibilities on her own account. "Elise thinks that her playing has been affected her playing, and that has brought back the anxieties she had in Lutèce before Myrica Mavor persuaded Charles and Mariette to relocate to Mnemosyne, when she thought that she was being haunted. As for me, I seem to have lost the vital connection between my eye and my hand. I finally put that to the crucial test today, after procrastinating for weeks, and it didn't go well. In fact it went so badly that Elise only had to take one look at the painting before…well, at least it prompted her to tell me what was wrong. Not that I was able to help. I might already have made things worse for her, accidentally, by telling her the story of Eirene Magdelana's long-lost son, so that the idea of morpheomorphism was bound to leap to her mind…and as soon as she'd opened up to me, I must confess, I couldn't get it out of mine."

Madame nodded her head. "That is one of the forms of magic most likely to have an effect, albeit a vague and haphazard one. If the Marquise de Mesmay is taking some such malevolent action, especially with the help of Charles Parenot's art…but that's an action we can oppose, and ward off. Now that I know about the possibility, I can make arrangements of my own…"

I wished that I had the confidence to laugh at the suggestion, but I didn't. In fact, I was grateful for it. I realized, reluctantly, that I had more in common with Madame than I would have liked to think. I had no intention for the moment of telling Mariette what Madame had just told me about Charles, and no intention of telling Elise what she had just told me about the possible effectiveness of the Marquise's magic. Did I really have the right to complain, then, about her inclination not to tell me everything?

"Wouldn't the Marquise be better employed using whatever magic she has against the Dellacrusca brothers than against us?" I said bitterly. "Their vendetta against her is surely a much more urgent matter of concern than her petty vendetta against us."

"Undoubtedly," Madame agreed. "But it's perfectly possible that she thinks that the two are intimately connected—especially if she has caught wind of Tommaso Dellacrusca's intention to come here. She seems to have tried to have you killed, remember, as soon as you'd finished the triptych, because she merely suspected you of having been in league with Dellacrusca. Everything that has happened then since has probably reinforced that suspicion. And it might well become a self-fulfilling prophecy."

"Because you intend to make a treaty with Tommaso, in which I shall be involved, tacitly if not explicitly?"

"Let's not get ahead of ourselves. I don't know yet what Tommaso intends to offer—but the idea of an alliance is certainly attractive, and not simply to neutralize the Marquise and her cabal. When his father was alive, it was convenient, for him and for me, to be in opposition, in order to maintain an equilibrium of opposed agencies. Things have changed, and not just because of Dellacrusca's death. The Empire is under threat from new forces, in an unprecedented fashion. It might be the ideal time to unite against a common threat. If Dellacrusca were still alive, I don't think there would have been any possibility of that, because of the kind of man he was and the inertia of history, but now...as I said before, you might be able to weigh up the brothers better than I can. Obviously, I can't trust them...but that doesn't necessarily mean that I can't work with then, for a while, and if I can do that...well, much depends on how like or unlike their father they really are."

"When you say new threats," I said, just to make sure, "you're not talking about earthquakes? You mean steam power, and electricity? What other people call progress?" It was a discussion we'd had before, albeit briefly; she had mentioned the issue during our very first conversation, although there had been so many other things in that conversation that needed my urgent consideration that I hadn't given that one much thought.

"It's not the technologies that are dangerous but the corollaries of their usage," Madame said, "Dellacrusca understood that very well, and tried with all his might to maintain control over their deployment, but the implications were simply too far-reaching. Even when you were young, let alone when I was young, the potential boundaries of the Empire were relatively stable. Communication with the Far East was manageable, the heart of Africa was cut off by the Sahara, and the trans-Oceanic continent was purely legendary until little over a hundred years ago—another world, in effect. It's not another world any more. Commerce, of all kinds, is increasing dramatically. The plagues we're exporting seem to be doing more damage than those we're importing, for the moment...but that's a danger in itself. You know about the plagues?"

"Only rumors," I said. "Far travelers are said to be bringing back diseases that the Empire hasn't seen before, from the east and south as well as the other side of the Ocean. There have been epidemics in numerous major ports, as well as Lutèce."

"That's true—and the traffic is worse in the other direction. Settled peoples seem to build up immunities to their endemic diseases, but when they begin to travel afar... Mnemosyne is vulnerable because of its annual influx of summer visitors, but even the Island of Dionysus can't be completely secure, no matter what precautions I take. Nor is it just a matter of external threats. Railways and the telegraph are changing the internal order of the Empire is a way that politics can't control. And they might be just the beginning. Even if the Cult of Dionysus and the Cult of Orpheus do join forces, their combined might be impotent to slow down the deluge of change that's building... but if we don't, the days when a balance of forces could maintain a certain political equilibrium are over."

"Does it really matter that much?" I asked. "Even if provinces began to break away from the center..."

"Don't be naïve, Master Rathenius," she snapped. "The Empire's citizens might have forgotten that there was history before the reign of the Divine Julius, and have forgotten the cost in bloodshed of the early revolts, but true scholars know what happened to all the Empires that preceded ours. Secessions and civil wars are things to be avoided at all costs, if humanly possible. Dellacrusca knew that, and Antoine de Mesmay probably knew it too...but I'm far less confident about his widow, and the twins."

I had never known Aethne de Mesmay well; my impression had always been that she lived meekly in her husband's shadow, as aristocrats' wives were supposed to do, having a somewhat colorless personality and somewhat lacking in intelligence—although that, I suppose, must have been a side-effect of my awareness of her occult interests—but I had never studied her with my gaze, let alone painted her. Now I had to assume that I had been mistaken, and that she was actually strong-minded and manipulative. As for her understanding of history, that was a different matter. Her aunt was a great scholar, but the two of them seemed to be at odds now, so the possibility of Aethne taking any advice from Ursule seemed remote.

"Do you really think that the dispute between the Mesmay cabal and the Dellacruscas could turn into a civil war?" I asked.

"Yes, I do, if it escalates" she said. "And if it does, it could start a domino effect that will bring countless other old resentments to the surface, all the way from Brest to Byzantium and Scandinavia to Nubia. We stopped the split becoming an open wound at the bacchanal, but the rift still needs to be healed, if possible. It's possible that my siding with the Dellacruscas might make things worse rather than better...but if the Marquise is convinced that we're already in league, or even that we might be...we'll have to defeat her quickly...if we can. Even that would only be a beginning, with the worst challenges yet to come..."

"So if Tommaso makes you a seemingly-reasonable offer," I said, by way of summation, "you won't be able to refuse."

"In terms of the long game," she said, cautiously, "if it's possible for me to make a secure alliance with the Dellacrusca twins, assuming that they really can pick up the pieces of their father's fractured organization, I would very much like to do so. But I really don't know whether it's possible. Their reputation suggests that it isn't, but reputation is sometimes an unreliable guide."

"So what do you want from me?" I asked her, curt-ly.

"That depends on what you can offer," she said, "and what you're willing and able to do."

"That doesn't answer my question," I observed.

"Of course not. I don't know the answer, yet. I'll have a better idea when I know what Tommaso Dellacrusca wants from you...assuming that you'll be willing to tell me."

"Or able," I pointed out. "He's just as likely to feed me a string of lies as he is to feed you one."

"Indeed. But he must want something from you, or he wouldn't have asked to see you before anyone else. Either he thinks that you're the most reliable source of information to which he'll have access here, or he thinks that there's something specific you can do to favor his schemes. I presume that we can take it for granted that he does have schemes, of a typically Dellacruscan na-ture."

"Probably," I agreed, dryly. "I can't help wishing, though, that he'd leave me out of them."

"He can't," Madame said, bluntly. "You might not like being a pawn—nobody does—but whether you like it or not, you're on the board and in play. You do have freedom of movement, though, within the limits of cir-cumstance."

"Really?"

"Do you doubt it?"

"If I had freedom of movement," I said, "I wouldn't be here, would I?"

"Of course you would. You arrived a little sooner than you would have done if Helen had had time to give you a full explanation and make you a formal offer, but she thought—and rightly so—that your life was in danger and that swift action was necessary. She would far rather have brought you here by invitation, I'm sure...seduction, if you like...but as you've observed, she was afraid of disappointing me. I'm by no means as terrible in disappointment as she might think, but I have had to cultivate that reputation, for practical reasons, just as Lord Dellacrusca was obliged to do. Over the centuries, I've become habituated to it. Mine has been, as I suspect that you're on the threshold of being able to understand, a lonely existence, and experience taught me a very long time ago that it is safer and more reliable to dominate by fear than by love, even if it's safest of all to rule by means of a deft combination of the two. But you know now, do you not, that the Island of Dionysus is where you belong? This is the only place of earth that offers you the possibility of a secure and fruitful future, as a Macrobian. Only the possibility, alas...but that is considerably more than you could have anywhere else."

She was jumping to conclusions. I had jumped to the same conclusions myself when I had first arrived on the island, in spite of the inconvenient circumstances of my arrival, but I had had second thoughts since then, and the summary of my existential situation I'd sketched as I was climbing the mountain had the opposite implication, An earthly paradise the Island of Dionysus might be— but precisely for that reason, it wasn't where a man like me belonged.

Even if I had agreed with her judgment, though, I would still have resented the fact that she was manipulating me, and the way she was going about it. Perhaps it was inevitable, given her situation, that she had fallen into the same habits as Lord Dellacrusca, albeit with more velvet glove and less iron fist, but that didn't mean that I had to sympathize.

"You could have issued an invitation ten years ago," I pointed out. "If Helen suddenly found herself forced to take urgent action, it's only because you had been watching me for years without every taking the trouble to inform me that you even existed."

"True," she admitted. "Force of habit. In hindsight, it was a mistake. Had I known then...but I didn't. This is now. I might need your help. Would you like to paint me?"

That seemed, in the circumstances, to be a low blow—and also a belated one.

"I don't think Mariette would approve," I said, dryly. "And in any case, I seem to have lost my touch."

"Would Mariette's disapproval stop you, if you wanted to do it?" she asked. I wondered whether it might be a sincere question, asked because she didn't know the answer, and would like to know.

"Yes, it would," I told her, wondering myself whether it was the truth, or just a move in the game. I remembered Helen's damnation with the faint praise that, although there was no such animal as a trustworthy man, I had at least a spark of decency. Perhaps I had.

Madame shrugged her shoulders. "That's what I thought," she said. "Personally, I'm far too old for a grand amour, and perhaps for any amour at all, but you're not there yet. While not taking yourself seriously enough in the respects that matter, you take yourself too seriously in the ones that don't. Don't bother to contradict me—I'm well aware of the fact that what matters to you is whatever you think matters to you, and that you're still too young to have formed a mature attitude to such matters. And it's no bad thing, from my point of view, for the nexus formed by you, Mariette and Elise,

82

to be more tightly bound, even if the knots have become uncomfortable."

""I'm glad it pleases you," I said, putting as much sarcasm into the remark as I could contrive.

"It does," She told me. "Partly for magical reasons—but mainly because you'll go into your meeting with Tommaso Dellacrusca thinking of others as well as yourself. You'll be thinking of what might be in Mariette's interests, as well as your own...and Elise's. Not to mention Hecate Rain's."

Again I remembered Helen's embarrassed attempt to obtain a promise of protection from me. I understood now that it was because she thought that Tommaso Dellacrusca might be harboring a grudge against her—as, indeed, he might be. Perhaps, though, the more interesting aspect of her move was that she thought I might really be able to provide her with a measure of protection—that I might actually have some influence over Tommaso. Evidently, Madame thought the same.

And perhaps they were right. He had tricked me, over the matter of the Orphean manuscript, but it was at least possible that his subsequent apology had been sincere, and that he did feel remorse—that he really did have a measure of respect for me, and that the reason he wanted to see me even before seeing his niece was that he wanted, and valued, my advice about what he should do, both about Elise and about Madame.

I had to bear in mind, though, that that might only be my vanity talking.

"What do you know about the Dellacrusca twins' relationship with Eirene Magdelana?" I asked Madame.

"Only that they went to see her, every summer. You probably know more about it than I do."

"I didn't even know that much," I confessed. "It came as a complete surprise when Helen mentioned it."

"Is it important?" she asked. Her tone suggested that she was prepared to believe that it might be. Helen had not been on Mnemosyne during the Ragan Barling fiasco, but Madame must have had reports of it, and must, in any case, have had reports of Eirene's morpheomorphic talents."

"I don't know," I said. "But if Eirene was working on the boys' dreams...well, she was a real artist, and they consented to be taken under her wing...effects of that kind can last a long time."

"Was she as mad as her reputation suggests?"

"Alas yes, poor thing. She'd long ago lost the distinction between dreams and reality—an occupational hazard among morpheomorphists. But there can be art in madness, as well as madness in art."

"And magic in madness, as well as madness in magic."

"Presumably. But the point is that if the boys came under Eirene's influence, however slightly, that influence might well have been benign. More so than mine, at any rate."

She could have suggested that I was underestimating myself again, but she wasn't in a flattering mood.

"I've sent a message to Tommaso agreeing to his requests," she said. "I proposed that I send a boat to collect him at daybreak tomorrow, and I told him that I would request that you meet him, in accordance with his wish, and make arrangements to see his niece, but that it would be a matter for your decision. His reply should reach me very soon, and I shall then be able to send a further message confirming your agreement. I've proposed that you meet him in one of the inns on the waterfront of the harbor, but I can change that venue if you wish in my next communication. Is there anything you would like me to add?"

"Will he come alone and unarmed?"

"Of course. I've given him a guarantee of safe conduct, which I fully intend to honor."

"Do you have any objection to his coming to the house to see Elise—assuming, that is, that Elise is willing? I assume that she'll not only be willing but eager, although I'll have to check that. Mariette will almost certainly want to be present, though."

"That's perfectly agreeable to me. In that case, do you have any objection to my coming to the house to meet him, once he's had a chance to talk to Elise? It might me more comfortable for both of us not to meet here. What will happen thereafter, of course, depends on the specific proposals he makes. That's when complications will inevitably set in…and perhaps conflicts."

"But he'll hardly be in a situation to make demands," I pointed out. "Even if his steamer is armed and carrying soldiers, he'll only require one glimpse of your Sileni to persuade him that he has no possibility of using force."

"My earnest hope is that any conflicts of interest that might arrive can be settled without any threat of the present or future use of force," she said. "Even if we can't reach an agreement, I'd like him to go away satisfied that we mean him no harm."

"And if he wants to take Elise away?"

"That's up to Elise and Marianne…and you. If she wants to go with him and he wants to take her, I won't interfere. Helen really did bring her because she thought she was in danger. Do you think she was wrong?"

"Perhaps not," I conceded. "I thought I wasn't in any danger until I was actually stabbed. Once that had happened, I was frightened myself that I might have made a mistake in telling Elise that the Marquise couldn't possibly want to hurt her. Given what you've just told me, though, it might have been a mistake to leave Parenot behind."

"Perhaps," she agreed. "But there were questions of practicality as well as the detail of the instructions given in advance. Helen did what she thought best..."

She broke off because she had been interrupted. The message whose imminent arrival she had just announced had arrived, brought in by a Silenus. Madame read it. She didn't show it to me, but she nodded in satisfaction.

"Everything is agreed so far," she said. "When I receive a reply to my reply, everything will be settled. I'll write it now. Will you wait for a few minutes?"

"I'd rather relay the information to Elise and Mariette," I said. "I don't think they'll raise any objection, but if they do, you'll need to know about it quickly. If you have any further instructions...."

"I haven't given you any instructions," she interjected. "I have no intention of doing so. You're free to act as you see fit. We really are on the same side."

She was probably right. I certainly wasn't about to contract her. The sun was already setting, and twilight didn't last long in the latitude of the island, I didn't want to have to go down the hill in the dark, although the path was safe enough, and was even fitted with lanterns at intervals, which the Sileni were careful to light.

VI. Tommaso Dellacrusca's Proposals

I was up bright and early, although I knew that the
boat that would fetch Tommaso to the island wouldn't
be able to make the two-way journey until the sun was
high in the sky. I hadn't had much sleep, mostly because
Mariette hadn't been able to sleep at all. She was the
only one who seemed frightened; Elise, as I had anticipated, was both excited and intrigued by the prospect of
a visit from her uncle—an uncle who had only spoken to
her once, with the utmost politeness and charm. She
wasn't afraid at all, all the more so because I had empha-
sized the fact that it would be entirely up to her to decide
what she wanted to do as a result of her conversation
with her uncle, if anything. Not unnaturally, that assertion hadn't reassured Mariette, but had merely added to
her anxiety.

Equally naturally, Mariette had bombarded me with
a thousand questions, hardly any of which I could answer, at least until I had seen Tommaso and had some
idea of why he had come and what he wanted.

The tavern in which I was to meet him seemed eerie
in its emptiness. Apart from a single waitress there was
not a human to be seen, although there were Sileni posted at the door and others within earshot distributed
around the harbor, where the usually daily activity was
distinctly muted.

I sat down at a table in the middle of the room,
which would normally have had others close by but
around which an eccentric *cordon sanitaire* had now
been contrived. I had a bottle of wine uncorked and two
glasses placed on the table, and I waited. I had turned up

early enough to become distinctly fidgety, but I refrained from pouring myself a glass of wine, thinking that it might be as well to keep a scrupulously clear head.

Eventually, he came in, abandoned by his escort at the door. Inevitably, he took a long look at the stony faced Sileni before coming to take his seat, but he didn't make any comment on them. He was dressed in the conventional fashion of the young Empire aristocracy, but wore the black jacket, frilled shirt and red cravat with elegance and authority. Many of the young men who strutted around Mnemosyne during the summer season looked like fools and fops putting on an act, but Tommaso seemed born to the role—as, indeed, he had been, although no one would have been able to tell three years before. It struck me for the first time that he was an exceptionally handsome young man, and that his newfound aristocratic attitude set off that masculine beauty perfectly.

I only hoped that Elise didn't fall head over heels in love with him at second glance.

"Thank you for agreeing to meet me, Master Rathenius," he said, while I filled his glass and mine. "I must confess that I find your presence quite reassuring. I really didn't know what kind of reception I was going to get, and the sight of the hairy fellows in the square outside didn't reassure me at all. Satyrs?"

"Sileni," I told him, but didn't pause to explain the difference. "You're perfectly safe here, Tommaso. No one has the slightest intention of harming you."

He smiled, faintly, and then said: "You have no reason at all to trust me, Master Rathenius after…you know when…but believe me, a lot of water has flowed under the bridge since then. My world has been turned upside-down, and yours too, I think. I would really appreciate it if we could make a fresh start."

I nodded, making no promises.

Then, without any forewarning, the surprises began. He took a sealed envelope out of the inside pocket of his impeccable jacket. "First of all," he said, "I've been asked to give you this. You might not be able to believe me, but for what it's worth, I swear that I haven't had it opened, and I don't know what it contains. It's from Hecate Rain."

I suppressed my amazement and unsealed the envelope. I took out the single sheet of paper within it and opened it, in such a fashion that Tommaso couldn't read it. He made no attempt to do so, ostentatiously. There was an exceedingly short handwritten message on the page, which read:

Axel. It is absolutely imperative that you return as soon as possible. Remember the dark petals fallen into the pool of Mnemosyne. Hecate.

I had not an atom of doubt about the note's authenticity, not because of the handwriting, which could have been forged, but because of the second sentence of the missive: a line from a poem that, so far as I knew, I was the only person ever to have heard recited. I was certainly the only person to whom its meaning had ever been explained. I assumed that it was there purely and simply to provide a guarantee of authenticity. As for the rest of the message, all the terms of endearment that were conspicuously missing from it were presumably absent in order to emphasize the utter seriousness of the instruction.

I folded the note up and put it away inside my own jacket.

"You've been to Mnemosyne," I observed.

"Yes—incognito, this time. It's not a safe place for me any longer. I had accumulated news of you from various sources, and while I was there I wanted to pass on reassurances to some of your friends, as a gesture of goodwill—needlessly, as it turned out. Your man Jean-Jacques had already received a copious letter, and so had Hecate. I couldn't reach Charles Parenot. You know why, I presume?"

"I've heard a rumor," I said.

"It's true. The Marquise has commissioned him to work on a painting in her house. I don't know any more than that for sure. If Hecate knows what's going on between the two of them, she wasn't about to tell me, any more than your man Jean-Jacques was willing to give me any information, although I suspect that he's a better spy than any of mine, on his home ground. There are some who think that Hecate is working with the Marquise on conjurations of some kind, as Vashti Savage seems to be, but the one thing Jean-Jacques was prepared to say to me, insistently, was that I shouldn't believe any gossip I heard about her. She'd been to see him too, to give him news and collect it. He insisted that she would never betray you. I believed him...but if he's right, she might be playing a dangerous game. She's been spending time in the Convent of Shalimar, and relations are very strained at the moment between the superior and the Marquise. She might simply be trying to smooth things over between the two of them, but I don't think so. Something is going on. Maybe you know more about it than I do now."

He nodded in the direction of my jacket pocket, although he must have known, even though he couldn't read it, that the note he'd brought me was terse in the extreme.

I nodded again, and waited. He was hesitating, although he had obviously come with a plan, and a script.

"I know that it was you," he said, simply, when the hesitation had finally run its course.

"What was me?" I asked.

"It was you who stopped me killing the Marquise on the night when your picture sang. Most of the people there, my men as well as hers, thought it was a trick on the part of the Marquise, but I knew. So did Hecate Rain. Nobody else heard it, I don't think, but I heard her say "Adieu," and I knew that she was saying it to you. But I'd have known anyway, because of the dream."

"Dream?" I echoed, mystified.

"It's a long story. I'll tell you—but first, you knew, didn't you, what Lorenzo and I went to do that night? We were outnumbered, although not to the extent that we were on the night when my father was killed, but we didn't care. We were prepared to die, if that was what it took. There was a debt to be paid, and we had a list, by then, of the people who needed to pay it. Every one of them was in the room—including the second assassin that she sent after you, by the way. We intended to kill every last one, no matter what the cost. I was supposed to take out the Marquise. You knew that, didn't you?"

"Not exactly," I told him, "but Madame knew that there was a mortal danger, and she wanted to stop it. She used the portrait, and me, to work some kind of spell. I don't understand what happened, or how, but yes, somehow, in spirit, I was there."

He nodded, as if he had needed conformation of that, and was relieved to have it, in order to remove a stubborn residue of doubt.

"What dream?" I asked, again.

"I dreamed the night before that I saw you. I dreamed that you told me not to do it, that there was a better way than murder. I didn't know at the time that it was *the* dream...I thought it was just any old dream, just the product of ordinary anxiety. But when the picture started singing, and I knew you were there, I knew that it was *the* dream—the one I'd been told to expect, years before."

"By Eirene Magdelana?" I had no difficulty guessing.

A cloud of suspicion passed over his face. "How do you know that?"

"I learned yesterday that Madame's spies had reported that you and Lorenzo went up Snowspur to see her every year. It was news to me, but things are beginning to add up now. I'm amazed, though, that she told you years ago that you would one day have a dream about me."

"She didn't. I had no idea when she told us about the dream that it would involve you, and I don't think she did either. She just told us that they would come a time, at a moment of crisis in our lives, when we would have a meaningful dream, in which the unconscious part of our mind would communicate something to our consciousness, using as a mouthpiece someone we thought that we could trust, and that if we were wise, we would attend to what the message said. I didn't talk to Lorenzo about the dream until afterwards, but when I told him, he confirmed that he'd had the same dream, I'd never really believed until then that the old woman really could see the future—and even then, I suppose, it wasn't really seeing the future...because she'd told us that was impossible...but anyway I'd never really believed she could do anything magical, until then. But I believe now, and I'm truly sorry that she's dead."

"So am I," I murmured.

"The first time we met her," Tommaso said, "we just wanted to climb the mountain—not that it was really climbing, even for a couple of kids; just a long uphill walk, really, but tiring. Anyway, she found us, and talked to us—that was rare, you know. We were treated like lepers, and we didn't understand why. It was only years later that we realized that it was because people thought that our father was the devil incarnate...but that's old news, and you probably remember and understand better than we do how we reacted to the way people treated us. But the old woman didn't look at us that way. She told us that we were special because we were identical twins, that we had a shared soul, and that as long as we stuck together, and never betrayed one another, we'd always have twice the strength of any single soul.

"Looking back, I suppose that it was mostly just flattery, but it wasn't all nonsense, and she really believed that there was something to it. We couldn't understand most of what she said, which I now suspect is because much of it was incoherent, but what we did understand, we took aboard, She told us that she could teach us how to educate our dreams, how to make use of them. While we were children, she said, that would only help us to make them more pleasant, and help us to laugh at nightmares, but that if we stuck at it, when we were adults, it would become useful to us, because while our conscious minds were learning about the world by means of our senses, out unconscious minds were learning too, by what she called morpheomorphic resonance.

"We didn't understand the jargon, obviously, but we got the gist of the argument…and we really did learn, over the years, to generate pleasant dreams and laugh at nightmares. But she told us that there would eventually come a time, probably at critical turning point in our lives—the death of our father was one of the examples she cited—when our conscious minds would be in turmoil. At that point, she said, our unconscious minds would have a better understanding of the situation we were in than our waking minds could grasp, and that it would be able to make its understanding clear to us, by using the image of someone we thought trustworthy to tell us something that we needed to know, in order to save us from danger. The unconscious mind couldn't predict the future, she said, because the future was unmade and unfixed, but it could sense ominous possibilities, and offer warnings, which we'd be wise to follow.

"So, when I dreamed about you the night before we had decided to risk everything in order to obtain our vengeance, I didn't immediately realize that it was that sort of dream—but when I did realize, I knew, and I knew that what you'd said in the dream had to be true: that there was a better way than murder, and that I should wait. So I gave the signal to abort the plan, and Lorenzo knew immediately that something had happened. We withdrew.

"The Marquise thought she'd won, that we were giving in. But you were right. Since that night, we've found out a great many things that we didn't know then. In fact, we've found out more about our father in the last few weeks than we ever found out in all those years of living with him…or, at any rate, living in his house. He left us quite a legacy, although it took some finding, and it's going to take an awful lot of work to figure out how to use all the information profitably. It won't be easy, but I really do think that he's left us everything we need to take up the reins of his operation, if we're clever and careful, and to crush any opposition that presents itself, without having to commit suicide in the process."

He finally paused, and waited for a reaction. All I could think of to say, for the moment, was: "You trust me?"

He shrugged his shoulders. "I told you that before," he said. "You were the only person in island of Lutecian society who ever treated Lory and me half-way decently. There were times when you could have ratted us out, and didn't. You don't imagine, I suppose, that I could have dreamed about my father instead?"

On reflection, I didn't suppose he could.

"Well," I said, "I'm glad things have worked out for you—and glad, too, that I played my part, however un-wittingly in preventing a bloodbath. And now, I suppose, you want me to act as an intermediary between you and Madame, in the hope of forging some kind of alliance?"

"If that can be done, I'd be glad of it—but I'm not sure I could possibly trust her, given the history I've recently been studying with an intensity of which I'd never thought myself capable. I'll enter negotiations with her, obviously, but I'll be treading exceedingly carefully. No, that's not why I came, and not why I wanted to see you."

"It *is* because of Elise, then," I said, congratulating myself on my superior judgment—a trifle prematurely.

"Partly. I certainly want to talk to her, and discuss the best way to prepare for her future—but that's really up to her. I certainly wouldn't be happy, now, to return her to Parenot's custody, but rumor has it that Parenot's out of the picture anyway, and that you're now her guardian. If she's happy with that, then I'm certainly happy. If not, I'll be pleased to make whatever alternative arrangements we can both feel comfortable with. But there is one awkward complication, which is the real reason I'm here."

"Which is?" I said, warily.

"I'd like you to return to Mnemosyne, with or without Elise."

I felt an inevitable twinge of suspicion regarding the letter from Hecate, suspecting some collusion, but I suppressed it.

"Why?" I said.

"Because the one other person who knows for certain that it was you who worked the magic the night the Orpheus sang is the Marquise. She was already scared of you, which is why she tried to have you murdered, and the fact that you escaped with not much more than a scratch, and then disappeared, along with Elise, frightened her even more. When the picture sang...no matter how successful she was in convincing others that hers was the sorcery powerful enough to contrive that, she knows that it wasn't. She knows—or at least believes—that there's at least one sorcerer in the world more powerful than she is, and fully capable of scotching her schemes: you."

"I'm not a sorcerer, Tommaso. I was there, it's true, but I was just an instrument."

"Hecate said that you'd say that. She said that you probably believe it, that you simply won't admit to yourself that you're a sorcerer."

"Hecate said that, did she?" I said, dryly. It was easy to believe. I couldn't even hold it against her

"She says that you don't even believe that you're immortal, although you must be at least a hundred years old, and perhaps twice that. The best estimate that my agents have been able to make, after tracking your movements before you arrived on Mnemosyne, is a couple of years short of a hundred and thirty, but let's not quibble—the point is that you're a hell of a lot older than you look."

"I'm not immortal, Tommaso," I told him, keeping my voice quite level. "I stopped aging, it's true, some time in my late forties, but I could start against any time…and the only reason I escaped the Marquise's assassins is that one of Madame's agents was watching me, and got to me just in time to prevent me from sustaining a fatal wound. I could die tomorrow from a knife in the back, or a fall downstairs, as easily as the next man. And I'm not a sorcerer."

"I don't have to believe that you are," said Tommaso, very reasonably. "I just need the Marquise to believe that you are. She does."

"And you think that my mere presence on Mnemosyne will scare her to death?"

"Of course not. That's not the point."

"What is the point?"

"The point is that there's a very delicate balance now in the struggle between us for control of the cult. If we could take a roll call of her supporters and ours, we'd probably find that the numbers are now approximately equal, although she and Alectryon have total control on Mnemosyne, and we probably have a slight advantage in Lutèce at present. The real issue is the fragility of the support on either side. It's brittle, and a single fracture or defection could start a chain reaction that could tip the balance abruptly and catastrophically. Lory and I have the power of father's blackmail library on our side, but she has hocus pocus and Alectryon on hers.

"When I say that, I don't mean that I believe that she's a real magician, but even if she is, I've seen with my own eyes that you're better. It seems to me, though, that it doesn't matter much if you're both charlatans, and it might be more convenient if you are. The point is that the glue that's holding her cabal together is her followers' belief that she really can do magic. That's partly based on the mistaken belief that she worked the tricks on the evening of the unveiling, but it's shored up by that fact that she has a free hand to keep on working supposed magic in circumstances where she can organize her own trickery, with regard to Vashti Savage's séances and the like, and make claims that are difficult to check. That will change if she has to face a real challenge: if circumstances force her to bring her magic to bear with all her supposed might…and she fails. If that happens, her support will melt away like snow in a heat wave, and it's possible that Lory and I might be able to take over the entire organization without a shot being fired. A better way than murder, as you put it in my dream. I need you there to provide that challenge, to force her hand."

"In brief," I said, "You want me to be a target."

"No, I want *her* to be the target—but you won't have to fire a shot. You just have to take aim."

"And what happens if whatever magic spell she launches against me actually works?"

"It won't. As I say, even if her act isn't all mumbo jumbo, yours is better. It was you, not her, who made the painting sing. I know it, and you know it. So there's nothing to be afraid of, is there?"

"And what if I don't want to take the risk?"

.

98

"Then we'll have to go back to the original plan: armed assault. Blood everywhere, perhaps including ours. But you won't chicken out, because you want the better way as much as we do, and you know, even though you're probably the only person in the world who does, that our reputation for evil malevolence is misleading. You know what we're really like."

The naivety of it all was astounding, and so was the presumption—but it was also rather touching, in a way...and not fundamentally inaccurate.

"And how do you propose that I go about issuing a challenge to her that she'll have to meet...in some other way than just paying a handful of hired maenads to come after me with daggers?"

"She won't do that. Everyone will know that it's a test of her magic, and you can make it obvious easily enough."

"Can I?"

"Yes. It's up to you, obviously, but I have thought of a plan, just in case. I think you ought to you to paint her...and to let it be known far and wide that you're painting her. She'll believe that you intend to use the painting in question to hurt her, by magic, mentally and physically. I don't suppose for a moment that that would scare her to death, but I think it might very well drive her mad, since she's already half way there, and I'm certain that it would distract her attention away from her quiet war of attrition with us, and very probably—*very* probably—lead to her losing all her authority over the other members of her jittery cabal. We can make our own contribution to that, by applying our own pressure to the house of cards. But you need to be there in order for the pressure to be effective. It's a matter of show-manship, you see. But that's always been your forte—

and even though you're not an Italian, you do understand the concepts of vendetta and poetic justice, don't you?"

I was stunned. "You and Hecate cooked up that scheme up between you?" I queried, hardly able to believe it.

He frowned. "Hecate had nothing to do with it," he said. "Lorenzo and I cooked it up, just between the two of us. We thought it would appeal to you."

"Come off it," I said, taking the folded letter out of my pocket and showing it to him. "She's come clean."

Tommaso took the piece of paper from my hand, opened it, and read the letter. Either he was genuinely surprised, or he was putting on a good act—but I knew that he was capable of that.

"I've no idea what this means," he said. "What pool? What petals? And why would petals in a pool make it imperative for you to come back to Mnemosyne? I swear that I didn't breathe a word to her about our plan—I didn't dare, in case it got back to the Marquise. To me, this message sounds more like Eirene Magdelana or Vashti Savage than Hecate Rain. I honestly hadn't read it, and it's nothing to do with me. Whatever reason she had for asking me to give it to you, it was entirely her own."

I looked at him long and hard, and eventually decided that I had no reason not to believe him. If he had cooked up his bizarre plan in collaboration with Hecate, there was no reason why he shouldn't simply say so.

So why, I wondered, did Hecate think that it was *absolutely imperative* that I return?

"But still," I said, "if I do go back with you, I might be in danger."

"I'm not saying that there's no risk at all," he said, "but the thing to remember is that she really does believe that you're a sorcerer, and she's certainly not the only one. It would take a brave man to try to kill you, after what happened last time. Anyway, do you really think that you're safe here? She knows where you are too, by now. Maybe there is more risk in confronting her at close range—but I don't think you're a coward, Master Rathenius. I know you didn't run away after you'd been stabbed. You had to be drugged and carried out of the Sprite unconscious. Do you remember how the townspeople reacted when they knew you were under threat? If you go back, you'll be a hero. Stand up to the wicked witch, and you'll have the entire proletariat of the island behind you. They wouldn't get behind the Dellacrusca twins in a thousand years, but you're a living legend now. Mnemosyne is where you belong, Master Rathenius—and that's not just my opinion. You might have been hounded out of places in the past under suspicion of being a sorcerer, but times have changed, and so have circumstances. If my plan works, and the Marquise comes unstuck, they'll probably carry you through the streets in triumph. I don't know what *this* means"—he handed Hecate's letter back to me—"but she's right. It *is* imperative that you go back, as soon as possible. And I just happen to have a fast steamer a couple of hours away by rowboat."

I stared at the letter. His plan, I knew, was simply grotesque—a magnified version of the idiot pranks that he and his brother used to play as children, and by which I'd been foolish enough to be amused. But Hecate's letter was something else. If it was genuine—and I couldn't doubt that it was—then it was serious. Hecate was a poet, with a poetic turn of mind, but she was no fool.

Tommaso could see that I was thinking about it, but he probably had no doubt as to the conclusion I'd eventually reach.

"Which pool does she mean?" he asked, curiously. "Mnemosyne's got hundreds of them, inland and along the shore."

"It isn't a pool on the island," I said, absent-mindedly. "It's a reference to the mythical pool of Mnemosyne."

"Don't know it," he said. "The mythical Mnemosyne was the mother of the Muses, wasn't she? That's probably why some wit took it into his head to found an artists' colony on the island, way back when."

I doubted that, but didn't want to debate the point. "Mnemosyne means memory," I told him. "The mythical Mnemosyne had a pool in Hades: the pool of memory. The ancient Greeks believed that souls drank from the River Lethe—the river of forgetfulness—before being reincarnated, so that they could start again with a clean slate. But the rare few who could drink instead from the pool of Mnemosyne were able to carry their memories of the previous life forward into the next one, sometimes straightforwardly and sometimes cryptically encoded, thus equipping themselves to be great sages, or great poets...or great madmen. The reference is only in the letter to prove its authenticity, though. Hecate once improvised a poem in my presence, in which dark petals falling into the pool of Mnemosyne could confuse and corrupt the process of memory transfer from life to life. She imagined herself at the time as the victim of some such confusion...she was subject to occasional dark moods. I helped her through more than one. It was a poem she never published, but she knew that I'd remember it."

"Oh," he said. "You mean that she took it for granted that I couldn't be trusted—that if she didn't take some such precaution, you'd automatically assume that I'd had the letter faked?"

"Don't take it personally," I said. "The point is that she wanted me to be sure that the letter was from her because she wanted to me sure that she meant what she said. But why, if she isn't party to your crazy scheme, does she think that it's imperative that I return?"

"I have no idea," he said, "unless it's simply a matter of great minds thinking alike. Maybe she came up with my idea independently as a way of defeating the Marquise."

I didn't laugh, although the notion was ludicrous, even assuming that Hecate wanted the Marquise defeated. I put the letter away again.

"Time's getting on," I said. "Mariette should be waiting outside by now, with a escort of Sileni. She'll take you to the house to see Elise."

"You're not coming?"

"I'll be there a little later. There's something I have to do first."

"Give Madame Minerva a report of this conversation, you mean?"

"Yes. Have you any objection?"

"No. But you are a free agent, I suppose? You can make your own decision as to whether to go back with me."

"Of course. But I do need to discuss it first—and not just with Madame."

"Naturally. Parenot's a complicating factor, I suppose—a loose cannon. It might be better for Elise and her mother to stay here…just for a while. But that's up to them, and you." He paused, and then said: "How is she?"

"Adorable," I said curtly, "but with more than a hint of Dellacrusca steel about her. Your father would have been very proud of her, and rightly so...but that wouldn't have stopped him ruining her completely."

"He didn't ruin us," said Tommaso, perhaps assuming a little too much, "but I suppose it wasn't for lack of trying. If there hadn't been two of us...well, no matter. Thank you again for listening, Master Rathenius...whatever you decide to do."

He said it like a man who had every confidence that I would make the decision he wanted me to make. He thought I'd have done that anyway, even without Hecate's letter. Perhaps he was right. I had always had something of the showman about me. On the other hand, I had once sworn to myself that I would never use my art as Claudius Jaseph once had, in a manner that drove his sitters mad, and what Tommaso was asking me to do seemed suspiciously similar to that.

Then again, I couldn't help thinking, Claudius Jaseph had succeeded, either by virtue of art or magic— and if a second-rater like him could steal a sitter's soul, what might not a genius like me achieve, if he brought his full artistry to bear?

Immediately, though, I knew that that was stupid vanity talking—and a vanity that was no longer unassailable, as it once might have been. Claudius Jaseph had painted from life; somehow I doubted that the same intensity could be achieved painting from memory. I doubted that the Marquise de Mesmay would actually consent to sit for a portrait, even if I had the audacity to turn up at the manse and request the privilege. I could see the logic of the twins' notion, but there had to be a better way; if I took on the role he wanted me to take, I'd need a better plan of campaign.

Then I remembered that, at present, I didn't even seem to be capable of producing an adequate representation of a sitter. And suddenly, Elise's hypothesis that she and I were the victims of some kind of distant magic seemed even more ominous...and if, there really were a competent art of magic, far more probable.

Perhaps the Marquise de Mesmay hadn't waited for me to issue a challenge; perhaps she'd already attempted a pre-emptive strike...which had worked.

You bitch! I thought, with a twinge of reflexive wrath, that I had not felt when I believed that she had only hired two thugs to cut my throat. Bloodshed was one thing; attacking my soul was another. *If that's the kind of war you want, my dear, you can have it!*

VII. Mariette's Anxieties

When I got to the house, having left Madame in her palace on the hill to gather a few materials before following me down, Mariette was there on her own. Elise had wanted to speak to Tommaso alone, and had taken him for a walk on the headland, albeit under the watchful eyes of the Sileni,

"She'll be fine," I assured her, glad to be able to muster confidence on that subject, at least.

"I know that," Mariette replied. "I'm just upset because she excluded me with such casual ease—and it felt as though she wasn't just banishing me from her presence. I'm no longer family, it seems. I've been replaced by a popinjay."

"Of course you're still family," I said. "It's precisely because you're her real mother that there are things she feels that she can't say in front of you. It's not unusual, believe me. If you knew how many girls her age have told me things while I was painting them that they would never have been able to say in front of their mothers..."

That was careless of me; I should have known that she'd take it the wrong way.

"They probably wanted to screw you too," she snapped, "And probably succeeded, even if you were already screwing their mothers. Esp—"

"Leave it there, Mariette, I beg you," I said. "It's nothing of the sort. Elise is confused about a lot of things, with good reason. It helps for her to be able to ask questions, and not just of me. Even if no one can answer them, making enquiries helps her to sort things out in her mind. Believe me, she isn't trying to seduce me—or vice versa."

"And can you say the same for that young rake?"

"She's his sister's daughter, his father's grand-child."

"And you think that makes a difference."

"Yes, I do. Anyway, Tommaso doesn't want to take her away. He just wants to make sure that she's safe and reasonably content—and to help her to arrange a future for herself, when the current ferment in the Empire has settled."

"And you honestly think that she'll consent to stay here if you leave? Even if she's sailing into danger on a ship crewed by murderers?"

"Why not?" I said. "If you're here..."

Again, I should have known that she'd take it the wrong way. And she did—but this time, she stopped herself. She didn't accuse me of waiting to leave her already. Instead, she made a strenuous effort, and reverted to her old self—the self I'd seen on Mnemosyne; the self to which I had been magnetically attracted, and still was. She looked at me, and suddenly, she was all beauty, just like her portrait: the way I wanted to see her, as Elise had shrewdly observed, and the way she wanted to see herself.

Such was my state of mind that my imagination immediately began to run away. If Elise and I really were the victim of malevolent magic, implausible as it seemed—and I had to admit that it seemed less implausible now that I'd referred the matter to Madame for a second time, and had seen her, once again, prepared to take it seriously—than Mariette would certainly have been included in the curse too. Was it true that the recent exaggeration of her innate tendency to jealousy wasn't

107

entirely her own fault? And if so, was the fact that she had just made an effort to suppress it evidence that the curse was so weak that it had only been able to obtain any purchase at all by taking us by surprise?

"I'm sorry, Axel," she said, "I'm being silly. It's just that...I've been out of sorts, unbalanced, and new things keep coming along to unsettle me further. Why didn't you tell me last night that Charles is screwing the Marquise de Mesmay?"

I must have been looking at her intently, seeing her the way that I wanted to see her while wondering, uneasily, whether it might really be possible that she was under invisible assault, and might really be repelling it. Responding to the question provided a distraction of sorts.

"We don't know that he is," I told her, firmly. "We don't know anything—not even what kind of picture she's commissioned from him."

"Well, it won't be a picture of me, will it?"

"Probably not," I agreed, hoping that she was right...and unable to help hoping, reflexively, that Elise and I were not included, if it were. "She's already got one of those."

"As Eurydice—safely in Hades."

My mouth grabbed hold of my thoughts—thoughts that it might have been better to suppress, or at least keep quiet. "It's more likely a picture of me," I suggested, "if the Marquise thinks along the same lines as Tommaso and Lorenzo, and wants to use it as a magical target." I tried to make it sound like a joke, but couldn't. Continuing the attempt, I added: "But portraits of middle-aged artists aren't Charles' forte, are they?"

"Mythological symbolism wasn't yours," she pointed out. "You adapted—very well, it seems."

"Artistically speaking," I agreed, wondering now whether I could really claim the credit for it. When I had obtained the belated spark of imagination that had given me the key to the triptych, that the inspiration—the magic, if it were possible to believe in magic in that instance—it had appeared to come from outside, if not from Orpheus himself, or from Dionysus Zagreus, then from some more numinous and mysterious source, with which, according to Eirene Magdelana and the doctrine of morpheomorphism, the unconscious mind can sometimes resonate.

"But it wasn't just a painting, was it?" said Mariette. She had been initiated into the Cult of Dionysus alongside me. She had been a part of Madame's summoning. She had some notion of what had happened during the bacchanal. Even before that, while I was still working on the triptych, she had probably been aware that more than just a painting.

"If only you'd arrived on Mnemosyne in time to deflect my attention," I muttered, "I could have painted you and Elise instead accepting Mesmay's commission."

"And the Marquise could have commissioned Charles to paint the Orpheus," she observed. "Could he have done it as effectively, do you think?"

My reflexive vanity wanted to say no, but I was well aware that she's used the word *effectively* deliberately. And that was the key question, at the heart of the matter. I was a better portraitist than Charles Parenot, but I had been a better portraitist than Claudius Jaseph, too, and that hadn't made his secret exhibition any less pernicious, as black magic. His dark dreams, too, had found a resonance, and a force: a force that he couldn't control, and which had sowed dire distress in all directions, but a force nevertheless summoned by his art.

When I didn't answer, Mariette went on: "What *should* have happened, in a sane world, is that Dellacrusca ought to have told us who Elise was the moment he saw her viola, and taken her away from us in Lutèce, whether politely or brutally, without going about things in such a bizarre roundabout way."

She was right, of course, but Dellacrusca hadn't been insane in any real sense. He had simply had a niggling obsession, tiny in itself, but which had been gnawing away in his soul for years: a vendetta. It hadn't been enough for him to find his granddaughter; in a sense, that hadn't been the real issue at all. He had still required some kind of vengeance—purely symbolic, given that the artist he considered to be responsible for his loss was long dead. I had been a substitute for poor Almeras, now beyond his reach, whose murder had not slaked his thirst. *That* aspect of his scheme had been utterly insane, in spite of the fact that he was, in all other matters, a monster of cynical calculation.

Tommaso, it seemed, was his father's son. But was I, deep down, any different? Was anyone, I wondered? Didn't we all have those bruised seeds of obsession, waiting to germinate into bizarre designs and moments of sheer madness? Could I claim that my own excrescences of that sort had always been benign?

I made an effort to concentrate on the conversation, which seemed a lot safer, as well as saner, than my runaway thoughts. "If Dellacrusca had reclaimed Elise in Lutèce, you and I would never have met," I pointed out, "and you'd still be with Charles.

"You and I might never have met," she conceded. "But as to the other…that's a different matter. Without Elise to hold us together…"

"But you did love him," I reminded her, "and he loved you."

"Oh yes," she said. "But hasn't Elise told you that it was the wrong kind of love? She's too clever for her own good, sometimes. In the beginning it was...well, you might call it convenience, but it was more like desperation even then. You've seen at least one of his paintings of me—the Eurydice. If that painting and the portrait you've just painted were set side by side, it would be obvious to anyone looking that they were pictures of the same face, one a few years older—but anyone with an artist's eye would be able to see that they'd been painted with different kinds of lust."

Or, as Elise might put it, the way I had wanted to see her was not the same as the way that Charles Parenot had wanted to see her. Mariette hadn't used the word *lust* instead of the word *love* by accident. She didn't believe that either of us loved her in the way she wanted to be loved. And she was right. I wasn't sure that either of us was capable of that kind of love...or that anyone was. Perhaps Helen was right, and there was no such animal as a trustworthy man, but merely a few possessed of a slight spark of decency.

"You don't have any regrets about the separation from Charles, then?" I queried.

"Few enough to be ashamed of not having more," she said, with a sigh. "It would have been far more difficult if we'd had to go through the painful business of tearing ourselves apart, when the time came. That's not a problem you have, I gather?"

I contrived a hollow laugh. "I've been working on it for a hundred years," I said. "Harder, since I realized the necessity forced upon me by my longevity. I can't say that I've mastered it yet." Unbidden, my right hand touched my torso, not above the heart but above the pocket where Hecate's letter was still tucked away.

She nodded her head—not because she thought she understood, but merely in recognition of the fact that there was a problem. She was still thinking about herself, and anticipating the day when, as she saw it, I would cast her aside and move on to my next object of temporary passion. She was by no means the first woman I had ever known who had allowed that kind of anticipation of the future to corrupt her enjoyment of the present.

"You know," she said, thoughtfully, "on the first day we spent here, when you went for that long walk with Madame, I was sure that you were going to…paint her instead of me. I only had the vaguest idea of what you both are, but I couldn't help thinking that you were made for one another…that she was the only kind of woman that you could really love."

I ought to have been able to contrive another hollow laugh, but I couldn't. I simply said: "It doesn't work like that, Mariette. Even I know that, and she's had a further nineteen hundred years to absorb the lesson. The real trick must be learning to love the ephemeral, to value and appreciate the moment to the full, no matter how fleeting. But knowing what the necessity is, and adapting your feelings to it, are very different things. And if I did become the kind of person who could simply move on, and on, and on, without pain or regret…I'm not all at sure that I could admire myself for it."

I didn't add that in my darker moments, I couldn't admire what I actually was, either. There are some thoughts that can't be voiced to anyone, although they can sometimes be committed to uncaring paper.

"But if she had…commissioned you to paint her...,'" Mariette began, and then stopped, manifestly abandoning the thought, so that I didn't have to remind her that euphemism has its limits, and that I'd painted literally hundreds of women without ever doing anything but painting them, whether on my own inspiration or in response to a commission…or even a command.

With a visible wrench, she redirected her train of thought. "If Elise insists on going back with you," she said, "as I'm sure she will, I'll go gladly. I can face Charles...and any danger the Marquise de Mesmay might pose."

"You seem to be as sure as Tommaso is that I will go back," I observed. "Wouldn't you rather we all stayed here? You could demand that, after all."

She didn't bother to contrive a hollow laugh, or even raise an eyebrow. "The boy told us about the letter from Hecate Rain. He didn't seem to think that it was particularly important, but I knew that you would. I'm sure that you could turn down his crazy scheme with consummate ease, if you wanted to, but Hecate's appeal is something else. I can't pretend to understand what there is between the two of you, but if I were the jealous type..." She laughed at herself then, even though she knew that it wasn't funny.

"It's not personal," I said, pensively. "The summons to return, that is. If it were just a matter of personal feelings, she'd want me to stay here, out of harm's way, no matter how much she might be missing me. It's something else. Hecate doesn't use phrases like *absolutely imperative* lightly. She's not that kind of poet."

"But you have no idea what it might be?"

"None," I said, half-truthfully. "I asked Madame whether she had any clue, but her spies haven't sent back anything that offers a substantial hint."

She detected the half-truth. Unlike Elise, though, she didn't think that she had any right to demand complete honesty from me. She simply said: "Why didn't Hecate simply tell you straight out what the reason is?"

"Because she was afraid that the letter might be read. She didn't trust Tommaso—understandably. She probably doesn't trust Madame either...again, understandably. In fact, she probably feels that there isn't anyone she can trust, even the Sisters of Shalimar, in spite of their common loyalty to the great Bardic tradition...which must be an uncomfortable situation for her."

"And from which you feel obliged to rescue her? I've seen your reflexes in action, remember. Don't worry, though; I know that if you hadn't managed to get Charles to his feet and hurl him into the fray, you'd have carried them both back by yourself. Elise knows that too. She thinks that it was you who saved her life, not Charles."

"That's a trifle unfair," I said. "He only needed a shove because he hadn't realized what was happening. If the positions had been reversed he'd have been the one shoving me." That was less than half a truth, though, and she knew it.

"That couldn't have happened. I can't imagine Charles running into gunfire willingly, even to save Elise...let alone me."

"Well, perhaps he's not such a reckless fool as I am," I suggested. "It was just a reflex action."

"I was admiring the reflex action," she said, deliberately echoing Hecate, on the night in question. I was

114

glad to see the flash of humor, even though it was a trifle sardonic—but she hadn't forgotten that I was being deliberately economical with my presumptions. "You do have some idea why Hecate wrote that note, don't you?" he said. "I wish you thought that you could trust me enough to tell me the truth."

Perhaps there was a little of Mariette in Elise too, as well as a hint of Dellacrusca.

"It's pure conjecture," I said, defensively.

"I still wish you'd tell me," she said. "I'm involved, after all…even if only temporarily."

She was more involved than she probably knew, or imagined.

"Hecate and I are very different, in some ways," I told her. "I used to think that our affection was a kind of attraction of opposites, but that's just an empty cliché. Nor is it just an effect of the fact that I'm a painter, working in visual images, and she's a poet, working in words, and it would be misleading as well as simplistic to say that she's always believed in magic and I…didn't. Hecate is a mystic…

"Anyway, the point isn't that she believes in magic but the kind of belief she has. She has a lot in common Eirene Magdalena, who has been dead for some time now, but who seems to have left a last thing impression on this tangled affair. Eirene, as I've told you, was a morpheomorphist—a dream-shaper. She seems to have taught the Dellacrusca twins something of that art, and Hecate has had reason to study it too…but that's another story. The point is that although Hecate added a second sentence to her letter as a certificate of authenticity, there might well be a reason why she chose that particular identifier."

I took the letter out of my pocket again, and handed it to Mariette.

She had been living with a painter addicted to mythological themes for ten years. Unlike Tommaso, she recognized the reference to the pool of Mnemosyne.

"Dark petals falling into the pool of memory," she said. "Symbolic of some kind of confusion, or obscuring, of the memory."

"Not memory in the usual sense," I said. "Something transmitted across incarnations, from the distant past. Nothing as specific as the memory of an event, or a item of information, more pertinent to the unconscious part of the mind than the conscious part: the source of dreams, and artistry...and magic."

Mariette frowned—at herself, for not being able to see where I was going. "Does Hecate believe in reincarnation, then?" she asked.

"Not in the crude sense in which the notion in popularly understood, but in the sense of transmission of a kind of understanding, yes."

"The kind of understanding that you incorporated into the triptych? The spirit of Orpheus?"

"Yes. Also the kind of understanding that Charles incorporated into his Eurydice—and, more pertinently, the kind of inspiration that Hecate and Elise, in collaboration, incorporated into their interpretation of the same story, while trying to rediscover the suspiric language by means of poetic inspiration. All of it obscured and confused by the dark petals...but all of it emerging, nevertheless, from the pool of Mnemosyne, the true source of what most people call magic, although it might not be the best word, because it has taken aboard too many misleading implications."

"And you think that the reason Hecate considers it imperative that you return to Mnemosyne has something to do with…the pool of Mnemosyne?"

"And the dark petals, Yes, on reflection, I do. As I say, it's all conjecture, but I'm beginning to think that what we've seen, perhaps inevitably, as a haphazard sequence of events, each with its own particular cause or trigger, might more accurately be seen as aspects of the same event, like bubbles or ripples on the surface of a pool that are separate on the surface, but which all originate from something in the depths—a stirring in the mud, a release of gas…or the movement of some aquatic monster.

"Hecate already had a connection to the unfolding phenomenon, more peculiar than my painting, or Parenot's, which she tried to express in that strange poem in the language of sighs. I suspect that she has continued the development of that connection, partly by working with Vashti Savage and the Marquise on their magical endeavors, but also by working with Sister Ursule in the Convent of Shalimar—which she seems to have continued in spite of the fact that Ursule and her niece are at odds. She might be the only person capable of putting all the pieces together and glimpsing the whole picture..."

"I doubt that, Master Rathenius," put in a voice behind me.

Having been carried away by my discourse, I hadn't noticed Madame come into the studio, so I had no idea how much she had overheard, but it was obviously enough.

I turned to face her. "Do you mean that you doubt that Hecate is capable, or simply that she isn't the only one?" I said, a trifle testily.

"The latter," she said. "I can't presume to know your friend as well as you do—but if you're correct, and she has contrived to obtain the kind of…connection that you're describing, the effect might have been disturbing. If you have been having bad dreams, she might well be suffering even more intensely."

She made a signal through the doorway to someone waiting outside, and a Silenus came into the room in order to deposit a wooden box on the carpet. It contained objects wrapped in paper, whose nature I couldn't determine from the shapes of the packages.

"I've included a few books," Madame said. "They are, without exception, the ignorant attempting to lead the ignorant—if there have ever been any great magicians fully capable of living up to their reputations, they have not been much inclined to committing their secrets to manuscript—but the texts might help to refine your thinking. I do hope that you will still have time to learn something about during the voyage. It will be a serious inconvenience if you suffer from sea-sickness again."

Madame had already lent me several of the old bound manuscripts from her library in order to assist the education that she had hardly begun to provide, but I had found them difficult to read, difficult to comprehend, and far from convincing. The prospect of trying to decipher more, especially aboard a lurching ship, was not attractive.

"You're assuming that I'm going to go with Tommaso?" I queried, slightly resentful of the fact that everyone seemed to be making that assumption, in spite of the fact that I was a free agent, capable of choosing otherwise.

"Having considered the matter carefully," Madame told me, "I consider it to be imperative. Were you not explaining that to Mariette yourself as I came in?"

I realized that I had been hoisted by my own petard. I had only been dealing in conjectures, but Madame, it seemed, had already progressed beyond mere conjecture.

"What...?" I began—but she stopped me with a gesture.

"Not now," she said. "Dellacrusca and Elise are on their way back—they saw me coming, just as I saw them. It's imperative that I talk to Dellacrusca now, with the utmost seriousness, and delicacy. There will be time for further discussion later, before you board the ship."

"You're not coming with us yourself, then?" I asked, sarcastically.

"I dare not," she replied, simply.

That surprised me. I couldn't imagine that she was afraid to face the Marquise de Mesmay in the kind of contest in magic that Tommaso Dellacrusca's imagination was picturing, so I jumped to the obvious alternative conclusion.

"Your seismograph is giving you cause for anxiety?"

"Yes, and not simply the machine. I wish I were more certain of what its implications are, and how seriously I need to take them, but I have a conviction that some kind of catastrophe is imminent...call it a premonition, if you wish. I have had such feelings before, and I know that they ought not to be ignored." She brushed that matter aside with a gesture and redirected my attention to the box that the Silenus had deposited. "There is something else in there that might be advantageous to you, when you reach Mnemosyne."

"What's that?"

"You ought to have a telegraph cable run to your house, now that you can do s overtly. You should be able to hire workmen to do it quickly. That way, you will be able to communicate with me—not directly, alas, but with a delay measurable in hours rather than weeks. The necessary receiving and transmitting apparatus is all in the box, ready to function as soon as it's connected, provided that you have an electric current generator. If not, you'll need to acquire one of those too."

"But I don't know the tapping code, let alone your personal ciphers," I reminded her. "Or am I supposed to learn that, as well as studying all your books on the voyage, assuming that I don't come down with sea-sickness again?

"Helen knows the basic code, and the ciphers necessary to ensure confidential communication. She will be your link, not just to me but to the Dellacruscas."

"You're sending Helen with me? Isn't that dangerous—for her, I mean?" I didn't dare look at Mariette to see her reaction to that item of news.

"Not while she is under your protection," Madame retorted, phrasing the reply in a way that was certainly not calculated to ease Mariette's anxieties, which Madame evidently considered irrelevant. I realized that she was not only taking it for granted that I would return to Mnemosyne with Tommaso, but that Mariette and Elise would go too.

"And has Helen volunteered to accompany me?" I asked, with a hint of asperity.

"Of course. I wouldn't seek to constrain her."

"Oh, never—but she wouldn't want to disappoint you, would she?"

"Or you, Master Rathenius." Madame turned to Mariette. "You have nothing to worry about, Mariette.

Helen knows how to be discreet. She would never attempt to come between you and Axel."

"I'm not afraid of Helen," said Mariette, with all the contempt she could muster. "And Axel's a free agent, in any case."

I said nothing, contenting myself with the hope that the clash of sarcasms wouldn't escalate.

It didn't. Madame had other things on her mind. She turned back to me. "I shall be truly sorry to see you go, Axel, but I have every faith in your ability to handle any dealings you might have with the Marquise in a reasonable manner. I have every faith in Dionysus, too, of course...but even the gods are subject to Ananke." She raised her hand again to suppress any possible response, although I had not even begun to formulate an objection.

Elise and Tommaso Dellacrusca made their entrance into the studio then, having come through the garden and the dining-room—and when I say that they made their entrance, I mean it in the theatrical sense. I had already made the observation that Tommaso had dressed to impress and wore the costume of authority well, but his manner, when he came into the tavern on the harbor, had been a trifle tentative. Now, he was very obviously and very consciously stepping into his father' shoes. He was trying with all his might to look like the power behind the Imperial throne.

Tommaso was too young, of course, and perhaps too handsome, to match his father's demonic majesty but he was putting on quite a show, for Elise's benefit as well as Madame's, I supposed. He was trying to demonstrate what it was to be a Dellacrusca, in order to inform Elise of the tradition whose belated heir she was, and to inform Madame of the fact that he was a man of intelligence and authority, who had to be taken seriously. He was certainly not, as Mariette had spitefully suggested, a popinjay or a rake, and had, in fact, already acquired much of the authority of the title of which he was the joint heir. I only hoped that he would not acquire the implacable cruelty that his father had cultivated over the decades.

As he cast a long glance around the studio I wished that I had removed the canvas from the easel, but his gaze hardly paused on it, evidently only taking in the fact that it was far from finished. It lingered for considerably longer on the completed portrait of Mariette. He had been looking at Elise as they came into the studio, and he looked at her again once he had finished his swift survey, as if to affirm a common cause between then, before he redirected his attention to Madame. The manner in which he did that was pure showmanship, clearly intended to carry the implication that theirs was a meeting of equals, in spite of the vast difference in their ages.

Madame, of course, had had hundreds of years of practice in confrontation. She also had a Silenus by her side, the one who had brought in the box of books having immediately stepped to her shoulder, where he was looming impressively. There was an implausible graciousness in her smile as she inclined her had very slightly toward her visitor, and said: "Be welcome, Lord Dellacrusca. Shall we walk? I believe that you have something to ask of me."

Madame's second Silenus had also come in, and was looming over Tommaso's left shoulder. Both of the unhumans were perfectly impassive, but there is more than one way to loom, even for creatures of flesh feigning the diffidence of statues.

Tommaso didn't flinch or blink, refusing to show the slightest sign of intimidation. "I do, Madame," he said, with the utmost politeness, "and I'm very grateful to you for giving me the opportunity, as well as your patience. You will understand, I think, my need to put family matters first."

"Of course," said the woman whose family, such as it had ever been, had been extinct for two thousand years.

And the two of them fell into step, as if they were following the movements of a familiar dance, and disappeared. They went across the corridor, into the dining room and out into the garden, presumably aiming for the privacy of the headland. The Sileni fell into step behind them, at a distance they presumably considered respectful and discreet, although I suspected that Tommaso might obtain a different impression.

Mariette and I both looked at Elise, curiously.

"I like him," she declared, flatly. "And to think that there are two of them!"

It was, in fact, a striking thought, all the more so if Eirene Magdelana had been right in telling them that they shared the same soul, and would always have twice the soul of other men, provided that they remained united. But I also remembered them as small boys, full of mischief and malevolence, deliberately subversive of the whole society of Mnemosyne's aristocratic summer visitors. They had not abolished the legacy of that past in my mind, nor its dark petals of confusion.

"What did you talk about?" Marianne asked, uneasily.

"All kinds of things," she said. "Future possibilities...and present difficulties. He didn't treat me as a child. He listened. When I explained that I couldn't possibly stay here or go with him if the two of you returned to Mnemosyne, he accepted my judgment, and even complimented me on it. It was, he said, exactly the determination that a Dellacrusca ought to show. He wants me to play some music for him when he's settled things with Madame…I only hope that I'll be able to recover my touch."

I had a few suspicions about the motives for which Tommaso might have flattered her in that way, but I didn't voice them. Marianne wasn't so shy.

"Don't be misled by his appearance and manner," she said. "His father had a reputation for the utmost deviousness, and he's inherited more than his father's wealth."

"Oh, don't worry," Elise said, blithely. "I've heard the song that you and Helen sing a thousand times. There's no such animal as a trustworthy man. I know the chorus by heart, and Master Rathenius says the same, even though it's reminiscent in his case of the proverbial Cretan who declared that all Cretans are liars. I don't suspect my uncle of decency—but I can still like him. And when all's said and done, my eventual future does depend on him and his brother, doesn't it?"

She looked at Marianne brazenly, but Marianne didn't flinch.

"If that's what you want," she said, simply.

Elise didn't ask her where she thought her own future lay. Perhaps that was kindness, or perhaps it simply didn't occur to her.

"It might not be wise for either of you to return to Mnemosyne," I said, knowing full well that it was swimming against an irresistible tide. "I'd feel better about going into possible danger if I knew that the two of you were safe."

"With Helen by your side," observed Marianne, waspishly.

124

That was news to Elise. "Helen?" she said. "But not Madame?"

"Madame is needed here," I said. "She's expecting an earthquake or a volcanic eruption, and she wants to be able to protect her island as best she can."

Elise didn't question the reason, or ask how Madame expected to be able to protect her island from disaster, in the event of an earthquake or eruption. She looked at the crate containing the parcels.

"Madame thinks that I need to continue my education in ancient wisdom as best I can in her absence," I told her. "She also wants me to install telegraph apparatus in my house, so that I can keep her abreast of my progress...and other things. I only hope that I have a little time to read during the voyage. She knows I'm a terrible sailor, but I don't think Helen managed to make the true horror of that clear to her."

Elise was still possessed of the blithe optimism of youth. "We've got used to it now," she said. "It won't affect us a second time."

I didn't bother to correct the misconception. Nor did I think it worth trying to persuade Marianne that there was no danger to her in my taking a long sea voyage in close contact with Helen while she remained elsewhere, with her adoptive daughter.

"Madame has yet to make a treaty with Tommaso," I pointed out, instead. "They might not be able to reach agreement."

"They will," said Elise. "He told me why he hopes that the Marquise would be intimidated by Axel's presence, and I think he might be right. Her support will melt away, and she'll capitulate without a whimper, let alone a fight."

Her native optimism had obviously encountered a counterpart in Tommaso's. She had found nothing alien or absurd in the logic of his argument. She had no conception of the face that it was not, in fact, a matter of logic, but of vendetta. I had a strong suspicion that if the Dellacrusca twins would have no rest until they were able to tell one another, and agree, that their father had been avenged, one way or another. That perceived necessity was twisting their view of the situation and its possibilities, all the more so because of the complication of the advice Eirene Magdelana had given them regarding the value of dreams.

I wondered whether the Marquise might thinking in a similar way, and whether she too would have no rest until she could satisfy herself that she had made someone pay for her husband's death. And even Charles Parenot, although he presumably had no more Italian blood in his veins than the Marquise, was probably not immune to vengeful passions. Even in the absence of a commitment to the idea of vendetta, the two of them were presumably party to the Gallic tradition of wrath that had generated the mythology of the *crime passionel*. Charles had no real reason to hate Marianne, or even me, but if he really had joined forces with the Marquise, it was unlikely that the alliance had been motivated merely by a commission to paint her portrait, or by everyday lust.

Just as Madame had a feeling stirring in the unconscious part of her mind that a disaster was in the offing, against which she could only make feeble defensive provision, I had a muted conviction that, if I did elect to return to Mnemosyne, and throw down a figurative gauntlet inviting magical attack, the Marquise and her new associate might well make whatever reckless use of magic they could...or, more accurately, allow magic to make what reckless use of them that it could, in its own mysterious and malign fashion.

It did not make me feel any better to know that Madame expected me to prepare myself as best as I could with the aid of a handful of unreliable texts, in a desperate hurry, while I might be vomiting uncontrollably, and also having to wonder about the mystery that lay behind Hecate's message, and the possibility that she might be in danger because of it.

It was difficult, in those circumstances, to look forward to my homecoming.

VIII. Laudanum

Elise's optimism proved, not unexpectedly, to be completely unfounded, at least in my regard. I could not carry forward the adaptation I had made during my first sea voyage. Perhaps I was not quite as seasick as I had been the first time, but it certainly did not feel any less painful, perhaps because I had been drugged in advance the first time, and had been delirious even before the illness gripped me. On the homeward voyage, the sickness was able to come upon me in a casual and wholly conscious fashion.

Elise, unsurprisingly, did not come to my cabin to express her sympathy, although I gathered from second hand reports that her prediction had worked out a little better in her own case. Marianne had fared better that either of us on the outward journey, but she was forced to give her first priority to taking care of Elise, even if that left the task of cleaning up after me and dosing me with laudanum largely to Helen. At least she was able to be confident that I was at my least seductive and Helen at her most diplomatic.

Before the disorder plunged me all the way into the abyss of delirium and despair, I expressed my surprise at the fact of Helen having volunteered for the mission.

"Do you think I had a choice?" she parried.

"Yes, I think you did," I countered. "Madame doesn't seem to me to be as much of a tyrant as you imply. Did you even ask Madame whether you might stay on the Island of Dionysus?"

"No," she admitted. Sarcastically, she added: "But what does it matter, since I have the promise of your protection as well as hers, and Master Dellacrusca has even offered me his? What enemy can possibly strike me now?" She certainly did not give the impression of believing herself to be unassailable. I might have taken offense at that lack of confidence, as Madame and Tommaso would surely have done, but I couldn't.

"The Dellacruscas really aren't holding a grudge against you," I said. "In fact, I think they're genuinely grateful to you for removing his niece from a possible danger, and they probably fell about laughing when they heard that you drugged my wine in the Sprite and sneaked me out under the noses of Madame Auger and Nicodemus Rham's vigilantes. As for the Marquise, her magic is mostly charlatanry. Even if it weren't, she has far bigger targets in her sights, and doubtless considers you irrelevant."

"When a poor archer takes aim at the gold," she said, seemingly quoting a saw, although it wasn't one I'd ever heard before, "the blue is not out of harm's way."

"All the more reason for staying behind, then," I suggested.

"I don't like to disappoint Madame," she said

"I can't believe that you're in some kind of magical thrall," I said.

"I know," she said. "You don't believe it of yourself, either, but here you are, doing as she wishes."

I didn't bother to tell her that I was doing as Hecate Rain wished. It wouldn't have cut ay ice—and in any case, I could feel another attack of nausea coming on.

"Would you like a dose of laudanum now?" she asked; and she added, still wanting to make a point: "Madame has given me permission to supply as much as you need."

I would have liked to say no, simply in order to be perverse, but I didn't dare. My stomach would never have forgiven me, and would undoubtedly have intensified the violent reprisals that it was already brooding.

"Is it mixed with sailors' rum?" I queried.

"And kaolin," she told me. "You'll be spewing up pale mud for hours...perhaps days...but if you want to make a start on learning the supposed secrets of magical self-defense, you need to get through it and find your sea legs."

She was right, of course. I didn't believe that I was under any kind of magical thrall. I didn't believe that the Marquise de Mesmay and Charles Parenot had put some kind of curse on me, which had interfered with my presence of mind when I had set out to paint a portrait of Elise. I still thought it far more likely that it was a delayed after-effect of the rite in which we'd taken part, or a subconscious sensitivity to distant tremors in the earth's crust, and in either case, that its explanation was purely psychological rather than supernatural.

Indeed, I had even started to wonder the kind of unconscious resonance that Madame was experiencing, and which she credited to tensions building in the earth's crust, gestating earthquakes and eruptions, might be affecting Hecate Rain and Aethne de Mesmay too, rumbling away imperceptibly in the depths of all our various anxieties. Hecate, I knew, was unusually sensitive to atmospheric changes, and it did not seem at all implausible that she might have a kind of internal seismograph, whose deviations she could not begin to understand, but which nevertheless filled her with foreboding. It was not at all implausible that Vashti Savage had one too, and if the two of them had now formed some kind of nexus with the Marquise, the three of them might even be caught up in a kind of *folie à trois*.

Everything had, after all, begun to grow crazy when Hekla had erupted, and set about distributing such visible omens as the black snow and the pillar of fire, and even if the eruption had now died down, the sea bed round Iceland might still be restless, sending its barely-perceptible ripples all the way to the Empire.

With those hypotheses very much in mind, I was convinced that the causes of the hallucinations into which I was plunged by the combination of seasickness and laudanum were a straightforward combination of the physical and the psychological, without any genuine supernatural intervention—and I clung to that conviction, repeating it to myself frequently in the intervals between my dreams and fits of nausea. Any occult inspiration involved, I felt sure, was coming from the unconscious part of my mind, not from the incantations or operations of any sorcerer or sorceress.

I also had in mind, of course, the possibility that that was a distinction without a difference. If the dogmas of morpheomorphism had any real foundation, and the unconscious part of the human mind was capable of some sort of resonance with some kind of pool of memory that extended beyond the items sorted into that storehouse by personal experience and sensation, and if the unconscious mind was capable of feeding the implications of that resonance into the arena of consciousness via dreams, then it made very little difference whether I thought of the ultimate source of my hallucinations as the real underworld beneath the earth's surface, the realm of Hades, or simply a mysterious *beyond*. They were coming from *somewhere*, and there was potential in their arrival for a measure of enlightenment as well as alarm, horror and distress.

There was also potential in their arrival for the infliction of harm, even extending to madness or death.

It was not obvious that attaining a measure of enlightenment would afford any protection against those possibilities, and it was likely that any enlightenment I thought I received while I was in no condition to make rational judgments would be pure delusion. It was even possible that ignorance might provide better protection than knowledge—but what thinking man could possibly prefer that alternative, or resist the temptation to grasp at any straws of apparent wisdom there seemed to be within the toils of chaos?

I had taken laudanum enough times, in my long life, to know that it is unwise to deliver oneself to opium dreams while thinking hard about problems and prospects, lest the substance of those intense thoughts become subjects of baleful obsession. Mental effort can become a torture itself, in the grip of delirium and hallucination. Philosophical speculation regarding the nature and import of dreams can offer ironically perverse fuel for dreaming.

I can no longer remember very clearly what I dreamed under the effects of the laudanum with which I tried to numb the effects of my sea-sickness, but after-effects inevitably remained. The symptoms of seasickness are, in any case, intermittent, continually giving way to periods of consciousness and relative calm, which seem perfectly lucid. In such periods, one can make determined attempts to process the substance of the obsessions that have possessed one's nightmares. Perhaps that, too, is unwise, the rationality thus brought to bear being partly illusory.

But I had no alternative, in the circumstances. And I can still remember some of what I thought and dreamed, and what I then thought about what I had dreamed, even if any coherency and consistency I now find in the memories in question is a belated superimposition.

So, while I experienced nightmares, I strove with all my mental might, in every interval of lucidity I could attain, to find some sort of meaning in them, and some kind of sense. I knew, even as I was doing it, that it might be futile, not only because the vast majority of the dreams might be meaningless, but because my consciously-accessible memory might well forget everything that I thought I saw or imagined that I understood, but I had to try.

I was a free agent, but I had no choice. The opportunity was there, and I had to take it. If there was one thought that obsessed me more than any other during that interval of hell, that was it.

There were characters in my laudanum dreams; I saw faces. I saw Elise, Mariette, Madame, Helen, the Marquise de Mesmay, Lord Dellacrusca, Claudius Jaseph, Eirene Magdelana, Lucian Sombre, Nicodemus Rham, Charles Parenot and Hecate Rain. I also saw people I didn't know, black faces and white, and various shades of brown. I saw Orpheus and Eurydice, Dionysus and Pan. And not one of them—not one, out of the entire chaotic parade—could answer my urgent questions, or volunteer any remark that was not anodyne, gnomic or pure gobbledygook.

I cursed myself, because I knew they were all just images, and that I was really questioning myself, in the faint and possibly stupid hope that I might know something that I didn't know that I knew, and could somehow persuade myself to cough it up, if I could only phrase the question correctly.

I saw other images, too, which seemed somehow less cynical in their refusal to make any clear declaration of verity, although not necessarily comforting in their muteness. I saw the Devil's Rocks and Lucifer's Light, and dead men's fingers dangling in the crevices that were only uncovered at rare low tides. I saw the crest of Snowspur, and swirling clouds full of ominous shapes and muted lightning. I saw Conrad Othman—or something pretending to be Conrad Othman—playing the Rose Duet with Dorothea Rosa...

But I did not hear the music...

I thought at first that I simply could not remember it, and cursed myself again, and added an extra curse because I was convinced that I could not remember, either, what music Davida Amalek had placed for Candida Kracy to sing on the night that Eirene Magdelana had found her long-lost son and lost him again after one brief embrace...

But it occurred to me, as a corollary to that conviction, that perhaps there was more to the omission than forgetfulness...that the forgetfulness itself was more significant than mere omission.

It was then, seemingly after a very long time, although that might have been a purely subjective impression, that I really became fully aware of a significant absence within my hallucinations, which ought to have been conspicuous from the outset. I realized that I had seen Elise, with her viola da gamba and her bow, but that I had not heard the sound of her playing. I had seen Sisters of Shalimar equipped with marine trumpets and harps, but I had not heard the notes emerging from the reverberation of the strings.

Was that really surprising? I wondered, when I was capable of wondering again, no longer under the brutal cudgel of the drug and the rum. I was a painter, after all, not a musician. My mind and my imagination were intently focused on visual imagery, my mind was primarily a storehouse of pictures, not sounds. In addition, I was aboard a steamship, and the throb of the engines was ever-present in the air and the very walls that surrounded me, tyrannical and imperious, drowning out all other sounds, with a mechanical insistence with which mere music and the beating of hearts could not be expected to compete.

Except that, in my hallucinations, when the laudanum had me fully in its opiate embrace, I could not hear the engines either. I had the sensation of being insulated from all vibration, cushioned within the bleak infinity of my own soul, alone.

And it was in those intervals of apparent mental isolation, or not so far away from them, either in time or imaginary space, that I sometimes saw a dark pool, which I knew to be the mythical pool of Mnemosyne, and thus to be Mnemosyne herself, who did not require a human form to be properly symbolized, and did not profit from attempts to give her one, because she was not a person in that way, but memory…not *a* memory, or even *the* memory, but merely memory.

A pool, not a person…but a pool with its own innate invisible turbulence, and a murky, muddy, slimy bed, similarly invisible, and strange life-forms, also invisible…and floating petals, which could not only be seen, but which carried implications in their slow drift of what might be going on beneath, and of whence they might have come.

What sort of petals were they, I wondered, afterwards, when I tried to remember and refine the substance of my opiate dreams? I could not tell, but I suspected that they were the blossom of trees…of very old trees…and that the patterns on their surface, of spots or streaks, might be a script of some kind, or a cryptogram.

I could not remember the exact words of Hecate's poem, which she had improvised while the two of us were together, resting after a walk along the clifftops, looking out over the sea—not the high cliffs overlooking sea to the east, beyond the headland on which the house was situated, but the low cliffs fringing sea to the west, in the direction of the Ocean. So far as I knew, Hecate had never written the poem down; I had no idea whether she might have been able to remember it herself, or to reconstruct something similar from scattered fragments of lines or rhymes. But what I did remember was the images that she had evoked.

Hecate did not believe that she had "lived before" in any simple sense, or that she would "live again" after her death, if and when some immortal fragment of her being invested itself with a new body and a new existence. But she did believe, poetically if not dogmatically, that she was connected to the past and the future of the human race, and to the great tide of time itself. She did not think that her personal universe was bounded by the meager limits set by her memory of things that she had done and heard and the eventual cessation of that secretion. She believed that she was connected, materially and psychically, to her parents, and her ancestors, not merely all the way back to the dawn of human self-consciousness and rational thought, but to all her prior ancestors: mammals and fish, worms of many designs, infusoria and protoplasts.

She had never given birth to a child, and knew now that she never would. She had long been aware that she was barren, in the crude physical sense. But she did not think that the great chain to which her being belonged would end with her. For one thing, she was a poet and the best of her words had been printed, although she did not think that it was necessary for her poetry to have been printed, and for those printed texts to be reprinted and copied again, in order for it to have made a contribution to the threads of meaning that imagined words contributed to the sum of being. For another, she knew that the substance of her body—of the many bodies that had replaced her physical substance within the frame of her identity, the plan of her soul—was returning to nature even while she lived, carrying something of her back into the atomic flux, the everlasting metamorphosis of matter.

More importantly, she did not conceive of her poetry as entirely her own, something created by her mind *ex nihilo*, any more than her physical self had been created *ex nihilo* and entirely shaped by her. She thought of the threads of meaning to which she and her work contributed as aspects of the world's metamorphosis that extended far beyond her own being, in both directions of time, and in communication too. She had said more than once that I was as much an author of her poems as she was, but that I ought not to derive any vanity from that. because I was merely the closest at hand, albeit perhaps the most beloved, of a multitude of co-authors.

But I *had* derived vanity from that, vanity being one of my more obvious flaws, and I also took pride in remembering the images contained and evoked by her poetic representation of the pool of Mnemosyne, the essence of memory, which contained so much that was invisible on the sluggish surface, and was blurred and obscured even in that surface by stray petals tumbled from elsewhere: fragments of flowers, whose role in the ordered pattern of existence was to attract pollinating insects in order that their parent trees might live, but which, in that process, added beauty and poignancy to the world; petals that might, by obscuring and confusing memory, make their own strange contributions to the never-ending metamorphosis.

And with a poetic impetus of my own, I added the notion that even in making the vision of memory murkier and more frustrating, those dark petals were multiplying the facets of life, life being something that could not abide too much order, too much clarity, or too much smoothness, but which required shadows to emphasize enlightenment by its absence...and not just any shadows, but shadows pregnant with the significance of previous light, previous color, and previous allure: the shadows of petals.

All that had been in the poem, I felt sure, implied if not explicitly stated, but it had all been symbolic. I couldn't remember the exact words, but I remembered the meaning that I had read into them, and the meaning that I reconstituted in the intervals of my sickness and delirium.

The most important thing of all, though, I remembered, was the conclusion of the poem; its final stanza and its final suggestion.

Again, I couldn't remember the exact words, but I remembered the gist. The pool of Mnemosyne is within us; it is a private well from which we draw the water of thought; but it is not only within us, because its waters are connected, more or less distinctly, with all the waters beneath the surface of human consciousness, past as well as present. We remember, but in that process, we are remembered. We are among the petals ourselves, among the confusions; in the ultimate analysis, we are mere fallen fragments, inscribed with mysterious texts, unconscious of our own reality and our own necessity.

As I had mentioned to Tommaso, Hecate had been in one of her darker moods when she improvised the poem—but that didn't mean that the vision was wrong. It had always seemed to me that it was in her darker moods that Hecate saw most clearly, even if she required consolation for what she saw.

When I resynthesized all of that, later, after having recovered completely from the effects of the laudanum and the effects of seasickness, I probably embroidered it a good deal, because that is what memory does when it reconstructs: no one can remember the same memory twice, any more than he can step into the same river twice. But I knew that it didn't matter, because I knew that there was as much significance in the embroidery as the backcloth. Conscious remembrance is a creative process, and it is in the interstices of that creation that enlightenment sometimes appears to dawn.

We should not, however, take undue pride in that creative process, because we are not so much remembering as being remembered, not so much creating as being created. We are merely fallen petals, cast adrift on the surface of mystery.

But that was all incidental. The bottom line was that when I was no longer feeling horribly sick, and the hallucinatory effects of the laudanum had worn off, I thought I knew what I needed to paint, in order to describe, and perhaps to challenge, the magic that was brooding on Mnemosyne: the magic that was using the Marquise de Mesmay, Charles Parenot and Vashti Savage as its instruments, as well as Madame, Mariette and Elise—and, of course, me. I had in mind the embryo of the image that I needed to produce in order to counter its confusions: not to bring order to the chaos, that being a task far too vast for any mere human, but at least to provide some means of partial rescue from the ongoing catastrophe of the world.

I couldn't see the finished painting in my mind's eye, and I knew that I wouldn't know exactly what it looked like until I had actually applied the last brush stroke, but I knew what its subject would be, and what its symbolism ought to imply. I knew what it had to say—or sing, or perhaps scream, in the suspiric language—with all the force and clarity that my artist's eye and hand could give it.

And in spite of the lesson I had taught myself, I couldn't help feeling pleased with myself, in anticipation of the strange masterpiece that I was about to produce.

Vanity of vanities, as the prophet is reputed to have said, all is vanity.

By the time I was able to get out of my bunk and stand up with perfect steadiness, and go for bracing walks on the deck of the ship, and even entertain visitors in my cabin, I thought I had guessed what Hecate Rain was doing in the Convent of Shalimar, and why my presence of Mnemosyne was, in her mind, absolutely indispensable.

I had made it up, of course, but I had also seen it in the pool of Mnemosyne, and read it in the drifting petals.

Hecate, I thought, had put the pieces of the puzzle together, and although there were some still missing, she had glimpsed something in the implied image that had frightened her. She was the most sensitive of us all, and doubtless felt the threat of imminent danger more intensely than anyone else. She could not know exactly what the danger was but she felt—she *knew*—that my presence on Mnemosyne was indispensable to oppose or appease it.

Perhaps she was wrong, and perhaps my feeble presence would be impotent do achieve anything but enable her to think that she was no longer alone. But that was more than adequate to justify my answering her appeal, and making every effort I could, however eccentric, to supply the need. Over the years, I had become indispensable to her consolation, when her dark moods came upon her, and I could not leave her lacking.

The first person I went to see was Tommaso. "I thought I ought to let you know," I said, "that I won't be painting the Marquise de Mesmay, as you suggested. I'll leave that to Parenot, if that's what she's commissioning him to do. I have a better idea."

"You're the artist," he said, equably. "Paint whatever you think most appropriate." He didn't really think it mattered what I painted, as long as the Marquise knew that I was painting something, and was alarmed by the implications. He was wrong. It did matter; I was convinced of that.

"As I understand it," I said, "although neither you nor Madame has taken the trouble to spell it out exactly, the agreement you've made with her doesn't go much further than a non-aggression pact, a let-and-let-live agreement?"

"No, there's much more to it than that," he said, "but the full implementation depends on contingencies. Lory and I have to obtain complete control of the organization before we can go to the next phase, and then we'll have to proceed carefully."

"So you really are aiming at an explicit and elaborate alliance?"

"Yes. It's tricky, of course. She doesn't trust us and we don't trust her; she isn't going to submit to our authority any more than we're going to submit to ours. Then again, even if we can march in step, sing in harmony, or however you want to put it, we can't really control what happens within the Empire, let alone what happens elsewhere in the world. As long as we can work together, though, I'm optimistic that we can save the Empire from collapse. That was what father was always trying to do. I know you didn't like his methods, and I'm not going to make you any promises about ours, but for now, the knives are sheathed, and I'll be happy if they can stay that way."

"But?" I prompted, when he stopped without having followed his thoughts to the end.

"But the Marquise and the people who actually plotted my father's murder can't get any advantage from it. Maybe they don't actually have to die, but they have to be defeated. A point has to be made. We'll welcome all the genuine defectors with open arms, but if the Marquise is permitted to live, she has to come out of it with all her ambitions shattered. If there's a better way to achieve that than cutting her throat, it's up to you to find it."

He looked at me warily. I knew full well why he'd waited until we were on the ship and only three days or so from Mnemosyne to spell that out. He knew that he had only dreamed my speech telling him that there was a better way, and that for him to demand that I fulfill the promise made to him by my simulacrum in a dream was a trifle unreasonable…but if his dream really had been *the* dream, that was what he felt entitled to expect, It

142

wasn't my own promise to him that I had to keep so much as Eirene Magdelana's; but that didn't make the obligation seem any less forceful, in my mind.

"I'll do my best," I said. "How does Charles Parenot figure into your calculations?"

"He's not on our list, obviously," he added, in a carefully neutral tone. "He didn't have anything to do with father's death, and he pulled my niece out of danger, although I gather that he needed a stern shove in order to do it. I have nothing against him—but if you do…?"

"Don't be ridiculous," I said. "The man's an artist. I don't wish him any harm."

"He might not feel the same way about you."

"Probably not—but if he thinks I've harmed him, that's all the more reason for not compounding the offense. I wouldn't have anything against Aethne de Mesmay either, if I didn't suspect that she tried to have me killed. She paid me what she owed me for the triptych, even though it was her husband who'd made the deal."

"She did try to have you killed," he assured me, although I wasn't convinced that even he could be certain of that. "You can't have any objection to her being paid in her own coin, especially as she'll undoubtedly try again, if only with inappropriate and ineffective means."

I wasn't entirely convinced of that either. I had a much greater capacity for doubt than Tommaso, who had the arrogance of youth and Dellacruscan vanity shielding his convictions.

"I'll react to that in my own way," I told him. "Don't include me in your vendetta." I kept my tone strictly neutral. "In respect of your request that I issue some kind of challenge to the Marquise, however, there's one item of publicity that might be useful, although I didn't think of it in time to seek Madame's permission."

"What's that?" he asked.

"It might be as well to make my affiliation to the Cult of Dionysus public—even to give me the status of a Hierophant—a high priest, that is."

"I know what a hierophant is," he said—but he was more amused by the idea than offended. "Father wouldn't have liked it—but then, Father didn't like you, and that's partly the reason why Lory and I do. No one on the island will believe it, though—not of you."

"Aethne de Mesmay will," I assured him. "In any case, it's the symbolism that's important. I'll have difficulty believing it of myself, but if you want me to oppose myself to the Marquise, it's a useful item of fancy dress. It would be helpful if you and Lorenzo went along with it. In letting the fact be known to the members of your organization that you've made a pact with the Cult of Dionysus, it might even be an advantage to identify me as the figurehead with whom the pact has been concluded."

"It would certainly attract attention from Alectryon and his satellites. You do know that he hates you at least as much as Father did, I assume?" he asked.

"I'm well aware of it," I confirmed.

"All right," he said. "Perhaps it would be usable propaganda capital. I must say, though, that I'm surprised. What made you think of it?"

"I had a dream," I told him.

I knew that explanation would satisfy him. It wouldn't have satisfied ninety-eight men out of a hundred, but he and his twin were the other two. They had fallen under the spell of Eirene Magdelana at an impressionable age.

"I see," he said. "Do what you think best, then. Lory and I will go along with it. We wouldn't do it for anyone else, mind. You should feel privileged."

"I do," I assured him.

Next, I went to see Mariette, who was feeling much better herself now that Elise had recovered from her illness, without the aid of sailor's laudanum, and was also up and about. I didn't tell her exactly what I intended to do, or what I intended to paint, or why—I felt that I was becoming more like Madame every day—but I did try to set her mind at rest.

"How are you feeling?" she asked, with the falsely sympathetic air that someone who has not been seasick inevitably adopts to lesser individuals devoid of her fortitude.

The attitude was, however, mere bravado. She had not taken any laudanum, because she had not been seasick, but that hadn't saved her from having bad dreams, or from trying to measure the symbolism of these dreams in the light of what she now knew about their possible origins. The after-effects of that that self-interrogation had not left her any less fearful, although she seemed to be resolute, or at least resigned.

"Much better," I assured her. "Fighting fit, in fact."

"Are we going to be able to get through this safely, Axel?" she asked

"Yes," I told her. "I know what I need to do now. Anyway, the Marquise can't hurt us."

She was prepared to take my word for that, but she had meant more by "getting through this safely" than simply getting through it unharmed by any malevolence on the part of the Marquise de Mesmay.

"You and I will still be together," I told her. "Not forever, but for as long as we need to be. And Elise will stay with us, for as long as she needs to be. I have Tommaso's word on that. I believe, now, that I'll be able to stay on Mnemosyne for as long as I need to, because rather than in spite of the fact that everyone will know my real age and will think that I'm a sorcerer. I'll feel uncomfortable at first, I think, having to shed my old image, but it was always a pretence, after all. I am what I am, and can't help that."

"I know," she said, in a melancholy tone. She was still thinking about the inevitable transience of our present relationship. No matter what assurances I gave her, she had her own view of what it meant when I said that I was what I was, and couldn't help it.

"I need to make some attempt to read the books that Madame gave me," I said, preparing my excuses for what she was bound to see as neglect of her. "I painted the Orpheus triptych without a word of scholarly instruction in magic, and the painting sang anyway—or, at least, provided the channel for the song—so I could probably do the same again, but I it will probably help if I know a little more about the symbolism I'll be incorporating into it."

"I thought Tommaso wanted you to paint the Marquise, so that you could burn the painting, like one of those dolls that African sorcerers are supposed to use to commit murder by proxy."

"He did have something of the sort in mind, but I have a different approach."

"Another mythological paining? Dionysus rather than Orpheus? Do you want me to pose as a Bacchante?"

"No," I said, "that won't be necessary. I won't be using a model. It will be a mythological painting, of sorts, but not like the ones Charles used to paint, always casting you as the heroine, the nymph or the goddess."

"I could take that as an insult," she observed.

"Don't," I said. "And don't take it as an insult, either, if it turns out that Charles is now casting the Marquise in the same role he used to award to you. It's just a limitation of his imagination. Believe me, it's better to be painted as you are, as I painted you on the Island of Dionysus, than as any kind of avatar."

"As I am?" she queried. "Elise says that it's how I wanted to be and how you wanted me to be…for the moment. She's right. I don't even know who I really am, or who I want to be. I'm not even Elise's mother, and no matter what promises Tommaso Dellacrusca has given you, she's already left me, in that sense."

"You're wrong," I told her, flatly. "You'll be her mother for as long as she needs one…and that will be forever. I can't guarantee that she won't leave Mnemosyne eventually, but I think there's a good chance that she'll decide that it's where she belongs. You might well make the same decision."

She didn't seem to think it likely, but it wasn't a thought to which she dared to raise any objection.

Next, I went to see Elise. She had a cabin of her own this trip, and a more capacious and comfortable one than mine—she was a Dellacrusca, after all, and no mere commoner in present company. She was playing her viola da gamba—somewhat imperfectly, but only because the sea wasn't calm and the motion of the ship was disrupting her movements, much to her annoyance. She seemed glad of the excuse to set the instrument aside.

"I feel better now," she said. "How are you?"

"Much better," I assured her. "There's something I'd like you to do for me, if you're agreeable."

"Of course," she said. "Anything—within reason."

"When we reach Mnemosyne, I intend to ask Hecate to come and stay in my house for a while. It will be crowded, I fear, given that Helen will be staying too—poor Jean-Jacques might end up sleeping in the stable and Luzon in the larder, but I suspect that Hecate is suffering and that it will make her feel better to be close to me. In any case, I need you all to be there. I'd like you to collaborate with Hecate on a new work, if you and she are willing."

"Like the one based on the fragmentary Orphean hymn?"

"In a way, and perhaps still in the language of sighs, but this one will have to go deeper into the pool of memory."

She nodded, as if that was only to be expected. "To reflect Dionysus, I suppose," she said. "I can do that, if Hecate's willing. I already have, when I was playing for the cycinnis during your initiation."

"Deeper than that," I said.

"Is there anything deeper than that?" she asked.

"Yes there is," I said. "I'll need to do some research in order to get a better grip on the symbolism myself, and perhaps consult another scholar, since I won't be able to hold any substantial conversation with Madame, even if I can set up a telegraph link to the house, but I already have the gist of it—enough to have the basic theme of the painting in mind."

"The pool of Mnemosyne?" she said, in order to demonstrate her precocious cleverness. "A still life with petals?"

"Not still," I told her. "The pool, yes, and the petals…but in order to bring out the full meaning, I'll have to bring something out of its depths. That's what I'd like you and Hecate to try to do as well. I'm not thinking of it as magic, although Hecate probably will; for me, it's simply art...but there's something it needs to reflect, if only to put me into the right frame of mind to do what I need to do."

"And what do you need to do?"

"I don't know yet—but if I'm in the right frame of mind, I'll know when the moment comes. I have Eirene Magdelana's assurance for that. When the unconscious mind needs to get its message across, because the crisis is at hand, it finds a voice. We just have to be ready to receive it, and decode it.

"Like a telegraph clicker?"

"Exactly,"

"And you think it will help if I can provide a musical accompaniment."

"I do."

"So do I. What do you want to bring out of the pool, then? A personification of Mnemosyne, modeled by Mariette?"

"No, I intend to paint Ananke, the symbol of Necessity. I won't attempt a personification, in any crude sense, although the Greeks did, following their invariable habit. They imagined her as a goddess, the daughter and consort of Chronos—the real Chronos, not the Titan Cronus—and the mother of the Fates. They sometimes associated her with Aphrodite Urania, the embodiment of celestial amour."

"Never heard of her. But Hecate will understand?"

"Yes, Hecate will understand very well. She's not only familiar with the symbolism, but habituated to using it creatively. If you associate her with the composition, it will help you to shape it."

"I know," she said. "I've done that before. I like Hecate a lot. It's not what Tommaso had in mind, though—will the Marquise understand the symbolism, and what you're trying to do?"

"Probably not, but I'm not sure that's a relevant issue. I've suggested an alternative way of provoking her attention, and Tommaso has agreed to go along with it. I'm going to pose as the figurehead of the Cult of Dionysus, much as she's employing the Duc d'Alectryon to pose as the figurehead of her cabal. I don't think Madame will mind—in fact, she might have suggested it herself if she thought I'd agree to it."

Elise didn't express any amazement of her own that I was willing to attempt such an imposture. She didn't know me as well as Tommaso Dellacrusca thought he did. She only said: "What do I need to know, in order to compose the music?"

"Hecate will be able to supply the detail of the mythology, and if her own scholarship is wanting, she only has to consult Sister Ursule. I'll probably have to consult both of them myself—but I already know that Ananke played a role in the theology of the ancient Cults of Dionysus and Orpheus. She's imagined in that context as having a serpentine form, enfolding the universe in her coils. That image might be enough to supply a seed, but if you need more, Hecate and Sister Ursule will have it in abundance. You'll know more by the time my painting begins to take shape, and as it develops, we'll be able to help one another, as long as..." I stopped, thinking that it might not be a good idea to pollute her youthful optimism with my doubts and fears, but I'd already gone too far.

"As long as we have time, you mean," she said. "You think we might not?"

150

"I don't know how imminent the danger is. Hecate obviously thinks that it's urgent, and I trust her judgment."

She simply nodded. "So do I," she said. "We'll just have to make the best use we can of the time we have." Selfishly, she added: "When it's over, will you be able to make another attempt at painting me...as I want you to see me? Tommaso will commission it, if need be."

She didn't mean commercial need. She knew that Madame had given me a supply of gold and gemstones in order to meet my expenses in my reestablishment on Mnemosyne, and also in order to create a debt that I would feel honor bound to repay in kind..

"Yes," I told her. "I'll paint you...as I want to see you."

She nodded again, but not in gratitude. She thought that was her due. "Does Mariette have a part to play in your grand plan?" she asked.

"She does," I said. "Perhaps, in fact, it might be the most difficult one, all the more difficult because I can't simply ask her to play it."

"Oh?" She was surprised. "What is it?"

"To begin with, it's imperative that she doesn't go back to Charles Parenot."

She laughed. "That's no problem," she said. "She's not as happy with you as I hoped and thought she would be, but there's no way in the world she'd go back to Charles now, even if he begged her on his knees."

"As he might," I said. "And it would be wise not to overlook the force of the past, as expressed in regret and remorse."

Elise took my word for it that there was some doubt on the issue. After a pause, she said, tentatively: "Would you really care very much if she did go back to him?"

"Oh yes," I said. "Make no mistake about that. Nor is it just a matter of pride, or masculine rivalry…or even sentiment, when you get right down to the muddy and murky depths of things. It's really a matter of symbolism—but everything is, so that isn't saying very much. I won't insult you by saying that you're not old enough to understand, but as yet, your experience is limited and confused. When you finally are able to understand exactly what I mean, you'll wish you didn't, believe me—and then you'll know why the innocence you'll have lost is something to be regretted. I need Mariette. Not forever, but for now. My plan won't work without her. She's a vital part of the nexus."

After another pause, she said: "There's always Helen…and Hecate."

"It has to be Mariette," I said, flatly. "For the moment, there's no possible substitute."

Elise considered the flatness of the statement, and then shook her head. "If you say so," she said. She thought about saying something else about Mariette, but thought better of it.

"What about you?" I asked. "Charles may not be your real father, but he's the only one you've had, and he's taught you most of what you know about music, art and life. And he did pull you out of the line of fire, on the night of your grandfather's murder."

She didn't raise any objection to those observations. "Yes," she said, after a pause. "Perhaps, if weren't such an unnatural creature, I'd be heartbroken about the split between Charles and Mariette, and would be desperate to see them together again. I do miss him…and I certainly wouldn't like him to be hurt. I've told Tommaso that. He says that he has nothing against him, and no intention of harming him."

"He gave me the same assurance," I said, diplomatically failing to mention the offer he had almost made me. "The fact remains, though, that Mariette mustn't go back to him, whether he begs or threatens...and it's possible that he'll put himself in harm's way, if he tries to harm me, or Mariette."

"He won't," said Elise, still possessed by optimism. "He's not that kind of man. He's far more likely to hurt himself than to harm Mariette or you."

I nodded, content for her to think that, even though I wasn't prepared to take her word for it, in the circumstances. I didn't bother to tell her that she wasn't an unnatural creature. I had promised not to lie to her.

"You can rely on me, Axel," she told me, "and Hecate." After a pause, she added: "You've always been able to rely on Hecate, haven't you?"

There was an implication of criticism in her tone, as if I'd somehow let Hecate down—but I hadn't. Not, at least, in the way that Elise thought. She thought that I hadn't loved Hecate in the way she really wanted to be loved, but I had; at least, I hoped so. And Hecate had loved me in the way that I really wanted to be loved. At least, I hoped so.

"Yes, I have," I told her.

"You said *to begin with*," she reminded me. "What else do you need Mariette to do?"

"She doesn't know it," I said, "but she's a medium, perhaps more powerful than Vashti Savage. That doesn't mean that she can summon the spirits of the dead, but it does mean that she can draw things from the depths of her unconscious mind, when the occasion demands. If the occasion does demand it, I'll need her support as well as yours. We form what Madame calls a nexus."

Or the victims of a folie à trois, I didn't add.

She nodded her head. "Thanks for treating me as an adult, Axel," she said—and for trusting me."

I could have said the same to her, and might have, if I hadn't thought that she would think it a flippant absurdity.

I went back to see Mariette again. This time, I didn't have to make small talk, or ask her any questions. It would have been nice, though, if her bunk hadn't been so narrow and so hard. Life on the Great Ocean isn't comfortable, even after you stop being seasick.

IX. Return to Mnemosyne

The steamer would have been too large and heavy to attempt entry to Mnemosyne's harbor, even at high tide, but Tommaso had never had any intention of doing so. The vessel didn't even drop anchor before releasing a launch, which ferried Helen, Mariette, Elise and me to shore. It was the middle of the night, and there were no laborers on the wharf. The Sprite was dark and silent, the Augers presumably being safe in bed, and the intermittent beam of Lucifer's Light seemed unusually bright by contrast. The quays were not entirely deserted, however. The advent of the steamer had not been announced by any kind of signal, but its approach had not been unperceived. Constable Clovis was waiting on the dock, in person, in order to cast an inquisitive eye over whoever might disembark.

There was no lantern on the boat, and although the sky was clear and starlit, the moon was a mere sliver. He couldn't possibly see who was aboard the launch while it made it patient way through the choppy waters, roped with mechanical efficiency by two skilled oarsmen, making excellent progress in spite of the rough water. I was profoundly glad when it passed the harbor entrance and stopped lurching violently, but I didn't throw up.

Helen went up the stairs first, followed by Elise, and then Mariette. Clovis didn't appear recognize Helen or Elise immediately, so it wasn't until the light of the nearest lantern on the quayside illuminated Mariette's face that the expression of suspicious puzzlement on his face began to change. At that point, he must have guessed who the fourth passenger was going to be.

To say that he welcomed me with open arms would be an understatement. For such a taciturn and self-controlled man, he demonstrated an amazing extravagance.

"Master Rathenius!" he gasped. "Thank the gods! I feared that you were dead, or at least gone forever! You have no idea how many rumors have been flying round."

I grabbed his right hand before he could actually fling his arms around me, and shook it heartily.

"It's good to see you, Clovis," I said. "Now I know that I'm home. Have you been looking after my island for me?"

It didn't occur to him for an instant to challenge my reference to Mnemosyne as *my* island.

"I have, sir," he said, "as best I could. I hope I've kept good order. There's a great many people who'll be very glad to know that you're alive and well...*are* you well, sir?"

"Never better," I assured him, "now that I'm back home."

"For good, sir?"

"I don't know about that, Clovis, but at least for now. You remember Helen, of course, and Mariette and Elise. You remember Constable Clovis, Mariette? I've talked about him often: the best man on the island, and the most trustworthy."

Mariette favored the constable with a warm smile, while he blushed. His gaze flickered from her to Helen, doubtless a trifle surprised to find them together in my company, even though the four of us had all disappeared simultaneously from the island.

"I need a coach to take us all home, Clovis," I said. "I want to reassure Jean-Jacques and Luzon as soon as possible that I'm well, and to ask them to prepare the

156

house for my guests. If you could send a man in search of one, I'd be very grateful. I'd also like you to do me another favor, if you will."

"Of course, sir," Clovis said. "But...."

I cut him off. "I'd like you to send one of your men to Hecate Rain's house, to inform her of my return. I'd also like you to refrain from informing anyone else, for the moment. The news will spread, obviously, but I'd rather not accelerate that spread unnecessarily."

"Of course, sir," he said. "I ought to inform Doctor Commonal too, sir, as president of the Town Council..." He hesitated, evidently aware of the possibility that that I knew that Fion Commonal was a member of the Cult of Orpheus, and not at all sure how that positioned him in my regard.

"Of course you must inform him, Clovis," I said, "but he's a busy msn, and a physician needs his sleep. There's no need to wake him; tomorrow morning will be soon enough, don't you think?"

"Yes, sir," he agreed, with alacrity, and was quick to add: "There's news, and a great deal of it, that it would be as well for you to know. If you'd care to step into the station, I'll give you the gist of it while my men fetch the coach and deliver your message."

"That's very kind," I said, and did as I was asked.

The first thing I noticed once we were inside the center of his operations was the thing that hadn't been installed the last time I was there: the telegraphic receiver and transmitter, connected by a new underwater cable to the mainland, and to several other points in the island, perhaps including the Mesmay manse, although that had had a covert connection for some considerable time.

The constable ran his eyes over my retinue with a certain unease, and even when I signaled to him that he could speak freely, he still seemed uncertain, but he immediately began to bring me up to date.

"First of all, sir," he said, "I wasn't able to apprehend the second of the two men who attacked you, but I have information from a usually-reliable source that he's now dead. The island was exceptionally busy, given the time of year, for some time after you…left, and there were a number of murders, for which I wasn't able to arrest anyone, but things have been much calmer these last few weeks, including the weather. The ash from the volcano is no longer falling, any more than the snow that came with it."

While he was speaking, he was gradually but insistently moving me away from my companions. They made no attempt to follow me, but cooperated with his intention by moving away themselves.

"The blonde lady's husband is living at the Mesmay house at present," he whispered. "He's said to be working on a painting there, but you know the sort of gossip that kind of situation generates. The house has been transformed into a virtual fortress, and there's a small army in the Duc d'Alectryon's livery camped on the hillside between the house and the West Bay. There are watchmen in the same uniform posted on Snowspur and the headlands, and the keeper of Lucifer's Light has been replaced yet again, much to old Nicodemus' disgust. Two negro women have also moved into the Mesmay house—identical twins, it's said. Sorceresses too, it's said, although you know I don't put much stock in that kind of thing. Vashti Savage is holding séances there regularly, supposedly conjuring all manner of spirits, real or imaginary. Niklaus Hylne attends them, and so does Fion Commonal. Davida Amalek did at first, but she and the Marquise seem to have fallen out. Your friend Miss Rain can doubtless tell you more.

"The summer season should be getting under way within the next couple of weeks, as you know, and I honestly don't know whether to hope that the visitors come or to hope that they stay away. Something's in the air, sir, and it's not just the smell of sulfur drifting from Hekla on the prevailing wind. I don't like it at all. I wish I could tell you that you'll be safe now from further attacks of the kind that drove you away, but I can't. Jean-Jacques has kept your house in good order, but it's no fortress, sir, and you might want to give some thought to precautions, especially with so many ladies in the house. I know twenty men who'd gladly serve as watchmen in shifts of three or four, for little more than the price of food and a tent, and it pains me to say it, Sir, but I think you might need them. The town is far from what it was this time last year, alas—it hasn't been right since that damned black snow fell. I know it was just ash from the volcano, but I have some sympathy with all those who still believe that it was an omen and a curse, and that the present calm is just an interval before the real storm bursts. The whole town is on edge."

"Thank you, Clovis," I said. "That's very useful to know. For what it may be worth, I have a strong suspicion that the summer visitors won't arrive this year, at least in any substantial numbers, but I have reason to hope that that things will return to normal eventually. As you say, there's still something in the air, even though the skies are clear for the moment and there's no longer any threat of snow—but I believe that matters can be settled, with the help of the gods. Mnemosyne might well have a hard time ahead, but she'll recover; trust me on that. And there's one more thing you need to know, which you needn't keep secret, although again, I'd appreciate it if the rumor spread slowly."

"What's that, sir?" asked Clovis, a trifle uneasily.

"Among the rumors you mentioned, it has probably been alleged that I'm more than a hundred and twenty years old, and that I'm a sorcerer. It's true. I'm also the Hierophant of the Cult of Dionysus."

He looked at me for a full five seconds as if I were insane. Then his face cleared. "I understand, sir," he said. "Fighting fire with fire, isn't it? You can count on me, Sir. I'll spread the word discreetly, as if it were a secret. I'll have half the island believing it within forty-eight hours, and the other half protesting its impossibility. If anyone asks me, I'll swear that I've heard it myself from a usually-reliable source, and that I have no reason to believe that it's not the honest truth."

He winked, in his most conspiratorial fashion. He was probably too simple-minded to be a good detective, but he was, as I'd ostentatiously told Mariette, the best man on the island, and the most trustworthy.

The carriage that the policeman had found for us wasn't a four-seater, so it was a trifle cramped even for the three women, and there was no possibility of taking all the luggage that the oarsmen had brought up on to the quay before setting off to return to the waiting steamer. I had to take the seat beside the coachman, but I didn't mind that in the least. The night wasn't cold, and the wind of our progress was pleasantly bracing.

"I'm sorry to have got you out of bed," I said to my companion.

"No trouble, sir," said the coachman, flicking his whip at the two horses, which were hauling the vehicle with difficulty. The nags seemed far more resentful than their conductor at being disturbed in their repose.

"Work's direly thin at present; any fare is more than welcome, believe me. Going to be a bad summer, they say."

"Perhaps," I agreed, with a sigh.

"Just as bad for you and the other painters, I suppose, sir," he observed. "We're all in it together. We won't starve, I dare say. There are always plenty of fish in the sea."

I hoped that he was right—but the island had had bad years before, and suffered numerous petty disasters. Its people had always pulled through. There were indeed, as all the native islanders were fond of remarking, always plenty of fish in the sea.

Jean-Jacques was twice as glad to see me as Clovis, but better able to control his enthusiasm. Luzon wasn't. She flung her arms around my neck in a manner quite unbecoming a woman of her age, let alone a servant, wept copiously and then told me, tearfully, that it did her the world of good to see me, but that I shouldn't have come back, because it wasn't safe, the island being full of murderers.

Jean-Jacques, in his quieter fashion, was not free from similar anxieties. "All the guns in the house are loaded, sir," he assured me. "If you wish, I can have a picket of riflemen around the house before dawn, working in relays, day and night."

"That's not necessary," I assured him. "I'm afraid I'm going to have to inconvenience you and Luzon, though. I don't want to put anyone to sleep in the studio or the reception room, and I need all the bedrooms for my guests; I'm expecting Hecate Rain to be staying here as well, with her chambermaid."

"That's no trouble, sir," he said, heroically. "I can sleep in the stable and Luzon will be fine curled up in the larder. I'll go into town at daybreak and fetch back supplies as soon as the market opens, if you can let me have a little cash. Do you have cash, sir?" He was worried, lest my sojourn in mid-Ocean had impoverished me.

"In abundance," I told him. "We'll all be able to eat like princes all summer long, even if the visitors don't come."

That eased his mind. "Will Miss Elise be sharing her mother's room?" he asked, warily.

"No," I said. "Elise will have her own room. Mariette will be sharing my bed."

"Very good, sir," he said.

"The luggage will be arriving when the coachman can cajole his horses into making the trip again. I've given him a good tip. The books are valuable and need careful handling. "

"Yes, sir."

Like Clovis, he took the first opportunity to detach me from listeners that he considered importunate, and accompanied me into the studio while Luzon showed Helen, Mariette and Elise to their bedrooms.

"You know about Parenot and the Marquise?" he asked.

"Yes."

"Miss Rain will doubtless be comfortable here, sir, but I have to admit that I've been anxious for her safety of late. Clovis has had men keeping an eye on her house, but she's keeping dangerous company, and although she wouldn't forgive me for saying so, she doesn't look well at all."

"As you say, she'll be comfortable here," I told him.

"One of the Dellacrusca twins has been on the island, sniffing round. I didn't rat him out to Alectryon's men, obviously, but I didn't tell him anything either."

"That's fine," I said. "If either of them turns up again, you can let him in. They're not our enemies."

"That's what I suspected, sir," he said, sounding relieved. "The enemy of my enemy, and all that. The Marquise *is* our enemy, I take it?"

"She's not our friend yet," I confirmed, "but things change, and I haven't given up hope of changing that. She's moved in two Nubian sorceresses, I hear— identical twins?"

"That's right, sir, except that they're not, strictly speaking, Nubians, having come from even further away. Definitely twins, though. As for their being sorceresses, I have my doubts."

"Very wise." I cast a long glance around the studio, where, as Clovis had promised, perfect order seemed to have been maintained in my absence. "Is everything ready for me to start work in the morning?" I asked, in order to make sure.

"Absolutely, sir. If any of the paints have deteriorated, just say the word and I'll bring back colors for mixing in no time. Can I take it that you won't want to be disturbed?"

"You can, but Mariette can receive any visitors— she's to be treated as the mistress of the house. Follow her instructions as you'd follow mine."

"Yes, sir." His expression suggested that he wasn't looking forward to giving Luzon that particular item of news, but they were both well aware of the protocols to be observed in such circumstances.

"There's something I else need you to do," I told him. "I don't need armed guards, but I do need to hire capable men to rig a telegraph cable from the Constable's station to the house. Can you arrange that?"

"Yes, sir. There are crews working on that all over the island. I'll hire the best of them. They'll have the cable in place in within three days—but it might not be easy to buy the clicker thing that you need to send and receive messages. You might have to send to the mainland for one of those—and a new generator, if the one we have isn't reliable enough to run permanently."

"The necessary apparatus is in the luggage," I told him. "The generator we have should be adequate, but it might be a good idea to obtain an extra one anyway, so do that. Helen's an expert operator, so as soon as the cable is in place and the apparatus is set up, we'll be able to receive and transmit messages, even in cipher."

"That's what Clovis thought," he said, "but he's been having trouble with the apparatus. I gather that it's not as simple as he imagined."

"Nothing ever is," I told him, "but the equipment and its users will improve, with time. It's a facility of which we need to make as much use as we can."

"Perhaps so, sir," he agreed, politely but dubiously.

Mariette and Elise were very tired, and only come back downstairs again to announce that they were retiring again. Helen's room wasn't ready yet, because Luzon had been sleeping in it during my absence, but she retired discreetly to the reception room to wait, after saying that she would help with the luggage when it arrived, and supervise the unpacking of the telegraph apparatus.

Before the coachman with the slow horses returned, however, a different carriage pulled up outside, carrying Hecate Rain and her chambermaid. I went out to meet it.

Hecate threw her arms around me, and I made no move to interrupt her intention or pull away. As Jean-

Jacques had said, she wasn't her normal ebullient self; she gave the impression of someone who hadn't been sleeping well for some considerable time, and was definitely in one of her darker moods, in need of consolation..

"Thank the gods you've come, Axel," she said. "I wasn't sure you'd understand my message, but I daren't make it any more explicit. The situation is very delicate, and I can't even trust my best friend—especially my best friend, in fact, if Vashti still qualifies for that title, as she certainly seems to think. Have you brought Elise with you?"

"Yes."

"Thank the gods. I daren't put that instruction in the letter, but I was sure you'd understand. And Mariette?"

"Yes."

"You're sleeping with her?"

"Yes."

Hecate simply nodded, as if that were simply something to be expected, and as if it were further cause for relief. She had predicted it, after all.

"Well," she said, "I'd like to be present when the news of your return reaches the Marquise and Alectryon, but it would undoubtedly be unwise. The Dellacrusca twins brought you back, of course?"

"Yes. They're hoping to pick up the pieces if I can frustrate the Marquise. But that doesn't matter. How are you?"

"Much better for seeing you," she said. "I really don't know what's wrong with me, and I ought to be much better able to bear up, but I can't shake off the terrible feeling that there's a danger hanging over the island. Perhaps it was wrong of me to ask you to come back, given that, but...I hope it's not just pure selfishness, but I have a strong feeling, too, that you're necessary…to the island, not just to me. I wish I could explain more coherently, but..."

I stopped her.

"It's not necessary," I said. "Not now, at any rate. It's better if we all get some rest."

Hecate was too impatient for that. She sent her maid inside, but she pulled me away from the door, into a quiet corner of the garden. It was dark, but she positioned us so that lamplight filtering through the kitchen window allowed us to look one another in the face. The sight of her did me good, and so did the touch of her hand

After studying me for a moment or two, with the hint of a tear glistening in the corner of her eyes, she sighed, and said: "I'm truly sorry to bring you back into danger, my love," she said, "but you can't imagine what's been going on at the Mesmay house. I wish I could believe that it's all masquerade and make believe, but...well, to put it simply, I'm frightened."

"I know that Parenot's moved into the house," I said, in order to abbreviate the explanation, "along with twin African sorceresses, and that Vashti is summoning spirits from the Netherworld with greater abundance than ever before. But apart from that, I haven't any hard information. I don't even know whether the Marquise is screwing Parenot."

"She is, but it's no great love affair. She treats him like a lap-dog, just as she treats Alectryon and Fion Commonal. I can't imagine why any of them puts up with it, and it almost makes it plausible that her powers of magical seduction and enthrallment aren't illusory. Parenot doesn't like it, and he hasn't forgiven her for burning his painting, but..."

"She's burned the Eurydice?" I said, sharply.

166

"Yes, but he's painting another, with a different model."

"The Marquise herself?"

"After a fashion—but it's not an accurate likeness, by any means, to judge by the glimpses I've been able to catch. Perhaps it's her as she'd like to be seen, but certainly not as she is. I've been able to come and go with Vashti, but I don't think I would have been allowed to do that much longer, even if you hadn't come back. Vashti's still besotted with me, and I've had to sleep with her to keep her sweet, but that doesn't cut any ice with the Marquise, as you can imagine. She knows that I've been spending time with her aunt. At first she thought she could use me as a spy, and I let her think so, but it wasn't me who stole the document for her, and the fact that I didn't..."

"Wait a moment," I said. "What document?"

"Oh!" she said. "I thought you might have guessed that. Ursule and I have managed to translate the Toustain fragment, but the Marquise has stolen the translation."

Mystified, I said: "But I thought that Sister Ursule's copy had been stolen weeks before I left the island."

"It had, but I'd already made a copy of my own. I kept that quiet, though—I didn't tell you, or anyone except Ursule. I thought that I had sufficient understanding of the language of sighs, thanks to Elise, to help her decipher it, and it seems that I was right, although it took longer than I had hoped. I thought that you might have deduced that."

"How could I possibly have deduced it since I didn't even know that you had a copy of the inscription?"

"Well, obviously I should have confided in you...but you were still keeping secrets from me, remember. Anyway, I daren't be more explicit in the letter, but I felt sure that you'd connect my reference to the pool of Mnemosyne to my endeavor in trying to reach back into the past to contrive the composition that I made with Elise, which we played to you the night you saved my life. I thought your thinking was sufficiently in tune with mine for you to catch the oblique reference."

At the risk of disappointing her, and even though I'd never made a promise to tell her the truth, I said: "No—that wasn't an inference I was able to take. But no matter; I got the message anyway. Why is the document important? When I asked Madame about it during our first long walk, she confirmed that it was a spell of some kind, but she didn't go into detail, and she didn't seem at all worried about the possibility of it being used, or even the possibility of it being deciphered. Obviously, she underestimated Ursule."

"This Madame is the mastermind behind the Cult of Dionysus?"

"Yes. Some of the people on the island call her Minerva, but she doesn't like that. She seems to take an odd pride in being nameless."

"But you're sure that she knows what the document is?"

I thought about it. "I can't be completely sure," I admitted. "She certainly gave me that impression...but she likes to give impressions. In any case, it doesn't matter. We already knew, or suspected, that it was written in the suspiric language, with which Orpheus allegedly charmed the dead, and even hoped to bend Hades himself to his will. Is it?"

"Yes it is, but in a more sinister sense than we imagined. It seems to be a spell for summoning and commanding Hades to emerge from the Underworld: a recipe for destruction."

"Ah! And having stolen your translation, she intends to use it against me?"

"I don't know for sure, but I think she intends to use it on the island where you've been…in hiding. That would have included you—but now you're back, that fact alone has confused the issue. The impression I get from Vashti is that she has attempted to use you—or, more specifically, Mariette—in targeting the curse she's been attempting to formulate, but she ran into difficulties."

"What difficulties?"

"As an Orphean hymn, the formula needs appropriate musical accompaniment if it's to work. First the Marquise tried to recruit the Sisters of Shalimar, but you can imagine how that went, and she won't get any assistance from that direction. Then she tried to recruit Davida Amalek, but when I told Davida that she intended to use her magic against you…well, Davida still owes you a debt for saving her from Ragan Barling's machinations, and she hasn't forgotten it. She's put the word around via her salon, and the Marquise is having difficulty recruiting any competent musicians. There are also problems with her African twins and the part she has in mind for them. Anyway, she's had to rethink her strategy for bringing disaster down on the island, and on you. Vashti seems convinced that she can do that…and also that if she can strike some such blow against the Cult of Dionysus, it will cement her power over the Orpheans, once and for all."

Once again, I felt the frisson that I had been feeling all too frequently of late. I was sharply reminded of Madame's instinctive feeling that disaster was imminent, and her hope that her seismographs might at least give her warning enough to save lives and to reduce the magnitude of the catastrophe. Ten years ago, of course, the Marquise and her associates would have had no way of knowing, at least imminently, whether any such spell had worked—but now there was the telegraph. Madame might only have to fall silent for the Empire's covert listeners to know that something had happened—and it might only require some kind of accidental technical breakdown, of a kind that was all too frequent, for the Marquise to claim that her magic was responsible.

"I see," I said. "But you think that the Marquise isn't ready yet to attempt to unleash destruction on the Island of Dionysus?"

"Not yet. Among other things, Parenot still has to finish his painting. The fact that you and Mariette have left the island will force her to rethink the details of the spell's supposed working, but it will only increase her sense of urgency.

"You said that there's also a problem with the African twins," I reminded her. "What's their role."

"The African twins are also supposed to be experts on killing by means of curses, but their reputation, enormous as it is in their homeland, might be exaggerated. In any case, the Marquise is still trying to master their language well enough to form a genuine conspiracy with them. They're not easy to deal with...fortunately, perhaps. I doubt that the Marquise will be ready to launch her magic thunderbolt for at least a week, but I could be wrong, and I don't know how she'll react to the news that you're back. In the meantime, though, there might be scope for you and the Dionysians to attempt some countermeasure, if you think that's necessary.

Ursule should be able to advise you as to how you might go about that."

"So Sister Ursule believes that the spell she translated might actually work—but surely she can't believe that it will actually summon Hades from the Underworld?"

"She's a follower of Shalimar, not Dionysus or Orpheus, but she also believes that it's only the symbolism that differs between religions. Bardic mythology doesn't include Hades, but it certainly has an Underworld, and anxieties about what might emerge therefrom, with or without the aid of Bardic hymns."

"So she thinks that the spell could have a real effect?"

"She's very much afraid that it might—but what scares her most of all is the probability that if it does, it might work all too well. The Marquise is convinced that she can direct any destructive force she can evoke against the targets she intends to hit, but Ursule says that once destruction is magically summoned, it tends to rebound on innocent bystanders, sometimes on a lavish scale—that there's no way to predict the consequences of the rite in detail. According to her, the Marquise knows too much to be harmless, but not nearly enough to have any substantial measure of control over anything she invokes."

"But she thinks that some kind of countermeasure might work too?"

"She hopes so, and she's convinced that if anyone can operate one, it's you, if only because the Marquise is afraid of you, fully aware of the potency of the magic you incorporated into the Orpheus triptych without even knowing what you were doing. The Marquise thinks that you've been studying magic on the island, and when she

171

hears that you've come back…well it will certainly alarm her, but it won't stop her. It will make her all the more desperate, all the more willing to risk everything on a crucial strike."

"Damn," I said, quietly. "Things are worse than I thought. But I do have countermeasures of a sort planned, and I'm no longer thinking of them as empty showmanship. I know I can't work magic...but I'm almost sure, now, that magic can work me. What I don't know, and what scares me even more that the mad Marquise, is what it might do with me. I don't think the force on which Madame drew, with the aid of her magic mirror and the triptych, is intrinsically evil, but I don't think it's intrinsically benign either. It has its Orphean aspect, and its Dionysian aspect, but fundamentally, it's Ananke…the blind, stupid force of necessity. I really do believe that I can invoke it…but what it might do, once invoked, I have no idea."

"But we have to do something, Axel," she said. "We can't just stand aside. It's imperative that we try. I've already been working with Ursule on a counterspell of our own, using the Sisters of Shalimar, and now Elise is here, she can probably help with the composition, as she did before…but you're the one whose art is proven. You've always contended that there's no genius that can match yours."

"That was my vanity speaking," I told her.

"I know," she said, a trifle faintly, "but if it hadn't been telling the truth, I wouldn't have loved it the way I always have."

That only increased the burden of expectation.

"I wish I'd been able to love you a little better than I have," I murmured.

The filtered lamplight was poor, but her surprise seemed genuine. "You've always loved me in your fashion," she said. "I know that."

"Not in the way you wanted to be loved," I said.

"Don't be ridiculous, Axel," she retorted, with a flash of her old flippancy. "Haven't you always loved me in exactly the way you thought I wanted, and needed, to be loved? Haven't I done as much for you...except, of course for not having been able to stop aging. But I can't help that, can I? Anyway, that sort of talk is a waste of time. Can I stay the night?"

"Yes, of course. Your bedroom should be made up by now. You can send for your luggage tomorrow. You'll move in here until this is all over, won't you?"

"Yes. I'll go to see Ursule first thing in the morning, and bring her here, if she'll come. I'm sure she will. With luck, you can confer with her before the news reaches the Marquise that you're here."

I wasn't confident about that, even though I knew that Clovis would keep his word not to let the news spread too rapidly from the police station. There was every chance that the Marquise already knew—or that she would be told as soon as she woke up in the morning.

I put my arms round Hecate and hugged her. "I've missed you," I told her.

"Of course you have," she replied. "Now go screw Mariette, if she's still awake—and do a good job. The last thing you want is for her to start regretting Parenot. Still, you've had a hundred years more practice, so he can't possibly be serious competition, can he?"

I kissed her on the forehead.

I really had missed her, and she was, as usual, right. She had loved me in exactly the way that I had wanted, and needed, her to love me—except for not having been able to stop aging, which really wasn't her fault.

X. Unexpected Developments

Early the next morning, Jean-Jacques took the cart into town in order to buy supplies; Helen accompanied him in order to help with the loading, and to make purchases of her own. Hecate and Elise set off shortly afterwards with Clementine, Hecate's chambermaid; Hecate and Elise were bound for the Convent of Shalimar and the maid for Hecate's house, where she had to pack for her mistress. Mariette took advantage of the opportunity to slip over to the old Toustain house, in order to collect possessions that had been left behind there when she and Elise had been abducted. The only other person in the house, therefore, when I went into the studio to begin making my preparations for the work on which I was about to embark, was Luzon.

I had selected, secured and primed the largest canvas I had in store, and was pinning it to the wall, for want of an easel large enough to contain it, when I heard the doorbell ring. I knew that Jean-Jacques had sent various messages around in order to recruit men capable of connecting the telegraph cable, and I assumed that Luzon had been fully informed as to what she ought to tell them. I was, therefore, slightly surprised when there was a knock on the studio door and Luzon came in, almost quaking with terror.

I thought she was alarmed by her temerity in having violated my instruction that I didn't want to be disturbed unless it was absolutely necessary, and opened my mouth to reassure her, but before I could speak, she said: "Oh, sir, I'm sorry, but I didn't know what to do..."

"It's all right," I assured her. Who is it?"

"It's…" She swallowed her saliva before continuing. "It's the Marquise de Mesmay!"

I'm sure that I didn't go pale, but the seizure of the surprise silenced me for several seconds. Then I assumed the utmost composure, and said: "Thank you, Luzon. Have you shown her into the reception room?"

Her eyes widened. "I didn't let her in!" she exclaimed.

I tried to be thankful for the small mercy that at least I had not heard the door being slammed in the unexpected visitor's face.

I pointed to an armchair and said. "Sit down for a moment, Luzon, and collect yourself. I'll take care of it."

The Marquise was on the doorstep. She did not seem unduly annoyed, or surprised, by the insult.

"I'm very sorry, Milady," I said, with the utmost politeness. "Please come in."

"In fact, Master Rathenius," the Marquise replied, in a tone that might have been thought honeyed if I hadn't taken it for granted that it was utterly insincere, "it might be better if I did not. Would you care to take a little walk with me? The weather is cloudy, I fear, and the wind a trifle sharp, but it's not unpleasant. We might walk to the tip of the headland, or go down into the cove, as you please."

I looked around. There was a carriage parked some thirty paces away, manned by a stout coachman who had dismounted from his seat, and seemed to be stroking the horses, as if thanking them for their exertions. There was no one else in the vehicle.

"I'm quite alone," she said. "After all, I'm in no danger here, am I?

"Indeed not," I replied. "Yes, I'll be happy to take a little walk. I've been away for some while, and it will be

176

pleasant to renew my acquaintance with my familiar sur-roundings in the sunlight. To what do I owe the honor of your visit, Milady?"

"I wanted to welcome you back to the island, on behalf of its population," she said, as we set forth along the path that led toward the sea. "Perhaps you don't real-ize how much you've been missed, but your absence has been a constant topic of regretful conversation, at all levels of society. It's impertinent of me, I fear, to appro-priate a prerogative that really belongs to Fion Commonal, as president of the Island Council, and he will doubtless call on you when his duties as a physician permit, but I have a personal interest too; I would like to commission you to paint another picture for me."

"Thank you," I said, a trifle numbly. "What kind of picture did you have in mind?" I had studied her while she was speaking, trying to penetrate the act she was putting on, but the performance was smooth and accom-plished: the perfect mask of someone who had spent the greater part of her life in the upper echelons of Lutecian society, fully adapted to its etiquette and automatic falsi-ty, and had then exported the carefully-honed aristocratic pose to the strange splinter community of Mnemosyne, where it became the voice of superiority, sophistication and, in its purest sense, Empire.

She smiled. "A portrait," she said.

"Of you?"

"Yes. The vanity might seem to you to be belated, at my age, but it is precisely when the sun of a once-glorious beauty is on the point of setting that one begins to feel a sense of urgency about the preservation of its radiance. The metaphor makes me sound very vain, I know, but you have known me for a long time, Master Rathenius, albeit distantly, and I'm sure that your artist's memory retains an image of what I once was, and that, while you were studying me a few moments ago, you were very conscious of the extent to which I have been changed by time. You are familiar with the psychology behind my desire, of course; I know that you have been commissioned over the years to paint many women of my...maturity. You doubtless prefer painting those in the full flush of their youthful beauty, but that has never prevented you doing justice—and more than justice—to your clients. I admire that, and that is why I know that I can rely on you now. I *can* rely on you now, can I not?"

I was familiar with the impulse that led women conscious of the fading of a once-spectacular beauty to want its residues preserved in paint of canvas as well as expert make-up applied to the features, but I had not expected to encounter it in the Marquise de Mesmay. Then again, I had not expected to encounter the Marquise at all, let alone in the role of a hopeful client—and I was sure that her enquiry as to whether she could rely on me was not simply reflective of a desire to be assured that my brush was capable of deft flattery.

Summoning up my own practiced social polish, I contrived to reply: "I do remember you from the days when you first favored the island with your presence, Milady, even though we rarely had occasion to converse in those days, certainly not in such intimacy as this. I can assure you that your beauty has only matured in the interim, as beauty does, gaining in majesty what it loses in naivety."

"Thank you for the compliment, Master Rathenius," she said, injecting a slight tone of melancholy into her contrived politesse, which might not have been entirely fake, "but I'm well aware of the toll that time takes—although it seems to me, in remembering you from the days of our first distant acquaintance, that you have not changed at all. Men are often more fortunate in that regard than women, I know. My late husband was still an exceptionally handsome man when he died."

With an entirely automatic politeness, I had allowed her to select our course, even though she had explicitly invited me to make the choice. She took the left-hand fork in the path, which led in a somewhat zig-zag fashion down into the cove to one side of the headland. The tide was out and there was a considerable expanse of shingle and rocks beneath us, with a plethora of rock-pools. There were a couple of ramshackle huts in the cove, used by fishermen to shelter tackle and nets, but there was no permanent habitation; although the inlet was in the lee of the island with regard to the prevailing wind. It was by no means immune to the effect of storms, and huts built there were inevitable smashed sooner or later by rough water whipped up by a storm.

"The weather has been very bad since you left the island," the Marquise remarked. "The winter was unusually prolonged, and the snow left behind a nasty black dirt. Fortunately, the first spring rains have washed it away, but they too have been heavier than normal. It's all due to the after-effects of a distant volcanic eruption, I'm told."

"So I believe," I confirmed, as we slowly descended the steep slope. She went ahead, while I remained respectfully behind her in the narrower sections of the path. It occurred to me that I only had to reach out a hand and gave her a shove, and she would take a tumble that might prove crippling, or even fatal. I could imagine Tommaso Dellacrusca's reaction to the news that I had had such an opportunity and had not taken it—but it seemed to me that I literally could not do any such thing.

It would not only have violated the code of etiquette that the Marquise was so casually invoking in her speech and manner, but also my own long-cemented principles, my own carefully-designed identity.

The awareness that the Marquise knew that—that she was absolutely confident that allowing me to walk behind her on the side of a cliff was not exposing her to any danger, believing that if she happened to slip, I would reflexively reach out to prevent her from falling—gave me an odd feeling of helplessness, of being obliged because of the freedom of my will rather than in spite of it.

In any case, I was exceedingly curious to discover the whole of what she wanted to say to me, and to measure the dimensions of the snare that she was weaving and setting out.

"You will paint my portrait, won't you, Master Rathenius," she said, as we reached the bottom of the hill and stepped on to the shingle above the high-water mark, a hundred paces away from the line where the waves were presently breaking, in a fashion that seemed surly rather than angry, but was certainly not serene.

"I fear that I will not be able to execute your commission immediately, Milady," I said, apologetically. "In three weeks, perhaps, or a month, if you have no objection to waiting...?"

"Of course," she said. "You have only just returned, I know, and doubtless you have other clients...although I far that the summer visitors might be slow in arriving this year, and might not arrive at all."

"So I hear," I said, in a neutral tone.

I was still a pace or two behind her, even though we were no longer on a narrow path. She paused in her stride, in order to match my step, and moved a little closer toward my side than the etiquette she was following so ostentatiously usually permitted, in terms of appropriate social distance. Her manner became more earnest.

"You will doubtless hear many other things, Master Rathenius" she said, in a quasi-confidential tone. "The island has always been a prolific rumor mill, of course, but imaginations have been running wild of late. That is, I confess, one of the reasons why I wanted to see you. Would you believe that the malevolent lie has been spread that I had something to do with the attempt on your life that was made on the evening of your departure?"

She had obviously researched that line, and probably thought that she could deliver it with the utmost feigned sincerity, but her composure faltered, her mask cracked, and my artist's eye perceived the truth—perhaps the whole truth.

Yes, the Marquise had instructed assassins to kill me, because she feared that I was an agent of Dellacrusca or the Dionysians, but she had done it in a moment of panic, still affected by her husband's death and the turmoil of trying to take over the reins of his conspiracy. She regretted it now.

My own reflexive reaction to that revelation surprised me. I wanted to tell her that I forgave her. I wanted to tell her that I understood her regret and remorse. I wanted to tell her that she had no need to fear any reprisal from me.

But I couldn't. How could she have believed me? Even if she had believed me, how could she have trusted her own credulity? And would she not have been correct? How could I trust the authenticity of my own reflex?

"Really?" was what I actually said, by way of a reply. "How strange! Why would anyone want to say such a thing?"

"I have no idea," she said—and then corrected herself, with a sigh. "No, that isn't true. I do have a notion. You remember the night of the planned concert, obviously, when my husband offered Lord Dellacrusca the use of our house in order that Hecate Rain and Charles Parenot's daughter could perform for him?"

"I remember," I confirmed, trying my utmost to maintain my composure.

She seemed to lose hers slightly—or, at least, to put on a show of doing so. "To my eternal shame and regret," she said, "I do not. I had never considered myself a weak woman, but one never knows how one will react in a crisis until the crisis comes. I remember a strange shriek, and then the Sisters of Shalimar undergoing a nightmarish metamorphosis, suddenly wielding daggers. My husband seized me by the shoulder and…I fainted. When I recovered consciousness, I was in my bed. Fion Commonal was there, with a bottle of salts, which he had used to bring me round. I was confused, but someone—one of the servants, I think—told me that Lord Dellacrusca and my husband were both dead.

"After that, things became even more confused. The Duc d'Alectryon appears to have taken charge, and he came to tell me, the next day, that, for political reasons, he and other influential people that he did not name did not want it known that Lord Dellacrusca had died in my house, or that he had been on the island at all. Since then…well, to be honest, life has become something of a nightmare. I have heard several accounts of what happened that night, but they conflict with one another. Although no one beyond our immediate circle is supposed to know what happened, everyone seems to have heard something, and everywhere I go, I seem to be regarded with fear and suspicion, as if I were somehow responsible, not merely for that but for other unfortunate events, including more than one murder.

"That fear and suspicion has, also, proved contagious. I no longer know who to believe, Master Rathenius. The only people I feel I can trust completely are Charles Parenot, Vashti Savage and Hecate Rain, precisely because they have no more idea of what happened than I do. Charles was entirely focused on the necessity of removing his daughter from danger. Vashti fell to the floor and kept her head down. Hecate was paralyzed by shock, and only saw guns being drawn in the audience before you carried her away. None of them saw Lord Dellacrusca and my husband die. I have spoken to my husband since, thanks to Vashti's evocation of his spirit, but he does not seem to know himself—and Lord Dellacrusca remains as enigmatic in death as he was in life. I hope you will not be offended by my curiosity, Master Rathenius, but would you mind telling me what you remember of the tragedy?"

All things considered, that was a very intriguing confession—if, in fact, it was a confession, and not a carefully compounded lie. I realized, to, that it was a challenging question, if answered with complete honesty.

"I fear that I saw no more than you or Charles," I said. "When I realized that guns were being drawn and leveled in the crowd, the one thought in my mind was that Hecate and Elise were in danger. I reacted exactly as Charles did. While he picked up Elise and ran for the exit, I seized Hecate. Once outside, I fear, we both kept running like rabbits. It was not until Tommaso

Dellacrusca came to the house later that night, in order to make sure that his niece was safe, that I learned about your husband's death. In the following days, I heard rumors and speculations, but as you say, even the accounts given by the people who were actually there were fragmentary and conflicting. Like you, I really did not know who or what to believe."

"It is an uncomfortable sensation, is it not?" she said. "To have been present at such a terrible event, and to have no reliable knowledge of it! I have been in a continual state of dread and anxiety since then, perpetually haunted by the vague feeling that something dreadful might happen at any moment. And nightmares...such nightmares! Many of my old friends seem to be avoiding me, but I have been very grateful for the ones that remain, and for the new ones I have made. Charles Parenot, in particular, has been a great comfort to me. He is presently a guest in my house. Do you know that his wife and daughter disappeared on the same evening that you left the island?"

"Yes, I do," I admitted.

"It has made us companions in distress. I have also become close friends with Vashti Savage since she held her first séance at my house. You were present then too, if you remember."

"I remember," I said.

"There were some remarkable manifestations, were there not? Lord Dellacrusca was an unbeliever, I fear, and thought that the evocations were all trickery—I believe he even suspected you of contriving them—but I knew differently. I realized then that Vashti is a medium of great sensitivity. We hold séances at my house regularly now. You might assume that the shock of losing my dear husband provoked that interest, and you would not be entirely wrong, but I have always had an abiding interest in the occult, and I like to think of myself as an assiduous explorer of its mysteries. I have two young African seeresses staying in my home too, lovely young women—identical twins. Perhaps I ought to commission you to paint them as well. I describe myself as an *explorer* rather than *scholar* because I have a more practical turn of mind than my mother's sister, who is a veritable scholar, and I have never been able to compete with her intellectually. You know my aunt, I believe— Sister Ursule, the superior of the Convent of Shalimar?"

"We met once," I confirmed.

"She disapproves of my interest, I fear. There was always a certain sibling rivalry between her and my mother, which she seems to have transferred to me, and which has only intensified with the years. I fear that I blamed her—unjustifiably, I recognize now—for the fact that my husband's assassins masqueraded as members of her community in order to gain access to the house. Even without that, however, I fear that we would have fallen out. The Sisters of Shalimar are quite benign, but also a trifle bigoted. She considers my explorations and experiments to be dabbling in black magic, inherently evil. I, of course, prefer to think of them as more akin to art.

"Hecate has been seeing a lot of Ursule lately, and although I don't like to speak ill of my aunt, I fear that she has infected your friend somewhat with her suspicions. I suspect that my aunt might even have begun to lend credence to some very ugly rumors regarding my possible involvement, not only in the attempt on your life, but also the murder of Lord Dellacrusca and my husband. That wounds me very deeply, as you can imagine. I loved my husband, in a way that…well, that a Sister of Shalimar could never understand."

She looked at me with an expression that seemed utterly sincere. "I fear that I must seem very garrulous, but I felt that I ought to tell you all of this, since you have been away from the island for some time, and presumably have no idea what was being said hereabouts in your absence. Now that you are back, you will doubtless hear a great deal of gossip from various sources, much of it ugly…and some of it, I fear, casting aspersions on my character and conduct. I hope that you will not judge me on the basis of that kind of hearsay. I cannot ask you simply to take my word for anything, but I do feel entitled to ask you not to believe anything simply on the basis of malevolent rumor. I feel that I am due that consideration. It might be the case that you have already been told that I am your enemy, but as you can see, simply by virtue of my being here, that is not true. We are not enemies, are we, Master Rathenius?"

That was a more difficult question than the ones I had been parrying without undue effort. "I can certainly see no reason why you should wish me harm, Milady," I said, carefully, "and I beg you to believe that I have absolutely no wish to do you any."

"Thank you, Master Rathenius," she said. "I will confess to you, because I believe that you will understand, that after my husband and Lord Dellacrusca were killed, I was in mortal fear for my own life. I felt obliged to turn my house into a fortress and surround it with armed men, which the Duc d'Alectryon was kind enough to supply. That contributed, I fear, to the poor opinion some people had of me…and still have. As I told you just now, my anxieties have not entirely eased. I am trying to be brave, and to suppress my anxieties, but

I really do feel the need to have friends around me. Charles and Vashti have been godsends. I have always treasured the company of artists—that is why I persuaded my husband to buy a house here and to take up permanent residence, rather than simply coming for the season, as we used to do. I would very much like, Master Rathenius, to have you for a friend too. Do you think that might be possible?"

"I hope it might," I said, wondering at my own sincerity, and feeling like a fool, even though, when analyzed rationally, there could surely be no better outcome to my present predicament than establishing a simultaneous amity with the Marquise, Madame and the Dellacrusca twins, in order that all of us might live in peace and harmony. I almost had to pinch myself in order to remind myself of the implausibility of such a dream.

"While you were absent," she said, "I commissioned Charles to paint a portrait of me, which is nearly finished. I cannot possibly tell him so, of course, because I love him dearly, but I am not very satisfied with it. I fear that he has not been able to capture my essence. I thought him a good painter, on the basis of the portrait that once hung in my dining room, but I am beginning to think that he could only paint his wife with any real precision or penetration. He does not have your all-encompassing eye; he cannot adapt, as you can. That is why I would like to commission you to paint me. I have not told him yet, obviously, for fear of hurting his feelings, but I honestly think that there will be no salvation for his painting if he does not find his wife again...and his daughter, of course. Such a tragedy. No one has the slightest idea what has become of them, it seems."

That, I felt sure, was a bare-faced lie. It was almost a relief to hear it, and to have that certainty.

"Actually," I said, feeling a slight moral superiority in sticking to the truth, albeit a carefully selected truth, "I believe I saw her going into to the old Toustain house shortly before you rang my doorbell...but I can't say how long she will remain there."

I wondered how long I could go on playing the game, and how long I ought to collaborate with her in maintaining the pretence. Although having been caught by surprise and somewhat slow on the uptake, I was beginning to see her objective, and the logic of what she was doing. It was difficult to break the spell she was casting, however, even though there was not the slightest hint of magic in it, so far as I could tell.

"That is good news," she said, equably. "Charles will be delighted. Did you see his daughter too, by any chance?"

"I don't believe she's in the house at present," I said, "but I'm certain that if Mariette has returned to the island, Elise must be here too."

It occurred to me then that the Marquise really might not have known that, having only been hurriedly notified of my own return, but I didn't criticize myself for having given anything away. If she had not been given the detail in question, she would surely have discovered it before noon. In any case, given that she doubtless knew perfectly well that Mariette and Elise had been with me on the Island of Dionysus, she could not have been the least surprised by what I had said, and I wondered whether she was exploring the strategy of my replies, trying to measure me accurately by the scrupulousness with which I was filtering the truth.

"I really would like to hear Elise play some day," she said, "in order to make up for the lost opportunity. Charles says that she will be a great artist one day. I would like to invite her to come to my house, but I fear that it might provoke bad memories for her. The rumors have not spared her either, I fear—but you're no stranger to that kind of slander yourself. You painted the Duc d'Alectryon's daughters once, I believe, and were caught up in the talk of black magic that followed poor Roxane's death. Wagging tongues are so malicious."

"They exaggerate, too," I observed, remembering the scandal in question only too clearly, distant as it now was.

"But not in the case of your reputation as an artist, Master Rathenius. The Orpheus triptych is a brilliant work of art, and a constant reminder of you. I really would like us to be friends, Axel...may I call you Axel? I feel that I know you very well, after all that Myrica Mavor, Vashti and Hecate have told me about you. Hecate, in particular, seems extremely fond of you."

"I do seem to be privileged in that regard," I admitted, curiously, wondering if the observation concealed a threat. I did not ask her whether I might call her Aethne, and she did not make any such suggestion. It was one thing for a Marquise to address an artist by his first name, but quite another for the favor to be reciprocated.

"She probably tries to conceal it from you," the Marquise went on still indulging her loquacity. "Women often try to conceal themselves from men...but they cannot hide their true selves from you, can they, no matter how hard they try?"

I was slightly relieved by that, the move suggesting a strategy far more subtle than any vulgar threat.

"It doesn't seem to prevent them from trying," I observed

"Of course not. It is a temptation to which I am probably not immune myself—because I really would like you to think well of me, Axel, or at least not to harbor unwarranted suspicions about me. You do believe that I'm sincere, don't you, when I say that I would like us to be friends?"

"I cannot imagine why you would want to deceive me if it were not true," I countered. In fact, I could simply have said yes, because I really did believe that she would have liked us to be friends. I believed that she wanted me to be on her side, perhaps even to lend my supposed sorcery to support hers. Whether she thought it was actually possible, I couldn't tell, but if she was only trying to sow confusion, she was certainly succeeding in that.

"I must telegraph Myrica in Lutèce to inform her that you've returned," she said. "I know that she has been worried by your absence."

I could believe that too, even though Myrica was one of the people to whom I had attempted to send a letter reassuring her of my safety, without actually telling her where I was.

"Did you know that the island now has quite an elaborate telegraph network." she added.

"Yes," I said. "I'm having an apparatus installed myself."

"Very wise. My late husband was a great believer in technological progress. Steam has changed the world, he used to say, and electricity will transform it. He used to play with a telegraph machine for years before the cable from the mainland to the police station was installed, but

I can't imagine what he used it for. He seemed to understand all that mysterious tapping. I don't. Do you?"

"Not yet," I admitted, "but I'll learn. One has to keep up with the times."

She bent down and picked up an empty whelk shell. I thought it interesting that she had chosen the relic of a predator rather than one of the countless harmless mollusks whose shells were distributed over the damp shingle, but almost all of the others were broken. Whelk shells are exceptionally hard, much more resilient than the shells of cockles or mussels. She inspected the chitinous spiral briefly, weighing it speculatively in her gray-gloved hand, and then dropped it delicately into a clump of wrack left behind by the tide and now shriveling in the sunlight.

"We had best climb the cliff again," she said, "or my coachman will be getting worried. I do hope your maidservant is feeling better. I thought she was about to faint when she opened the door to me."

"She's a little out of sorts, I fear—the shock of my return. I was not able to warn her of my arrival in advance. Please forgive her for her rudeness in leaving you on the doorstep.

"Of course," said the Marquise, as we set off up the steep path. "You're fortunate to have such good servants to look after your house in your absence. I admire a man who can command such loyalty."

We climbed in silence; no longer a young woman, as she had observed herself, the Marquise seemed slightly tested by the step ascent. Near the top, she paused and looked out over the distant sea, iron gray but flecked with white surf where it was whipped by the wind. There were a handful of fishing boats in view, their sails billowing in the breeze.

"What a fine sight it will be in mid-summer, she said, when all the yachts are here…if they come this year. Hekla will have a lot to answer for, if they stay away."

"We can hardly blame the volcano for erupting," I observed. "That is, after all, a volcano's reason for being. I have heard it said that they provide a useful safety valve for the magma beneath the crust, without which we might see much worse explosions, capable of blowing islands away entirely, and devastating continents. Nature's powers of destruction are terrible. We must be grateful for her temporary calms."

"You're quite the philosopher, Axel," she observed, as she resumed her uphill course, having recovered her breath. "I really must make an effort to enjoy your conversation more often. I'll wait with as much patience as I can until you're ready to begin my portrait. I'll gladly come to your studio, if you wish, although I would prefer to sit for you in my home. Will you let me know, please, as soon as you are ready to make preliminary sketches?"

"I will," I said.

As we walked along that path that led back to the house, Hecate Rain's carriage veered round the Marquise's vehicle. Mariette immediately came out of the house—my house, not the old Toustain house—in order to meet it, having evidently seen it from a window. Presumably, she had not spoken to Luzon since she had returned with the possessions she had transferred, and Luzon had not rushed to give her new mistress news of my unexpected departure.

Elise jumped down from the carriage and immediately turned to offer a helping hand to Sister Ursule, who was followed by Hecate.

None of them realized that the Marquise and I were only a few dozen paces away for at least five agonizing seconds, but during that interval, the Marquise did not say a word; and when the newcomers all turned round to look in our direction, and froze, as if they had seen a gorgon or a basilisk, the Marquise simply kept walking, as if it were the most natural thing in the world not only for her to be there, but for all of them to be there, stilled by respect alone.

"Madame Parenot!" said the Marquise. "How nice it is to see you again! And dear Elise! I was just telling Master Rathenius how pleasant it would be to hear you play, at last. I shall ask your father to arrange it as soon as possible. And how nice it is to see you out of your dusty convent, Ursule! Haven't I always told you that you should get out more? Good day, Hecate—your friend Axel and I have been having a very pleasant stroll down in the cove. He's going to paint my portrait. Will you mind, Madame Parenot, if I tell your husband that you've returned, or would you prefer to surprise him? He's painting my portrait too…you must think me very vain. He'll be delighted to see you—he really has been very anxious about you and Elise, and my attempts to console him have been quite inadequate, I fear. But I must be running along. I'm sure that I shall see you all again very soon. Have a very pleasant day."

And, without waiting for Mariette to reply to her question, she swept past them all, while her coachman leapt back on to his seat and picked up his whip.

Nobody moved until the coachman had pulled the horses round and urged them into a trot. Everyone was staring at me.

"It seems," I observed, "that I have been mistaken in my anticipation of the tactics with which this contest will be fought. I fear that I was caught on the wrong foot, and I have no idea what her next move will be."

"I think I have," said Sister Ursule. "May we go inside, Master Rathenius? I have a great deal that I want to tell you—and I can only hope, now, that you will not think me insane."

XI. The Meaning of the Orphean Manuscript

We all sat down in the reception room, which seemed oddly confining after my excursion to the cove. Luzon brought a pot of tea, but no one seemed very interested in drinking it.

"It appears," I said, "that the Marquise would like us to be friends. Perhaps, on reflection, I ought to have anticipated that possibility, but she caught me completely by surprise. She made some very interesting points, however, regarding the reliability of sources of information, and the desirability of keeping an open mind."

"But you didn't believe her?" said Hecate, incredulously.

"No, I didn't," I said "She knew that I wouldn't...but her objective wasn't to persuade me to believe her; it was to suggest that I ought to be wary of believing others. It's a fair point, given that most of what I know about her came from Tommaso Dellacrusca and Madame, who both have their own agendas."

"As have I," Sister Ursule put in, "as my dear niece doubtless suggested to you."

"She did—but like her, I have friends that I trust, and the most precious of those is Hecate. Since Hecate vouches for you, Sister, and does not trust the Marquise, I am entirely disposed to trust her judgment."

Hecate thanked me with a nod of the head, but Sister Ursule seemed oddly embarrassed. "In fairness to my niece," she said, "what she thinks of me is not entirely false. There are factors that go back to my childhood that prejudiced me against my late sister, and I am a member of a reclusive religious order, with little direct acquaintance with the world. I consider Hecate a good friend, and I am grateful for her trust in me...but I cannot be sure of the extent to which I can trust myself, where my judgment of my niece is concerned. It would not be unreasonable of either of you to conserve doubts about the value of my testimony."

I was impressed by her honesty, but I could certainly have wished her to be more confident in herself. The seeds of confusion and doubt that the Marquise had come to sow were already taking root.

I knew that I would have to ask myself some serious questions, when I had time to think about it, about what I really knew for certain. Had I any real proof that it was the Marquise de Mesmay had hired the assassins who had attacked me prior to my abduction, other than my own fallible intuition? Had I any real proof that she and her husband had plotted to murder Dellacrusca, or that it was Dellacrusca who had stabbed Mesmay and not the murderous maenads? As the Marquise had carefully provoked me into admitting, even though I had been present on the occasion of the multiple murder, I had seen very little of what had happened. Everything I thought I knew was a tissue of rumors and assertions, which already had an inevitable pattern of counter-rumor and counter-assertion.

Meanwhile, Hecate was looking at Sister Ursule quizzically. Typically, however, she focused on more practical issues "You can anticipate Aethne's next move, you say?"

"That's surely not difficult," said the superior. "You can certainly expect a visit from Charles Parenot within a matter of hours. He too will probably have been advised—or instructed—to feign ignorance of the circumstances of your disappearance and return. He will surely not have to feign delight at seeing his daughter again...or you, Mariette, although that might be more of a strain. If you were to confront him, Master Rathenius, you could probably crack his veneer far more easily than Aethne's...but it might not be wise to do that. Charles will undoubtedly demand an account of where you and Elise have been, Mariette, and much will depend on what you tell him...and on what you decide to do next."

Mariette looked at me, with frank alarm in her eyes. "What should I tell him?" she asked.

"The truth," I said. "At the very least, you should not lie to him. Tell him everything he wants to know...but it might as well to be careful only to tell him what you know for sure. It would be wise to refrain from reporting anything that is mere hearsay, whatever its source."

"You can rely on us," said Elise.

"That's kind, Elise, but I don't think you should say or do anything for my sake. You should consider your own interests, exclusively. Whatever you decide, I will respect."

"But if we don't give Charles the answers that the Marquise wants to hear," said Mariette, "it might put us all in danger."

"That's possible," I said, "but it's not a good reason for deception. You need not tell Charles everything, by any means, but what you do tell him ought to be true, for your sake and for his. If it disappoints the Marquise, so be it."

"Master Rathenius is right," said Ursule, support-ively, "not only as a matter of principle but of practicality."

"But she did try to have him killed...didn't she?" asked Mariette, obviously sensing the germination of her own seeds of doubt.

"I strongly suspect that she did," Ursule confirmed, "although I would certainly prefer not to think so."

"But she knows now," I said, "that when she sent assassins to murder me—if she did—she was acting on a false assumption: that I was an agent of Lord Dellacrusca. Her husband's spies had put a completely mistaken interpretation on the fact that Dellacrusca spent several hours in this house shortly before the planned assassination. She must regret that mistake bitterly, and I suspect that she really would like to repair it if she could. She surely will not try to harm you and Elise, even if any hope that she is nursing that Charles can lure you into her camp is dashed."

Mariette looked at Sister Ursule. She had never seen the Sister of Shalimar before, but there is something about the charitable Order, and especially its superiors, that instills confidence.

"I believe that Master Rathenius is right, my dear," Ursule supplied. "I had not expected my sister to come here, but since she has, I think you ought to see it as a genuine attempt to defuse hostilities. She has already made every effort to woo Hecate, via Vashti Savage, not only because of Hecate's own abilities but also because of her influence over you, Master Rathenius, which she probably does not understand but would nevertheless like to exploit. If she attempts any magical endeavor in the immediate future, it will surely be seductive, not hostile. With the Dellacrusca twins in Lutèce and the other potential target of her magical malevolence half way across the Ocean, the only rival seduction she presumably fears, for the moment, is mine...which she will regard with the inherited contempt that she has always had for me. If you want to be her friend, Master Rathenius, you probably could be."

"But I would disappoint you if I did?" I remarked, with a thin smile,

"Undoubtedly—but you might well feel that that there is no reason to pander to my residual sibling jealousy…and if you refuse my niece's offer of amity, you will certainly disappoint her. It's necessary, therefore, as you have just advised Mariette, that you have a far better reason for choosing your course of action than the risk of disappointing anyone. There are much larger issues at stake."

"So I believe," I said, quietly. "You have deciphered the Orphean manuscript from the copy that Hecate gave you, I understand?"

"I believe so, although I could never have done so without her intuitive grasp of the suspiric language, which she owes in large measure to Elise. I cannot be completely sure that my translation is accurate, given that it is written in an artificial language, and it might only be scholarly vanity that gives me confidence…and a similar illusion that gives my niece confidence. If I am even approximately right, however, there might well be a considerable danger in the understanding I have gained, and my sister's possession of that understanding."

"It's a spell to summon Hades from the Underworld and subject him to compulsion," I said, attempting to cut her loquacity short.

"It is," she agreed, "but if I remember our previous conversation correctly, Master Rathenius, you know that the matter is not as simple as a vulgar understanding of magic tends to assume. You appreciate the true complexity of such matters."

"I have a vague idea," I admitted. "What I learned, and did, on the Island of Dionysus added considerably to that appreciation, but I can't say that it clarified my understanding, or even suggested that any such clarification might be possible."

"I would very much like to hear an account of your adventure," said the superior, "but this is not the time. Yes, the text I have decoded appears to be a formula for summoning and directing destruction, via the symbolic person of Hades, which a vulgar sorcerer, or sorceress, would undoubtedly construe as an instrument that could be employed to wreak havoc upon a specific victim or an enemy. Such a practitioner would attempt to employ it in connection with of symbolic focusing device, usually an image of some kind, and appropriate musical accompaniment. I fear that my sister might try to do exactly that. Indeed, what Hecate has told me about recent events in her house convinces me that her preparations are already far advanced, even though no Bardic musician will lend support to her, and I believe that the musicians of the artists' colony are also reluctant."

"By preparations that are far advanced you mean the painting that the Marquise has commissioned Parenot to make?" I asked.

"No. Hecate has described that painting to me, and I believe that my niece intends, or at least hopes, to use it in connection with formulae of a different kind. It seems to be a portrait of the kind in which Monsieur Parenot has specialized in the past: a mythological painting, in which the Marquise is invested with the character of a symbolic figure from mythology, in this case, Eurydice."

"But he already panted Eurydice," Mariette objected, "with my face. The Marquise owns the painting."

""She did," Ursule agreed. "And she has burned it, symbolically. The Eurydice that she intends to substitute for it is an older one, and a markedly different one. Master Rathenius has explained to you, I presume, the amendment that he made to the existing legend in order to complete his own understanding of Orpheus and Eurydice."

"Yes," said Mariette. "In his representation, Orpheus is assumed to have killed Eurydice, in a fit of jealous rage, by means of the power of his lyre. Then, overcome by remorse, he went into the Underworld in order to bring her back, but coupled his remorse with a arrogance that made him believe that he could bend Hades to his will—although Hades tricked him. Orpheus' subsequent murder by bacchantes was the administration of the kind of divine justice that Greek myth tends to favor."

"Precisely." Ursule turned to me. "You never explained that to the Marquise, I assume?"

"It didn't seem necessary," I said.

"It wasn't—but, to judge by what Hecate has told me, she might well have discovered it. Perhaps she did so by intuition or intelligence, although it seems more probable to me that the information reached her via Myrica Mavor and Vashti Savage."

Myrica had, indeed, been present when I explained my thinking in regard to the triptych, and she was not reputed for her discretion. She and Vashti had been friends for a long time.

"That symbolism undoubtedly appealed to my niece," Ursule continued, "who probably found other suggestive parallels—for instance, the symbolism of Lord Dellacrusca's quest in the social Underworld for the redemption of his lost-lost granddaughter, and his murder by Bacchantes—which might well have encouraged her in the idea of appropriating Master Rathenius' improvisation for herself. If my guesswork is reliable, the theme of the painting that Charles Parenot is bringing to completion is Eurydice Redeemed, and it depicts a Eurydice delivered from Hades by her own efforts, without the need of any assistance from her murderer, and her assumption in the world of the living of the position of power and authority that was always her due. The ritual purpose of that painting is surely intended to be the celebration of the triumph of the Marquise over the remnants of Lord Dellacrusca's organization, and her assumption, via Alectryon, of a certain power behind the Imperial throne. I cannot be sure, but what Hecate has told me about Vashti Savage's séances in the Mesmay manse, and their surrounding circumstances, suggests very strongly that she intends to use the Orphean formula that she stole from me, reinforced by the supposed power of the twin sorceresses she has imported from the heart of Africa, for a different purpose, with the aid of a different symbolic work of art."

I looked at Hecate. "Have you seen this other work of art?" I asked.

"Sister Ursule believes so," she said, "but if she is right, I did not recognize it for what it is. It is a device that her husband imported from Italy after the black snow began to fall. A device called..."

Sometimes, one simply cannot resist the temptation to show one's cleverness. Reflexively, I stole her thunder. "A seismograph," I said—and immediately followed up the inspiration: "She's not planning to work magic at all! She's planning to put on a great pretence, just as she was planning to do on the night of my initiation into the

Cult of Dionysus. The Marquise and Madame have followed similar trains of thought to similar conclusions. The Marquise intends to pick up the early signals of a major earthquake or an eruption, which she expects to occur soon because such events tend to happen in series, and the after-effects of Hekla's eruption have not yet died down. She hopes to detect a major quake in time to put in a show of having caused it. By means of intercepted telegraph messages, she probably knows that Madame is anxious about the possibility that disturbances in the crust on the far side of the Ocean might cause a tidal wave capable of causing severe damage to her paradisal island. The Marquise intends to claim the credit for it, if and when it happens! It's all fakery!"

"That is a possibility, Master Rathenius," said Sister Ursule, equably, "but, knowing my sister as I do, I do not believe that she thinks of it as fakery. Nor, I will admit, do I. As I said, the matter is far more complicated than that."

"You really believe that the spell you deciphered actually has the power to cause an upheaval in the earth's crust?" I said, skeptically. "You think that the Marquise can somehow use her seismograph as a generator rather than a detector?"

"As I said," Ursule repeated, patiently, "the matter is not as simple as that. As you are using the term seismograph, I assume that the device you saw in the island where you have set the last few months is one that records a trace of the vibrations it picks up on a moving scroll of paper. That is, indeed, a recent invention, but related devices—seismometers, if you wish—are very old, predating the foundation of the Empire. Pendulums with attached styli have been producing what might be thought of as artistic representations of disturbances in

203

the Earth's crust for hundreds of years. The hope has always been that such designs might be useful as prophecy, that they might allow the prediction of disasters. Seismometric devices of various kinds have always been reputed, and used, as instruments of divination, perhaps inaptly, although, as you seem to have discovered, they really do have potential for that usage.

"The idea that magicians might be able to use seismometers, or the designs that they can be arranged to make, to provoke earthquakes, is the product of a naïve way of thinking. The idea that such designs might be potentially capable of anticipating earthquakes and eruptions, however, is not stupid. I am a scholar, who never makes any observations beyond the walls of my study, so everything I know about such matters is the result of reportage and rumor, which might be entirely fanciful, but there is a rich legendry that credits animals with the ability to sense impending events of that kind, presumably because the unconscious part of their minds recognizes subtle signals and generates anxiety. The unconscious part of human minds might also recognize similar signs, similarly transmitting them to consciousness as an anxiety—but human consciousness, not unnaturally, seeks interpretations of the anxiety in question in either rational or magical terms, or both.

"Enclosed in my study, in my convent, I have not had the opportunities to observe the social world as you all have, so I can only broach the hypothesis and ask you whether you have any supportive evidence to offer. Have you, in the last few months, since Hekla's eruption and for some time beforehand, seen signs both around and within you of an increased level of general human anxiety? Is it possible, at least, that the entire sequence of events that has led to the five of us being seated in this room today, discussing the strange predicament in which we find ourselves, is a reflection of some such increase in anxiety: a resonance within the unconscious part of our minds of events within and beneath the earth's crust, which really do presage some kind of critical fracture, and consequential catastrophe?"

I no longer had to ask Hecate what the larger picture that she had begun to grasp looked like. Sister Ursule had just set it out, with scrupulous attention to detail...and a certain amount of speculative embroidery.

At any rate, what she had said was certainly food for thought, which I began chewing reflexively, as the others doubtless did.

It was Elise, perhaps naturally, who intervened to bring the discussion back to the point.

"But Axel is still right, isn't he?" she said. "The Marquise is a fake. She can't really cause anything, even if she can detect it in time to pretend that she has, can she?"

"That way of thinking assumes that magic is simply the effect of a magician's instigation," Sister Ursule said, softly. "Seen from a different viewpoint, a magician is merely an instrument, and the true instigator of magic is something more remote, with which the magician's unconscious mind is in mysterious resonance. In the lore of legend and myth, such instigators are seen as gods and demons, but those are mere symbols. Indeed, everything in that realm of thought consists of symbols, because it cannot be represented consciously in any other way. Skeptics take it for granted that humans are utterly helpless in the grip of such forces, thinking that it is simply absurd to think that such a petty thing as human desire could affect or influence, even in the slightest, the forces of the underworld that determine such massive events as earthquakes and volcanic eruptions. Perhaps they are right—but I take leave to doubt it, and so, I assume, does my niece, perhaps for different reasons. I am not prepared to state, dogmatically, that the resonance that exists between the unconscious part of the human mind and the underlying, unperceived reality, can only work in one direction. Indeed, I tend to favor the principle that any such influence must, logically, be reciprocal.

"Undoubtedly, any such human influence must be tiny, even if it involves a nexus of human minds working within the framework of an appropriate focusing rite, but it seems to me that we are dealing here with phenomena of such a kind that a very tiny shift in circumstances could trigger a chain reaction capable of amplifying the effect, by degrees, into something tremendous. In view of that, I am not prepared to deny that Aethne's magic might not only be able to detect imminent upheavals that have been gestating for a long time deep within the planetary crust, but might be able to exert an influence upon them, which, although tiny in itself, might affect their development.

"If the circumstances were not already in place, and the situation already promised, she probably could not achieve anything, any more than an astronomer could conjure an eclipse if the Moon were not bound by its orbit to pass between the Earth and the Sun—but the Earth is already restless, and our anxieties are monitoring that restlessness via our unconscious minds. If my sister selects the moment cleverly enough, I do believe that she might be able to exercise a magical influence over the unfolding event. And by the same token, Master Rathenius, I believe—as she seems to do—that you might also be able to do so. You might see the choice of the right moment, and of the symbols that surround it, as a matter of art rather than magic, but from what Hecate tells me, you have believed for some time that that is a distinction with little or no difference. Why else are you here, planning to do what you are planning to do?"

She was right. That *was* why I was here, and what I as planning to do was, in essence, not so very different from what the Marquise appeared to be planning.

"You might think of it as mere performance and mere fakery, Master Rathenius" Ursule continued, "but that will not prevent you from bringing your artist's eye and your artist's soul to bear with full intensity...provided that the Marquise cannot deflect you from your purpose. She will doubtless attempt to do so. She is already trying, as you have seen, by means of methods cleverer than the crude ones that you anticipated, and more likely to be successful. But there is one thing that you really ought to bear in mind, if you hope to have an effect, however tiny, in this unfolding pattern of events."

A showman would have paused there for dramatic effect, but Sister Ursule was not a showman. She only paused to draw breath, because she was making a very long speech, before adding: "The principle of reciprocal influence. She hopes to create an opportunity to deflect your attention and confuse your allegiance. Inevitably, that creates an opportunity for you to deflect and confuse hers. None of you can prevent whatever upheaval is building in the earth's crust on the far side of the Ocean, but my belief is that everyone here present is potentially capable of intervening in the Marquise's attempt to influence its unfolding by magical means, by amplification or diminution, just as Vashti Savage and Charles Parenot are. She would certainly like to divide your nexus, if she can, but her own is not indivisible. If pressure is applied in the right way, at the right moment, it might disintegrate completely."

She left it there, perhaps because she was exhausted. She was far older than her niece, and by no means as strong physically, even though she was still full of life and intelligence.

It occurred me that if Ursule was correct, whatever we might do and whatever the outcome might be, we would never know whether or not it had made the slightest difference. If, in fact, all magic really was fakery and pretence, anything I might do would be a mere masquerade. But even if that were the case, the artistry of the masque would remain—and for me, at least, the artistry was necessary. Even if I were only responding to temptation, the lure was irresistible. For me, though, that was easy. I knew exactly what I was and where I stood. I merely had to take up my position and follow the logic of my imagination. Hecate would do the same. For Mariette and Elise, however, things were by no means as simple. They probably did not know, with any degree of certainty, who they were and where they stood—and within a matter of hours, Charles Parenot was going to put that to the test…and that would only be the first test to which they would be subjected.

Mariette was looking out of the window, deliberately, at the cloudy sky. Elise and Hecate were both looking at me. It was Elise's gaze that I met.

You selected me as your guardian, my own gaze said. *Trust me, and I'll do everything I can you bring you though this to the best of your advantage.*

Perhaps she understood, because she nodded her head, imperceptibly.

XII. Ananke and the Pool of Mnemosyne

When Charles Parenot arrived at the house that afternoon, asking to see Mariette and Elise, I was already busy in the studio, applying paint to canvas with a frenzied haste that was most unlike my normal earnest and methodical procedure. The Pool of Mnemosyne did not bear the least resemblance to a pond in a forest glade, or a rock pool recently filled and abandoned by the tide. It was not that kind of pool. It bore more resemblance, at least to the proverbial naked eye, to a black maelstrom, but an aerial rather than a liquid vortex. As for the petals, as yet I had barely begun marking their eventual positions with small dabs of paint; they might have been embryonic suggestions of almost anything, depending on the eye's interpretation of their backcloth: trees and roofs ripped from the ground by a tornado, the hulls of ships being drawn by a whirling route into the abyss, or people adrift in a void. Ananke, of course, had no face; she was ever-present, the darkness within the black, the impetus within the movement.

I had given strict instructions that I was not to be interrupted. I did not want to see Charles Parenot, and I did not want him to see me. Elise and Mariette were free and capable agents, and it was not for me to give them any further advice or permission regarding what they ought to say to him. Sister Ursule had returned to her convent, after making an arrangement to come see me again on the evening of the following day, in order that I could tell her everything that I had seen and learned on the Island of Dionysus. Helen had returned with Jean-Jacques from their massive shopping expedition, and was busy making detailed arrangements with him for the accommodation and establishment of the telegraph apparatus. Luzon was fully occupied in the kitchen.

Hecate was at a loose end.

"Tell me to go away if I'm inconvenient," she said, "or to sit and be quiet, if you can tolerate my presence but not my voice."

"You have never been inconvenient, Hecate," I told her. "Provided that you don't expect me to turn my head to look at you, I can listen and speak while I paint. Indeed, you are partly the author of this painting, so your presence is not inappropriate."

It isn't your usual style," she observed, a mistress of understatement for once. "It seems...rather abstract."

"I'm adaptable," I told her. "I've been stuck in a rut for far too long; I need to stretch myself."

"I know the feeling," she said. "It reminds me, somehow, of the composition I made with Elise before you went away."

"So it should," I said. "The sequel, I assume, will remain in suspense until Elise comes back from the old Toustain house? That might take some time, I fear."

"Elise doesn't love Charles," she said. "She told me so. I think she feels slightly guilty about it, though, as if it makes her an ingrate. She won't go back to live with him. Neither will Mariette, even though she did love him, in her way. No matter how difficult it is, they will tell him that."

"I hope you're right," I said.

"Parenot brought a letter with him. It's addressed to you. I have it here."

"Open it," I said. "Don't bother to read it aloud— just give me the gist."

There was a brief pause. "No surprise," said Hecate. "It's an invitation to dinner at the manse, for two evenings hence. There's no mention of other guests, but I dare say that a similar invitation will reach me, one way or another. Will you accept?"

"Yes, I think so. I'll ask Jean-Jacques to take a note."

"Do you want me to accept?"

"That's not for me to say, but I'd certainly feel a trifle exposed if I were there on my own."

"Does that mean that you want Mariette and Elise to accept, if they receive similar invitations?"

"That's not for me to say either, and I'd certainly understand if they don't want to go, after what happened last time, especially if Charles Parenot is going to be there. The Marquise has already mentioned the possibility that Elise might feel uncomfortable in the event of being asked to play at the Mesmay house, so she can't be offended by a refusal."

"You don't think we'll be in danger?"

"I can't guarantee that we won't, but I tend to trust Ursule's judgment; for the moment, at least, the Marquise is attempting seduction, that having been her most reliable strategy in the past. I suspect, too, that she's genuinely curious. When Parenot reports back to her what Elise and Mariette have told him about our sojourn on the island, she'll want to know more. She'll certainly want to know everything I can tell her about the night of the two initiation ceremonies, and about Madame."

"But you won't tell her?"

"I won't lie to her...but I'll be discreet."

"What will the Dellacruscas think, if they hear about your going to dine with the Marquise?"

"I don't know. I'd like to think that they trust me, and will assume that I'm simply playing a subtle game, but even if they don't, they surely won't think that I'm betraying them without much firmer evidence. I don't think they'll send assassins after me—and they certainly won't send assassins after you, Mariette or Elise. By then, in any case, the telegraph link ought to be established, and Helen will be able to communicate, albeit indirectly, with both the Dellacruscas and Madame."

"Perhaps I'll be able to pretend that it's just like old times," Hecate said, her voice and manner seeming firmer now. "How many dinners have we been invited to, and seated next to one another, sometimes with our current lovers to either side of us? And how many of Vashti's séances have we attended, holding hands in the circle? I lost count a long time ago."

"Me too," I agreed.

There was a pause, while I applied black paint to the canvas with such assertive recklessness that I splashed my smock and sent a few drips tumbling toward the varnished floorboards, which were uncarpeted close to the wall. I studied the pattern made by the fallen drops momentarily.

When Hecate spoke again, it was in a more hesitant tone. "You meant what you said last night, didn't you, about our always having loved one another in the way we wanted and needed to be loved? You weren't just being glib?"

"I meant it."

"Other people think that it's very strange—Myrica, for instance."

"Myrica isn't an artist. She doesn't employ her passions in the same way. When she exchanges lovers, it's merely out of boredom, not necessity, and she makes no attempt to keep her discarded lovers as friends."

"Whereas you and I are parasites, perverting our passions into painting and poetry." She simply couldn't resist the allure of the alliteration.

"We're artists," I insisted. "We're the true connoisseurs of passion. We're the least perverse of people. The fidelity that you and I have is the truest kind, untainted by jealousy or possessiveness. I don't say that artists are the only people capable of that, and it certainly isn't the case that very many artists are capable of it, but in our case, it has made us better artists and truer lovers. Myrica will never understand...and I fear that Mariette might not, either. Elise probably will, one day, but not yet. She hasn't had the formative experiences that will enable her, eventually, to take control of her passions as well as drawing upon them."

"That could take a long time," Hecate said, with a sigh. "I'm not sure I've got there myself yet, although my passions are already becoming futile. I couldn't have been nearly as sane and sensible these last twenty years without your example...and it wasn't until the night you went away that I realized, fully, that you had had sixty years of practice before you even met me. I thought, when that realization finally hit me—although I believe I'd known subconsciously for a long time—that I'd somehow been cheated, but I hadn't, obviously. I was just lucky."

"Luck," I said, "had nothing to do with it. We were made for one another."

"In spite of the difference in our ages?" Her tone was skeptical.

"Because of it."

"And when I'm dead, or senile, you'll find someone else who's made for you. And so *ad infinitum*.

"You're fishing for compliments, Hecate. Of course you're unique. Of course you're irreplaceable. Of course I'll remember you for as long as I live, even if I live to be as old as Madame claims to be." I hoped that she knew that I was only being glib out of habit, and that I meant every word.

"Claims to be?" she queried. "You don't believe her, then?"

"I'm not sure she even knows herself. I suspect that, over time, the identities that she made up when she was younger, when she had to keep reinventing herself, be-came confused with the one she synthesized for her own secret attention. I'm no longer entirely sure who I was, originally, and the age I attribute to myself already seems to be an arbitrary figure, which I might have made up. Most Macrobians don't seem to live much longer than two hundred years, and the older ones I encountered on the island were manifestly in the process of losing their minds. Madame is a very rare exception; I doubt that I can reasonably hope for another fifty years of sani-ty, let alone a hundred, and I could start aging tomorrow, so rapidly that I'll fall apart in ten. So there will never be another love like yours in my life, and when I die, it will be the most precious I have ever had. Does that satisfy your need for flattery, for the moment?"

She laughed. "That's a need that's never sated, Ax-el, as you well know, and I was never able to take your contributions to its satisfaction entirely seriously. Now that I can't fascinate virile young men any more, I'm pathetically grateful for the kind of awe I strike into Elise, and the crumbs of respect I get from Sister Ursule.

Vashti's infatuation, alas, leaves me completely cold, ungrateful bitch that I am."

"Now you're just playing at self-pity," I told her. "Not all the examples I've set you have been good ones, alas."

She laughed again. "I've missed this," she said. "You can't begin to imagine how I felt after you disappeared, thinking that you might be dead or gone for good. Or what a relief it was when I felt your presence, on the night when I agreed to be initiated into the Cult of Orpheus. Even then, I didn't know whether you were reaching out to me from beyond the grave. When your letter reached me, I still didn't know that you'd ever come back—and I didn't believe young Dellacrusca, obviously, when he told me that he was going to bring you back. I wrote the note because of what Sister Ursule had told me, but I'm not entirely sure myself whether that was any more than an excuse, and whether the absolute imperative I really meant was just my own feeble yearning. Could you forgive me, if that were the case?"

"There's nothing to forgive," I said. "You didn't have any more choice than I did. It was, and is, Ananke...and the pool of Mnemosyne."

"There really is going to be a disaster isn't there" she said, just to make sure.

"Yes."

"And we really can't do anything about it, except try to make ourselves feel better by enacting some empty ritual?"

"That's the worst case scenario, but I don't believe it. Sister Ursule is a wise woman. So is Madame. We can't stop the impending catastrophe, but we can certainly intervene, and we can certainly make a difference. Trust me."

I took a step back to appraise the painting. It had a long way to go, and an enormous amount of detail to fill in, but on the whole, I thought it was progressing well. It was the first time I'd ever tried to penetrate the soul of the world rather than a soul of a single person, but I was beginning to get a feel for it. It was just a matter of drawing the right symbolism out of the unconscious.

I heard the front door open and close. Hecate practically bounded to the studio door, moved by the spring of curiosity.

I don't know how much time went by after that; I was too deeply absorbed to keep track. When the studio door opened and closed again, I assumed that it was Hecate returning and didn't turn round. There must have been two or three minutes of silence, before Elise's voice said: "Hecate said that it would probably be all right to talk to you, as long as I didn't expect you to turn round. She said that it wouldn't be all right for anyone else, but that you'd make an exception for me."

"She was right," I said.

"Mariette didn't come back with me. She and Charles have adult matters to discuss. That's what they think, anyhow. Actually, they were striving with all their might to be adult while I was there. Now they've sent me away, they'll probably let themselves go. He'll beg, she'll cry; he'll threaten to kill himself, she'll tell him to go ahead. Eventually, they might start being rational...or not."

"You're very cynical, for someone who's only just fourteen," I observed.

"I grew up on Martyr's Mount. I've lost count of the times I've heard similar scenes played out. The walls are thin there, and the voices loud."

"Charles and Mariette are more level-headed and more even-tempered than that."

"Says the man who's been living with Mariette for a matter of weeks and doesn't know Charles at all, to the pretended daughter who's been living in uncomfortable intimacy with both of them for more than ten years. Don't humor me, Axel. You're my guardian now. I told Charles that. I told him that it was what I wanted. I thanked him for everything he's done for me, and I told him that I'd always think fondly of him, but I told him that I had to move on. I was trying to set an example for Mariette, but I did mean it. I hope you don't think I'll be a burden."

"I don't."

"He asked us a lot of questions—about what happened the night we were taken, about the island, and about you. Mariette told him the truth. So did I, when he turned his fire on me. He'll report it all to the Marquise."

"Good," I said.

"He says that she's invited you to dinner. She'll probably question you herself."

"Probably."

"She wants to come to the house—Charles's house, that is—to hear me play. Mariette said no, that it wasn't our house any longer. What should I do if she asks me to go to her house?"

"You can say no—that it would be too distressing to go back there, after what happened the last time."

"Is that what you want me to do?"

"It's up to you—and Mariette, obviously."

"She won't go—not if Charles is going to be there. He will, won't he?"

"I don't know. Perhaps what the Marquise has a mind is a tête-à-tête with me, and she won't invite you or him. It's her move."

"Charles doesn't love her, you know, even though he's screwing her. I can tell. He doesn't even like her—but while we're with you, he'll stay with her out of spite. And she'll carry on using him."

"Perhaps."

"And we can't save him. Well, we could, I suppose...but we can't. We can't put the clock back. Well, again, we could...but we can't. Not because we'd disappoint you, but because we'd disappoint ourselves...and, eventually, him. He can't win, can he?"

"I don't know," was all I was prepared to say

"It's a mess," Elise opined. "But it's not Mariette's fault. Or mine. Or yours. It's just...the way things are."

There didn't seem to be any necessity to reply to that.

"Should I play for the Marquise, do you think?" she went on.

"That's up to you," I repeated.

"No it's not. Didn't I just say that you're my guardian now? I'm a minor, so it's up to you—and don't brush me off with permission. Do you want me to do it or not?"

"I wish I knew," I said.

"That's no help."

"I'm sorry."

"Mariette will probably forbid it anyway. She thinks she can do that, because she's my mother.

"She is, and that makes her your real guardian. It might be wise to do as she says." I couldn't help adding: "Of course, we don't even know whether she'll come back here yet."

"I do. Are you really not sure?"

"Really."

"She does love you. Anyway, you and she both know now that her anxieties aren't really hers—according to the old lady, they're just resonances of something happening in the Underworld. She's right, isn't she?"

"I suspect so, with regard to their ultimate source—but once such resonances surface in consciousness, they become ours, to do with as…well, not as we will, or we please, but ours nevertheless."

"She'll come back. She loves you now, not Charles. Trust me—I know."

"I've been loved by a lot of women, Elise. It's never been a reliable guide to anticipating their conduct."

"I've only been loved by one substitute mother, but it's always been a reliable guide to anticipating hers."

"I hope you're right."

She didn't challenge the assertion, or its necessity. After a pause, she said: "That isn't your usual style of paining."

"No," I said.

"I'm not sure that you'll ever be able to paint me accurately. There's too big a difference between the way you want to see me and the way I am. It doesn't matter. Are you really going to paint the Marquise?"

"Why not? Commissions might be thin on the ground this summer, and if you're right, I won't be able to paint you to your satisfaction or mine. It probably wouldn't be wise for me to offer to paint Helen, so why not the Marquise?"

"Even though you still believe that she tried to have you killed?"

"I've never tried to paint someone who probably tried to have me killed before, so it will be an interesting experiment. Mind you, if looks could kill, I'd be long dead…and I have had more tangible threats."

"Yes, Charles mentioned that."

For the first time, my brush hesitated, and almost made a false stroke.

"What do you mean?" I enquired, in a level tone.

"He's not the only guest at the Mesmay house at present. The Duc d'Alectryon is there. Charles says said that you once seduced both his daughters, when the younger one was no older than me, and that the Duc would have challenged you to a duel if you had been a gentleman, and shot you dead."

"A lucky escape, then," I said. "In fact, Dian was seventeen, and I had no intention of painting or seducing her until the Duc asked me to do so. I say *asked*, but it was more like a command, albeit a trifle inexplicit. It was certainly a lot more forceful than permission."

"Really?" she said. "Why did he do that?"

"Because his elder daughter, Roxane, whom I'd already painted, and seduced, had committed suicide after becoming infatuated with a painter named Claudius Jaseph. Alectryon was mortally afraid that Dian would follow suit, so he asked me to seduce her, because he couldn't imagine any girl committing suicide over me— at any rate, Roxane hadn't. Afterwards, he conveniently forgot that he'd instructed me to do it, waxed indignant, and called me a vile seducer within earshot of everyone on the island. Fortunately, I already had that reputation, so it did me no harm. He's always been scrupulously polite when we meet in society, though. He and the Marquise have a lot in common."

"I knew that he was only telling me the story be-cause he thought it might frighten me, and that it proba-bly wasn't true. He doesn't know me at all. Do you still see the Lady Dian during the summer season?"

"Occasionally. She's very polite too, but she smiles much more convincingly than her father, albeit a little clandestinely. She's married now. Her husband doesn't like me."

"And what happened to Claudius Jaseph?"

"I have no idea. He left the island before that season ended, and I haven't heard mention of him since. Myrica Mavor was very disappointed—he was one of her proté-gés, and it was because of him that she became a serious agent. But Alectryon didn't shoot him—Claudius wasn't a gentleman either."

"Perhaps he hired someone to stab him in the back."

"Alectryon? Certainly not. He *is* a gentleman. An old fool, perhaps, but a gentleman. He probably believes every word the Marquise tells him, and would put his life on the line to defend her imaginary honor, if neces-sary. I doubt that he was on Tommaso and Lorenzo's assassination list. He might be in the Marquise's cabal now, but he would never have agreed to participate in a plot to kill their father."

"Do they still intend to carry out those assassina-tions if you manage to weaken the Marquise's support?"

"I hope not. Tommaso said that I appeared to him in a dream, told him that there was a better way, and that he believed me. He's not the most trustworthy of people, by any means, but if I find out that he's simply been trying to use me in a plot to commit mass murder more easily, I'll never forgive him. I'm hoping that doing what he wants of me might actually stop the twins murdering anyone, and settle for a softer revenge instead."

"But you wouldn't put your life on the line to defend the Marquise, if it came to that?"

Again, the brush hesitated in its stroke. "Probably not," I admitted. "As Alectryon says, I'm not a gentleman."

"*Probably* not?" Elise repeated. "That means you might. I think you would. Your reflexes would take over, as they did when you forced Charles to pick me up on the night my grandfather was murdered."

"I didn't force him. I just nudged him to make him aware of the danger. He saved you because he loves you."

"It's no good pretending that you're not a gentleman with me," she said, firmly. "I know you."

She didn't, but I didn't bother correcting her. She was only playing a game. Seeing her adoptive father had unsettled her, although she didn't want to admit it, even to herself.

The front door of the house opened again then, and Mariette's voice called: "Elise!"

"Thank the gods," muttered Elise. "You had me worried there, for a moment." I didn't know whether she was talking to me or to herself. She probably didn't either. She ran to answer the call.

More time passed. I was absorbed. The light was beginning to deteriorate, but it didn't matter. Faceless Ananke I could probably paint by lamplight, if necessary, but the detail of the Pool of Mnemosyne was a different matter, and I couldn't think of adding the kind of intricate detail and precise color that the petals would require in anything but the broadest of daylight. My arm was getting tired, though, and my eyes too. I told myself that I really ought to stop—and carried on painting.

I didn't hear Mariette come in.

"Axel?" she said, after the regulation hesitation. "Elise said you wouldn't mind, although I wasn't sure that she had any right to say so.

"She hadn't," I agreed, "but I'll make an exception for you. How are you feeling?"

"Utterly terrible: fathered by Cain on the whore of Babylon. But it had to be done. Not because of you, believe me, or even because of Elise. Just because."

"He'll get over it," I assured her. "The Marquise will do her best to console him."

"That old hag? I can't even believe he's screwing her. I thought he had better taste."

I didn't point out that that was her vanity talking. "She's a sorceress," I reminded her. "She doubtless used magic, as she has on Alectryon…and Fion Commonal too, if I'm reading the implications correctly."

"Are you really going to accept her invitation to dinner?"

"It would be impolite not to. And I'd far rather she played this game politely than with daggers drawn."

"And what if she invites us?"

"You can refuse, if you wish. She's already licensed the excuse that Elise might find it too upsetting, after her last visit. If the Marquise really wants to hear Elise play, it will be easy enough to find an alternative venue."

"Here?"

"Perhaps—but you can say no to that as well, if you wish."

"As well? You're assuming that I'm going to refuse her invitation, if she sends me one?"

"I had jumped to that conclusion. Are you thinking of accepting, then?"

"You are."

"Charles might be there, if she really is planning a party rather than a private chat."

"So what? I'm not afraid of him. It might help to convince him that it's over."

I didn't make any comment on that. The case was still hypothetical.

"Hecate will probably be there as well," she added, as if it were a casual observation of no significance.

My mind flashed back to a dinner, many years ago, at which I had sat between Hecate and Dian d'Alectryon. As Hecate had said, we'd been to other such dinner parties, at which I'd been seated between her and my latest mistress, with her own lover to her left—hostesses often seemed to think it was amusing—but that one was still stuck in my memory.

"Perhaps," I confirmed.

There was another pause. I knew that she was looking at the painting. Her silence spoke volumes. Eventually, she said: "When you painted me on the island, Madame had told you to do it, hadn't she?"

"I didn't need a commission," I said. "I'd already made up my mind on the steamer."

I didn't hear a sigh of relief. After a pause she said: "I looked terrible on the boat, and I was stuck in that stinking cell with poor Elise. I'd been seasick for days. You can't have been able to see me properly though that hole in the wall. I was convinced you were going to screw Helen. I still don't know why you didn't."

I didn't say anything. She hadn't actually asked a question, and I had my black brushwork to attend to.

"Anyway," she said, eventually, "it's settled now. Charles is history. If the Marquise sends him to see us again, or lures us to see him elsewhere, it won't make any difference. I can face him, if need be."

Again, there was no question, and no necessity for a reply.

"He asked us a lot of questions," she said. "I was honest, but discreet, as you recommended. He said some nasty things about you, but it was all just hearsay, so I ignored it.

"It's not entirely surprising that he's picked up denigratory gossip, in the company he's been keeping," I said. "Vashti Savage doesn't like me because she thinks I'm standing between her and eternal happiness with Hecate, and the Duc d'Alectryon holds it against me that I seduced his daughters."

"So that was true?"

"Not entirely. Charles seems to have been given an inaccurate account, and then added an extra twist of his own. I've explained it to Elise."

I stepped back again, in order to study my abstract vision of Ananke in the pool of Mnemosyne. There was way too much black in it for my liking, but my liking didn't come into it. I had to paint Necessity as I saw her with my mind's eye; it wouldn't have been honest, polite or artistic to do otherwise.

I had finished for the day—mercifully, because otherwise, I would have been seriously annoyed when the doorbell rang, and I was subjected to yet another interruption.

XIII. Another Welcome Home

Fion Commonal asked to speak to me in private. I knew there wasn't anything he could possibly say to me that couldn't be said in front of any or all of my house-guests, but I didn't want him to feel uncomfortable, so I took him into the studio, closed the door and invited him to sit down in what I could no longer help thinking of as "Dellacrusca's armchair," even though it had also been occupied by dozens of other people, including Sister Ursule

He turned his head sideways to look at the painting pinned to the wall.

"That's a new departure," he commented.

"Yes," I said. "I presume you've come to welcome me home, on behalf of the Island Council?"

He actually seemed surprised. "No," he said, "I've come to see how you are. You can't imagine how worried I was when you disappeared after I bandaged your arm and we had…our conversation. But if you like, yes, welcome home, on behalf of the entire population of the island. You've been missed—more than any of us would have imagined. You shouldn't have gone."

"As I remember it, Fion," I observed, dryly, "you were the one who advised me to get off the island as soon as possible. Surely you should have been glad that I'd taken your advice?"

"If I'd thought…," he began, and then stopped.

"It's all right, Fion," I told him. "I could see that you were in a state of some confusion when you gave me the advice. I knew even then that you'd been initiated into the Cult of Orpheus, but that the last thing you expected to come of it was that you'd see Dellacrusca assassinated before your very eyes. I took it for granted that you weren't involved, and that you were telling the truth when you told me you didn't know who was. Nor do I expect you to tell me now what you've learned in the interim, although I'd obviously be grateful for anything you can tell me without violating any oaths."

He didn't look as relieved as he might have been by those assurances.

"There are all kinds of rumors flying around about your return, Axel," he said. "Inevitable, I suppose, and mostly absurd. People are saying that you're the Hierophant of the Cult of Dionysus."

"That's true," I told him. "I've spent the last couple of months on the Island of Dionysus. I was initiated almost immediately, and promoted with flattering rapidity. Does it mean that you feel obliged to consider me an enemy?"

He tried to look at me as if I were mad, but he couldn't. He believed me,

"No, of course not," he said. "At least, I hope you don't consider me an enemy..."

"I don't," I assured him. "Indeed, the whole purpose of my being here is to negotiate a pact between the Orpheans and the Dionysians. I've already arranged matters with the Dellacrusca twins, but I understand that the organization has fragmented somewhat since Dellacrusca's death. Apparently, I'll have to negotiate a separate peace with Alectryon. Do you think that will be possible?"

He frowned, as if he had just had a flash of enlightenment, but he wasn't about to give anything away, as yet.

"Don't worry about it," I said. "I've had an invitation to dinner at the Marquise de Mesmay's house the evening after next. Alectryon will probably be there—I believe that he's staying in her house at present."

This time, he did manage to look at me as if I were mad.

"You're actually going to go?" he said, incredulously.

"Certainly. Do you know of any reason why I shouldn't?"

He swallowed. "I've had one too," he said. "An invitation to dinner, I mean."

"That's good—reassuring, in fact. The Marquise must know that you and I have been good friends for a long time. Alectryon's always polite to me, but there's always been a certain frostiness in his attitude to me, as you know. Your presence will help smooth things over. Do you have any idea who else will be there?"

Commonal shook his head. "I had no idea that you'd been invited," he said.

"Don't look so worried," I said. "I can't imagine that a gang of fake maenads are going to loom up out of nowhere and stab me to death. The Marquise came to see me this morning and she was extremely civil. She's always been a perfect hostess, to the best of my knowledge. Since it does seem to be a party, she's bound to have invited Vashti Savage and Hecate Rain. It'll be just like old times, won't it?"

The physician didn't seem convinced of that. "There are other rumors...," he began, hoarsely.

"No need to be shy, Fion. Yes, I'm with Mariette now, Charles Parenot's former mistress. She and her ward Elise are living with me here. I have the blessing of the Dellacrusca twins to assume temporary guardianship of their niece. Parenot is a trifle upset, as you can imagine, but we're all adults. It's not the first time I've stolen someone else's mistress, as you well know. You've described me as incorrigible yourself more than once. Just like old times, as I say"

"These aren't the old times, Axel," he said, having finally firmed up his tongue. "Things have changed."

"I haven't," I assured him. "It takes more than being appointed as the Hierophant of Dionysus to change me. As I said, my mission here is to smooth everything out. Having seen the Marquise this morning, I'm optimistic that it can be done."

His eyes went to the canvas hanging on the wall.

"Really?" he said, mustering a hint of sarcasm. "That doesn't exactly say optimism to me."

"What does it say to you?" I enquired. Although he was a physician, Fion was something of a connoisseur of the many arts of Mnemosyne.

"Looming disaster," he said, succinctly—and not entirely inaccurately.

"It's far from finished," I assured him. "That's just the backcloth. I haven't made a start on the petals yet."

"Petals?" he queried. "Those blurred dots, you mean?"

"That's right. It's an obscure reference, I'm afraid, to an image in one of Hecate's unpublished poems."

Almost on cue, the sound of music became audible, from the bedroom that had been allocated to Elise. She was playing one of the instruments she'd brought from the island: a cithara. I assumed that Hecate was with her.

"That's Elise," I said to Fion. "She's very talented. She'll be a great artist one day, and an honor to the Dellacrusca line. Hecate has taken her under her wing, but I'll have to search among the island's musicians for someone who can give her tuition on instruments of the lyre family, or at least stringed instruments of some kind. Davida Amalek might be able to do it, if she's willing. The Marquise is keen to hear Elise play, having heard so much about her from Hecate. Have you been to any good séances lately, by the way? I've heard that Vashti is excelling herself at present. Has she mastered the art of producing ectoplasm yet?"

"I've made up the numbers at séances the Mesmay house," Fion admitted. "I thought you didn't believe in that sort of thing."

"I always believed that Vashti had talent," I told him. "She and I merely disagreed as to the exact nature of the talent. I couldn't be more delighted to know that her abilities are blossoming, and I'm eager to hear what her spirits have to say, if she's going to perform after the dinner party."

Fion shook his head. "I'm sorry, Axel," he said, "but all this has caught me on the hop somewhat. I don't know what to say to you."

"What did you come to say to me?" I asked, blandly. "Apart from whispering another suggestion that I get off the island."

"I had just bandaged your arm because someone had tried to assassinate you," he said, defensively.

"And you had no idea who was responsible. Nor had I. Clovis told me last night that he hadn't been able to catch the man who escaped, leaving us all none the wiser. The only person that I can be certain that it wasn't is Lord Dellacrusca. He and I had a long chat shortly before, and he definitely wanted me alive,

"You and Dellacrusca had a long chat?" he said, trying to pretend that he hadn't heard. "About what?"

"Various matters, mostly his granddaughter and the Orphean text that Toustain had bequeathed to me. He told me the story of his daughter's elopement with poor Almeras, and I told him about my particular interpretation of the myth of Orpheus and Eurydice and my philosophy of art. I held forth for some time about the unconscious mind, and he listened very politely. But he was never a man for only doing one thing at a time. He asked me to do him a favor—a commission, of sorts. Do you think that might have been why someone tried to kill me?"

"I wouldn't be at all surprised," he murmured. "What commission?"

"I can't tell you that, I'm afraid. It was confidential then and still is."

"But it has to do with the Orphean manuscript?"

"I didn't say that."

Naturally, he took entirely the wrong inference from that perfectly true remark. "It's rumored that the document has been translated," he said, tentatively, still trying to pretend that he didn't know.

"That's right. Of course, the meaning was understood long ago on the island. Madame's long been familiar with the incantation and its possible uses."

He sat u a little straighter. "Madame?" he queried.

"The island's presiding genius, my initiator into the cult. She's a Macrobian, like me, but much older—perhaps as much as two thousand years."

"What's a Macrobian."

"A person who stops aging at some stage in his life and enjoys an extended lifespan. As I've always told you, I'm older than I look."

"How much older?" he asked, warily.

"A lot. You've surely heard the rumor?"

He nodded. "Yes, but I didn't believe it. You *are* a sorcerer then?"

"So far as I can tell, the longevity is a perfectly natural phenomenon. But Madame is certainly a sorceress, and although I can't claim to be an adept, she has employed me as an instrument in one of her operations. My role was passive, but interesting."

"You wouldn't care…?"

"Why not? It was the evening when Hecate and Vashti were initiated into your cult. I know you were there, because I saw you…in a vision, obviously. Madame employed me to establish some kind of link with my painting—the Orpheus triptych, that is. That's why she kidnapped me and brought me to the island. She brought Elise and Mariette so that they could participate in the same operation."

"Why are you telling me all this, Axel?" he asked, suddenly alarmed.

"Because I thought you might be interested. "It's not confidential—you can tell whoever you wish. They'll probably believe you, given that you're what Clovis calls a usually-reliable source."

"So…you're not a sorcerer?"

"I'm an artist. There's more similarities than you might imagine, but no, I'm not a sorcerer in the sense that I can perform magical operations, except as an assistant. I can't kill people by making dolls to represent them and throwing them in a fire, as the two African sorceresses who are staying with the Marquise at present are reputed to be able to do. You've met them, I presume?"

"I've seen them. They can't speak any language but their own, so I haven't had any communication with them. The Marquise is trying to learn their language, but it's not easy."

"I can imagine. You must have been very busy of late, with the unseasonably bad weather and respiratory problems caused by the dust emitted by Hekla."

Fion seemed grateful for the change of subject. "There have been problems," he admitted. "I've coped. Nobody expects many summer visitors this year, though, so I night have an easier time of it than usual."

"I hope not," I said, "but you might be right. Did you notice on your way out here that I'm having a telegraph cable run out to the house?"

"Yes. It seems to have become quite fashionable, but I don't trust the damn things myself, and everyone who has one seems to be cursing their unreliability. Do you understand all that clicking? I don't."

"Neither do I, but I have an operator who does. I'll soon be in communication with both Lutèce and Madame's island; it should make negotiating a treaty between the Dionysians and the Orpheans much easier, helping to put an end to hundreds of years of unnecessary rivalry. It's a pity that Lord Dellacrusca didn't live to see it."

"Yes," said Fion, "I suppose it is." He didn't seem convinced.

"Well," I said, "Doubtless you have things to do, having to combine your practice with your council responsibilities. It's very kind of you to take the time to come to see me, but I don't want to cause you any inconvenience. I'll see you again in two days' time, of course. I'll look forward to it."

He didn't give me a similar impression, but he saluted me with all due respect as he left. I saw him to the gate and then went back inside, where Hecate was lurking—although the sound of Elise's cithara was still audible from the upper floor.

"Another of Madame's spies?" she asked.

"I don't believe so—but it doesn't matter if he came here at her request, or if she interrogates him about our conversation. If she wants to know anything, she's welcome to the information. It will enable her to refine her questions for the dinner party."

"Will you have time to refine your answers?" she countered.

"With luck," I said, "I'll only need one, and I've had that ready since noon. I'll try to get as far as I can with the painting during the next two days, but I certainly won't be able to finish it—it's too complicated. I assume that your work with Elise will take longer than that as well?"

"I don't know. I'm sure that I can reconstitute the poem about the pool of Mnemosyne easily enough, but whether Elise can find the right music for it...well, we'll see tomorrow what progress we can make."

As we were about to go to dinner, a messenger arrived from the Marquise de Mesmay, with two sealed letters: one addressed to me and the other to Hecate. Mine asked me, with the utmost politeness, whether I could possibly bring Mariette and Elise with me to dinner, if it would not upset them too much, and whether I would ask Elise to play afterwards, if she were able to come. Hecate's was a simple invitation to the dinner, with a supplementary note saying that Vashti Savage would conjure spirits thereafter.

"The excuse is still viable," I told Mariette. "I can easily ask Jean-Jacques to convey a polite refusal."

Mariette looked at Elise.

"A Dellacrusca doesn't duck a contest," she said, "especially when it's a matter of vendetta."

"That might be a dangerous way to think," I suggested to her.

"Are you forbidding me to go?"

"No, I'm not," I said. "The more support I have there, the better, and if the nexus is intact, I think we'll be insulated against supernatural attack. And Madame will be there too, in spirit, as well as any additional guests that Vashti might summon from the Underworld, with Hades' generous permission."

"I hope she brings the spirits of Madame's bodyguards with her," murmured Mariette, intending it as a joke, "in case the ones Hecate's friend summons are hostile."

I assumed that the spirits Vashti might summon were unlikely to be friendly, given her attitude to me and the likely nature of any suggestions that the Marquise might give her. I also knew, however, even if Mariette didn't, that Vashti Savage wouldn't be the only person present at her séance capable of invoking spirits, although it was yet to be proven whether she was as specialized as her former idolater in shaping her inspiration.

Even that prospect didn't worry me. Even if the one shade that Mariette could bring to Vashti's séance was poor Eurydice, she couldn't possibly mean me any harm. If anything, by my reckoning, she owed me a favor.

XIV. The Dinner Party at the Mesmay Manse

As on the previous occasion when I had made the trip to the Mesmay Manse, there were four passengers in my sociable, Hecate replacing Charles Parenot on this occasion. The journey was tense. Hecate still seemed to be ill, and definitely in a dark mood, unconsoled as yet by my attempts at consolation. Mariette was distinctly unhappy too, and Elise seemed to be trying very hard to be putting on a brave face that did not reflect her true sentiments.

"We don't have to do this," I told them all. "We can go back, and Jean-Jacques can take our apologies to the Marquise.

Hecate looked at Mariette, and Mariette looked at Elise. Elise looked at me.

"I think, Master Rathenius," she said, "that we *do* have to do this. I don't know why, but we do need to do it. I don't think I'll be able to play very well, but I don't think it matters. We do have to be here, though—all of us, together."

Her voice didn't sound in the least hallucinated, but it seemed to me that it was the visionary speaking, not the child. I knew that I didn't have to bow to her judgment, but I didn't want to oppose it either, and I figured that it was probably wiser to have what might be a challenging meeting while none of us was yet ready to attempt any serious magic. I let matters take their course.

The Marquise was not as obliging a hostess as I might have wished, and her seating plan followed her own agenda. Hecate was not placed to my left, nor Mariette to my right. Mariette, in fact, was seated between

236

Charles Parenot and the Duc d'Alectryon, although the Marquise made a point of apologizing for an apparent slip of the tongue in addressing her as "Madame Parenot," and asking her if she would rather be addressed as "Madame Rathenius" instead. She did not address Elise as "Mademoiselle Dellacrusca," however, which was a mercy. I was seated to the Marquise's right, with Vashti Savage to my right. Hecate was seated to Alectryon's left, Parenot being on the Marquise's left. Elise, seated between Vashti and Fion Commonal, while Hecate was between Commonal and Alectryon, probably had the best of the arrangement.

The food was probably first rate and the wine excellent, but I didn't really pay much attention to either. I didn't have the opportunity to focus my attention on it; although there were nine of us at table, it wasn't the kind of party at which the conversation becomes fragmented and people make small talk with their immediate neighbors. In fact, it bore more a closer resemblance to a systematic interrogation, of which I was the focus. That was evidently the Marquise's intention: to measure, to test, and perhaps also to make a preliminary attempt to destabilize any opposition over which her own as-yet-unready schemes might stumble.

"I'm particularly glad that you were able to come tonight, Axel," said the Marquise, when everyone was seated. "You've been so sorely missed on the island—hasn't he, Fion?"

"Indeed," agreed Commonal, who had surely been sincere in telling me that he had regretted my absence, never quite having realized, over the years, how much of a fixture in his social life I had become.

"You really ought to have let us know where you'd gone, Master Rathenius," supplied Charles Parenot, who was, as anticipated, being scrupulously polite and thoroughly adult, at least for the moment.

"It would have been difficult," I said. "I was on an island in the middle of the Ocean, surrounded by Sileni."

"What the hell are Sileni?" asked Alectryon, whose age and status permitted him a certain latitude of language on polite occasions.

"In ancient lore, they were best known as companions of Bacchus, or Dionysus," I explained. "It was a Silenus who was captured by the legendary King Midas, who refused to release him until he revealed the secret of human life, and eventually confessed it."

"And what was it?" Alectryon demanded, never a man to miss a cue.

"That for a human, the best thing of all is not to be born, and after that, to die young. The Sileni had a dim view of human life—understandably, as they were almost a victim of genocide at human hands. Fortunately, a fragment of the Arcadian Golden Age survives on the Island of Dionysus."

"And how did you get there?" Alectryon asked, presumably being the only person present who hadn't yet been informed.

"On a steamship."

"But *why* did you go, Axel?" asked Vashti Savage, who was at least prepared to pretend not to know, and really might have been in doubt as to which rumor to believe.

"In order to be initiated into the Cult of Dionysus, as it turned out," I said, "although I didn't really have any choice in the matter, having been drugged and carried to the ship unconscious. Life is like that, don't you find? You think that you're in control, and then circumstances take hold of you and drag you away. I'm sorry that I didn't have a chance to say goodbye to you, Vashti, or to anyone else."

"The Cult of Dionysus?" said Alectryon, frostily—as well he might, being the titular head of one half of a rival secret organization. "I've heard of that, but it's always been a mystery to me. What is it, exactly?"

"It has, indeed, always been a mystery, Milord," I said, "and therefore incapable of exact description. It's a religious order, not unlike the Sisters of Shalimar, but much further from its origins, and much changed over time, in spite of a determination to hold on to its traditions, its rites and its magical intentions."

"And what intentions are those, Axel?" Fion Commonal put in, probably moved by natural curiosity.

"Salvation and protection," I said. "The purpose of all religion, it seems to me, although complications inevitably set in by virtue of the fact that, for poor human beings, there are so many forces in the world from which protection is exceedingly difficult and salvation perhaps impossible. But we must try, must we not, each in our own way? Even if the magic proves impotent, much of the time, there is often artistry in it, and sometimes heroism."

"And was it art, or heroism that drew you to the Cult of Dionysus, Master Rathenius?" asked the Marquise, silkily. She obviously felt comfortable—as well she might, being at her own dinner table, at a formal social occasion whose rules and etiquette she understood perfectly.

"The cult drew me, rather than vice versa," I admitted, "and rather brutally; but the chain of causation that led to my abduction began to exert its traction some time before that. Your aunt was one of two people who gave me the information regarding the cults of Orpheus and Dionysus that first intrigued me."

"I can only apologize for my aunt," the Marquise replied, smoothly, "but I'm sure that she meant no harm. If it isn't too indiscreet to ask, who was your other informant?"

"Lord Dellacrusca. He and I had a long chat about the Cult of Orpheus and its parental mythology shortly before his death. It was most enlightening."

"Dellacrusca?" echoed the Duc d'Alectryon, finding that difficult to believe, in view of what he knew about Dellacrusca's opinion of artists in general and habitual seducers of aristocrats' daughters in particular.

"That's right. I've known his sons for a long time, as you know, and they and I had a mutual friend in Eirene Magdelana. That helped to bring us together. I'd like to think that now I've been installed as the Hierophant of the Cult of Dionysus, I might be able to bring about a reconciliation between the sect and its traditional decriers. I discussed the matter with Tommaso Dellacrusca when he brought us all back from the island. He's enthusiastic about the idea."

"Tommaso Dellacrusca brought you back to Mnemosyne?" said the Duc, incredulously.

Almost simultaneously, Vashti Savage said: "You weren't alone there, then?" I couldn't believe that she really hadn't been briefed, by her hostess or rumor if not by her spirits, but she was apparently in quest of some kind of formal declaration.

"Mariette and Elise were with me," I said, as if it were the most natural thing in the world. "Surely you had all realized that we must have left and come back together?"

"I must admit," said the Marquise, smiling, "that it came as a complete surprise to me when Charles told me."

Vashti looked at Charles and Mariette, sitting side by side, then at the Marquise, and then at Hecate, as if her gaze were trying to draw an illustrative diagram.

"Perhaps I should have changed the seating plan," said the Marquise, disingenuously, "but one can't think of everything, alas." The sincerity was lacking, but she had surely never said a truer word.

Alectryon looked up at the ceiling, and shook his head—and then he looked at Elise disapprovingly, apparently having jumped to the most ungentlemanly conclusion possible.

Fion Commonal followed his gaze, but then immediately looked at Mariette. He knew me far better than Alectryon, and was not burdened by the same prejudicial memories. Nevertheless, he had more serious matters on his mind. "Are you really serious about having joined the Cult of Dionysus, Axel?" he said, incredulously, still unable to believe it. "I've known you for a long time, and you're the last person I would have expected to join any religious sect."

"I'm perfectly serious, as I told you two days ago," I said.

"As a result of conversations you had with Lord Dellacrusca and the superior of the Convent of Shalimar?" Alectryon asked, similarly unable to credit it, and similarly of the opinion that he had known me for a long time, although it was obvious that he had never actually known me at all.

"Partly, yes, Milord. It was Lord Dellacrusca who set the whole sequence of events in motion. He and Tommaso had me search for an Orphean document that my late neighbor, Toustain, had hidden in the binding of a book. I made several copies of it, one of which was forwarded to Sister Ursule. She has now translated it, but had not yet contrived to do so when she came to see me, in order to express her anxieties about its nature. She thought that I might be in danger as a consequence of having made the discovery—and, in fact, that proved to be the case. Circumstances, as I've explained, took me to the document's source, the Island of Dionysus, where its contents had been known for a long time. It's a fascinating place, and exceedingly hospitable; I would have stayed there longer had Tommaso Dellacrusca not come to collect me."

"Tommaso Dellacrusca made the journey specifically in order to collect you?" Alectryon repeated, giving the impression that the information was coming too rapidly for his slow brain to process, and finding it particularly difficult to accommodate the Dellacrusca twins to the narrative, still thinking of them as naughty little boys.

"That's correct. Tommaso's father had come to my house to collect the original of the document shortly before his tragic demise. I'm story, Milord—this is rather a complicated story, and responding to questions as they arise isn't conducive to its coherency. The document appears to be a magical formula. Lord Dellacrusca was very interested in having it translated, but he didn't live to see the task completed, alas. Tommaso and Lorenzo are attempting to carry on their father's work, naturally, and because Tommaso was present when I discovered the document's hiding place, he has a particular interest in it. In addition to the copy of the manuscript that I had Hecate pass on to Sister Ursule, I gave one to Niklaus Hylne, and Tommaso took another back to Lutèce, in order to submit it to scholars at the University—but that was unnecessary, as he obtained the information from another source."

"Sister Ursule," Alectryon supplied, trying to demonstrate that he was keeping up, although he was at least one step behind the evolving pattern of the story, and probably more.

"In fact, no. As I told you, the meaning has been known on the Island of Dionysus for a long time. I wasn't present during Tommaso's negotiations with Madame, of course, but she was perfectly capable of informing him as to the meaning of the document and its usage. Meaning no disrespect to your aunt, Milady, but it's possible that she was able to do so more accurately than Sister Ursule could have done, had she not been reluctant to make her own translation public."

"My late mother and I have, in fact, occasionally had reason to doubt the quality of my aunt's scholarship," said the Marquise, her tone neutral but her eyes slightly narrowed. That was one seed of doubt successfully planted.

"It's pure conjecture on my part," I hastened to add. "I wasn't party to the negotiation between Madame and Tommaso, and I have no knowledge of such matters myself."

"But you are a Macrobian, are you not, and a magician?" asked the Marquise. Alectryon opened his mouth, but she instructed him to shut it with an insultingly cursory flick of her left forefinger, most unbecoming of a mere Marquise addressing a Duc. The Duc seemed to be annoyed, but his reflexes obeyed the instruction. I wondered how long he and she had been lovers, and whether the Duc's opinion of Charles Parenot might be even lower than his opinion of me.

"I do seem to be what Madame calls a Macrobian," I confirmed, "although not by virtue of any conscious operation or effort on my part. I'm certainly no magician. I have only ever been an active participant in one magical operation, and even in that one I was guided by an expert."

"The Madame to which you refer?" supplied the Marquise. I inferred that she had, in fact, interrogated Fion about his conversation with me, as expected.

"Oh no," I said, blithely. "I'm referring to Eirene Magdelana, the morpheomorphist who worked with the Dellacrusca twins in their youth. She allowed me to assist her in a curious operation she carried out, in order to shape the dreams of an unborn child—but that was some years ago. Fion probably remembers the affair, although not that detail of it..."

Fion opened his mouth, but another curt gesture of the sinister forefinger closed it as effectively as the earlier one had closed Alectryon's, with similar authority, presumably obtained in the same fashion. I wondered whether the three lovers were aware of their rivalry, or whether they were willfully blind.

"You surprise me, Master Rathenius" said the Marquise. "Charles informed me that you had also participated in a rite on the island, in collaboration with Mariette and Elise. Is he mistaken?"

"No, he's correct—but we only participated in the capacity of passive instruments, at least in my case and Mariette's. Elise was playing a musical instrument, but she was only playing music; any magic there was in it was not of her making, but the work of the much larger nexus of Sileni and Nymphs, who were singing and enacting a ritual dance."

"But your own part, you say, was entirely passive?" the Marquise enquired, her tone pitched to feign the kind of polite and idle curiosity that a hostess is perfectly entitled to pursue at a dinner party.

"I believe so. Madame wanted me there in order to establish some kind of channel between her and your painting…the one that your late husband commissioned from me, before his tragic demise. Her purpose, so she said—and I believed her—was to try to establish a kind of spiritual communion between her rite and one that was being performed in your grand hall. It has long been her dreams to effect a reconciliation, perhaps even a fusion, between the Cult of Dionysus and the schismatic group known as the Cult of Orpheus, about which several people here undoubtedly know far more than I do."

No one answered that invitation to confession. The Marquise, in particular had no interest in stating what everyone knew. She was still in quest of information.

"And how was this supposed…spiritual communion established?" she asked.

"All that I did, as part of my initiation into the cult, was to look into the device that she calls the Mirror of Dionysus—and actual mirror, although its function in the initiation and the rite was essentially symbolic. I experienced a remarkable vision when I did so, doubtless due to the power of suggestion, amplified by a drug that Madame called cyteon, which I was given before the rite, and whose formula I do not know. In that vision, I was able to see the ritual that was being carried out in this house. The one truly remarkable thing about the experience is that two of the people here seemed to be able to see me, if only for a fraction of a second. Both of them have since confirmed to me that they did, indeed, have a coincident vision."

"Two people?" the Marquise queried.

"Yes Hecate and Tommaso Dellacrusca. Hecate, I believe, was still regretting the adieu that she had not been able to complete before my abduction, and Tommaso had seen me the night before in a dream."

Several glances turned to Hecate.

"That's correct," she said. "I did sense Axel's presence, although I naturally thought that it was a hallucination, generated by my anxiety in not knowing what had become of him."

"Tommaso, too, might have had a prior sensitivity to whatever force it was that Madame was endeavoring to transmit through me," I suggested, without venturing any hypothesis as to why that might have been. "Madame is, I believe, a remarkable magician—but she has been studying and experimenting for centuries, so that is perhaps to be expected. Speaking purely as an artist, which is all that I am, it was a remarkable experience. It really would have been interesting to stay on the island longer, and I might well go back some day."

"Why did you come back at all?" asked Alectryon, a trifle bitterly, having been granted silent permission to rejoin the interrogation at last, while Madame presumably paused for thought. I felt certain that she, too, had been aware of my presence on the night in question, but that she was now no longer certain that the inferences she had initially drawn from that awareness were correct.

"Tommaso Dellacrusca asked me to accompany him, Milord, in the hope that I might be able to persuade you to join the pact that he has made with Madame. Again, I am merely a passive instrument, but at his request I have established a telegraph station in my house, with which I will hopefully be able to communicate with both Tommaso and Madame—with the inevitable delays, alas, as the messages are relayed from station to station along the route. You're undoubtedly in communication with Lutèce already, but a third party is sometimes useful as an intermediary in delicate negotiations. My title as Hierophant is, I admit, purely for show, to grant me a certain quasi-official status. I am not really a priest."

The fish course—locally caught sole—had come and gone and we were now on the main course, which was some kind of beef ragout. I was eating slowly, really only pecking at my food, in order that chewing not did interrupt my narrative too much, although it was sometimes useful for the purposes of dramatic punctuation. I estimated that I had given the Marquise more than sufficient food for thought to justify her pause, but I still had my *pièce de resistance* in reserve. It was not something I wanted to save for dessert, though, so I felt a slight twinge of relief when she returned to the fray.

"You say that this Madame of yours has known the meaning of the Toustain document for centuries?" she prompted.

"That is my understanding," I agreed, not bothering to correct the implication that Madame as in any way *mine*. "She did not explain that meaning to me, however. I had no idea what it was until your aunt explained it to me two days ago. It was only then that I realized, belatedly, the significance of the apparatus that Madame had shown me in her laboratory, on the eve of my departure from the island."

"What apparatus?" the Marquise asked, demonstrating that Alectryon was not the only person capable of responding to a cue.

"Her seismographs," I said, with what seemed to me to be admirable panache. I let a full three seconds of pregnant silence elapse before adding: "Hecate tells me that you have one of your own, Milady. A wise precaution."

Alectryon had obviously seen the Marquise's seismograph, so he had no need to ask what the hell one was, but he did say: "A precaution against what?"

"Unlike Madame's island," I said, "Mnemosyne is not volcanic, and I'm unaware of any recent history of earthquakes in the region, but it is not immune, even so, to disturbances of the earth's crust—as evidenced by the recent effects of Hekla's eruption. The science of seismology is in its infancy, but it seems to be advancing all the time. Madame hopes that it might advance rapidly enough for her to be able to use her apparatus, in collaboration with the Orphean incantation, not only to be able to anticipate such events, but to suppress them."

This time, it was Hecate who responded to the cue—but I had cheated in that regard and given her prior notice.

"But according to Ursule," she said, "the formula is a spell for summoning destruction, not suppressing it."

"But if you remember, my dear," I said, "she also reminded us forcefully of the principle of reciprocity. Magical formulae, if they work at all, ought to be reversible, so a formula for summoning destruction must, *ipso facto*, also be a formula for inhibiting it, if the symbolism of its usage is suitably adapted. The seismograph is in its infancy, of course, so its effectiveness as a detection device is limited, as yet, but its role in any corollary magical operation is essentially symbolic. If the summoning formula works at all, it ought to work very well with Madame's seismographs, which really are quite impressive. I'd be interested in seeing yours, Milady, for the purposes of comparison."

The Marquise was in no hurry to assure me that she would be delighted to let me see it.

"So Madame's island is well defended, even against volcanic interruptions and earthquakes?" Mariette put in, obligingly.

"Insofar as any defense is possible," I confirmed, "it is very well defended indeed. Which is perhaps as well, as she told me that she has had a feeling for some time that some such defense would be necessary imminently. In two thousand years, she has learned to trust such feelings, and the Nymphs and the Sileni both have a special sensitivity to such subtle warnings, as well as being able to form a uniquely powerful magical nexus, especially in the context of a Bacchanal, with the aid of cyteon and the cycinnis—their ritual dance, that is. Primitive peoples often have such a sensitivity, of course, and the Sileni and the Nymphs are at least as ancient, and perhaps still as numerous, as the tribes of Asia and Africa reputed for their magical and shamanic skills."

"You seem to have given this matter a good deal of thought, Master Rathenius," said the Marquise, a trifle sourly.

"That's true," I said, "although I have only been able to put together the various pieces of the puzzle very recently. I've been painting intensely for the past three days, with a kind of quasi-automatic absorption that is conducive to letting one's mind wander and mull over ideas of which it seems to catch hold at whim—whims that presumably have a cause deep in the unconscious part of the mind. You'll be glad to know, Milady, that the painting is progressing rapidly. I might be able to begin work on your portrait sooner than I thought."

"What portrait is that?" This time, the interjection came from Charles Parenot.

"Oh, I'm so sorry," I said, apologetically, looking at the Marquise. "Should I not have mentioned it?"

That shot, at least, did not disturb her in the least. "We have no secrets here, Master Rathenius," she assured me. "I should have told you, Charles, but one can't think of everything. When I went to see Master Rathenius the other day, I asked him whether I might commission him to paint a portrait of me...I must plead guilty to excessive vanity, I fear. He told me that he was too fully occupied for the present, but would try to make time in the future."

It did not require a gesture of any kind to make Parenot shut his mouth, after briefly opening it and then changing his mind. Alectryon's jaw also twitched, perhaps shifted by a twinge of memory, but he said nothing either.

"You were right, Axel," said Fion Commonal, with a slight sigh. "You haven't changed. And this does put me in mind of some of the dinner parties were had back in the old days, when you used to hold forth at great length, and loved to demonstrate your cleverness." He did not seem to intend the remark as a compliment.

"But you were right too, Fion," I said, with a slightly heavier sigh. "Times have changed. I fear that my kind of shallow wit is going out of style, and I really must try to become more serious. I've outlived my era."

"You seem to be remarkably adaptable, judging by what I saw on your wall the other day," he retorted. "How is Looming Disaster coming along?"

"Please don't title my works, Fion—especially when they have titles already. The work to which you're referring is actually called Ananke in the Pool of Mnemosyne."

Alectryon didn't ask who the hell Ananke was. He probably knew, but if he didn't, he didn't want to admit it. Fion Commonal uttered a kind of suppressed grunt, which suggested very strongly that he still thought Looming Disaster a more appropriate title. He had only seen the black backcloth, not yet complete, with only the merest suggestion of the petals, but I knew that there wasn't that much difference between his flippant title and my more earnest one. The disaster was, indeed, looming, I felt sure—and perhaps on a scale that would not allow for any possibility of prevention or inhibition. There was still a decision to be made, however, as to how to face it, practically and symbolically. I had made mine, and I was still hoping that the Marquise might still change the direction of her own.

Having completed my own agenda for the evening, I was prepared to relax, but the Marquise still had her agenda to complete, and if she thought that her guns had been spiked, she was certainly not about to give me any indication of it. When the dessert arrived she was quick to ask Elise whether she would play for us before we retired to the small drawing room for Vashti's séance.

Elise still seemed to me to be putting a brave face on a nagging anxiety, but she replied affirmatively, with a decisiveness or a politeness that definitely had something of the Dellacrusca about it.

As her guardian, I felt entitled to be proud of her. Perhaps glimpsing that, Charles Parenot shot me a glance of pure hatred, but immediately resumed his mask of apparent impassivity. He was being patient. Evidently, he knew that the Marquise still had at least one shot in her locker that might be capable of upsetting my fragile nexus.

XV. Music and Spirits

Elise had, of course, come with the expectation that she would be asked to perform, knowing that she had been invited purely for that purpose. The Marquise wanted to measure her in the same way that she had wanted to measure me. Just as I had thought it a sensible move to allow her to obtain a more accurate estimation of me, I had thought it not unwise to enable her to judge Elise's musical ability, although there was probably a bigger risk in that. We had brought both her viola da gamba and her cithara in the carriage, and when a chair and a music stand had been positioned for her by a footman, Elise asked, very politely, which instrument her hostess would like to hear, and whether "Madame la Marquise" had any preference as to what she ought to play.

"The choice of your repertoire is entirely up to you, my dear," said the Marquise, "but I would like to make one small request. If I understood your guardian correctly"—Parenot winced visibly—"you played the music for a part of the Dionysian Bacchanal in which you took part. I believe he referred to a dance, the cycinnis. I would be very interested to hear a small sample of the music for that dance, if you can recall it."

I could see no reason to raise any objection to her compliance with that request, which seemed innocuous, and when Elise shot me a swift glance, in search of reassurance, I replied with an encouraging smile. I knew that Elise would have no difficulty recalling the rhythm of the dance; it was a very simple and repetitive tune. She

had no sheet music for it, of course, but she was perfectly capable of playing it by ear.

As she took her position, and picked up her cithara,
the door to the corridor opened, and two newcomers
slipped into the dining room, evidently in order to listen
to the recital. They were two young negresses, not yet
out of their teens, to judge by appearances, although
those might have been deceptive. They were possessed
of a spectacular beauty, which seemed further enhanced
by its uncanny duplication. They were exotically but
fully clad, in loose robes that descended from the neck to
the floor, with no belt to tighten them at the waist, but
which managed nevertheless to sketch their figures by
means of ingenious pleats. They sat down silently on the
carpeted floor, discreetly positioned in a corner of the
room, behind the table where nothing any longer remained but liqueurs and bowls of candied fruits.

I studied them, swiftly. They did not look to me like
murderous sorceress, and rather reminded me of the
Dellacrusca twins in their mischievous heyday, but I had
to assume that the appearance was deceptive, and that
they too had been summoned in order to take stock of
their potential opposition—or their possible targets.

Elise played.

The cycinnis was, in essence, a tedious piece of
music, unimpressive without the stately accompaniment
of the Sileni—which I could imagine, as Mariette and
Elise probably could, but no one else. Elise was apparently sensitive to that tedium, because she had only been
playing for two or three minutes before she seemed to
become a trifle impatient. I gathered that she was not
satisfied with her playing, because she glanced at me
again, not in quest of some signal of reassurance, but as
if to inform me that the problem she had felt while pos-

ing for me had not gone away: that she was still not at her best.

I glanced at the Marquise, but I could not believe that she and her twin sorceresses were trying to exert any disruptive influence on Elise's playing; their interest surely lay in the opposite direction.

I had not discussed any kind of program with Elise, perfectly content to leave the decision as to what to play to her own discretion. I assumed, while she played the notes of the cycinnis, especially given her apparent dissatisfaction, that she would put the cithara aside in order to take up the instrument with which she was far more familiar—the viola da gamba that her grandfather had once given her mother, and by means of which he had initially recognized her—in order to play a piece that she had practiced frequently, and mastered completely: an example of what is known as "chamber music," as polite, delicate and pleasant as an ideal dinner party.

She did not. When she felt that she had demonstrated the rhythm of the cycinnis sufficiently, she paused momentarily, shook her head slightly, and lifted the cithara a little higher, as if striking the pose that I had asked her to adopt in order to paint her. She did not look at me, however, or at anyone else.

When she began playing again, I thought for a moment that she had simply resumed the cycinnis, because the fundamental rhythm was so nearly identical, but within a matter of seconds she began to vary and complicate the pattern, without losing its basic cadence or theme.

The improvisation was ingenious, and I wished momentarily that there was a company of Sileni there, in order that I might see how they reacted to the variation, in terms of their own rhythmic movement—if, in fact they would have done that. The Nymphs, I was convinced, would certainly have responded, and provided some kind of kinetic translation of the notes. That hypothetical question vanished from my thoughts, however, as my mind was invaded by an anxiety. The impression grew that Elise was not merely weaving a musical scheme, but was extracting something more ambitious from her unconscious.

Did the music qualify as magical as well as artistic? The question was unanswerable, and I did not even try. A rapid glance told me that Alectryon was not appreciating it at all, and that Fion Commonal also seemed to find it rather alien to his taste, being insufficiently melodic. Hecate, on the other hand, was concentrating intently, and Vashti Savage also seemed fascinated by it, as well as puzzled. Parenot had tears in his eyes, but I didn't think that they were due to any pathos inherent in the music. I looked at the Marquise, but found that she was already looking at me, questioningly, and I did not want to lock interrogative gazes with her. Instead, I deliberately turned my head, and glanced at the African twins again. I looked carefully, but I could not measure their reaction at all. They were looking at one another, as if in secret and silent conference.

After a few minutes, Elise stopped that exercise, and simply announced, without consulting anyone, that she was going to play something else. She did not switch instruments, however. Nor did she say that what she was about to play was her own composition, but when she began, I certainly didn't recognize it. The music stand in front of her was still empty. Whatever music she had brought with her remained in the leather wallet beside the bulky case containing the viola da gamba. Whatever vague plans she had made in advance had been abandoned.

She was not simply playing music, and she knew it. She was endeavoring to make magic. Was that her own idea, or was she responding to some influence exerted by the Marquise or the twins? I had no idea. It was no part of my plan. Any illusion of control that I had had while holding forth in my customary glib fashion had vanished. From now on, others were in control: Elise first, then Vashti…but perhaps not only Vashti. I still thought I had a card up my sleeve in knowing that Mariette was a medium—something that she probably still did not know herself. But precisely because she probably did not know it herself, it was a highly unpredictable card, of unfathomable value.

I looked at Mariette, trying to judge what she was making of Elise's improvisation, but she did not seem to be reacting. She had heard Elise improvising many times before. To her, it seemed normal. Her eyes were dry, in contrast to Charles' rather tearful expression; but that was not surprising. She would be going home with Elise when the party was over; he was uncertain as to whether he would ever hear her play again.

I tried to focus on the music, to feel its significance. I tried to recognize it, although I knew that I had never heard it before. There did seem to be something in it that struck a chord within the unconscious part of my mind, but I could not obtain any symbolic echo of what that resonance might be, until I heard Fion Commonal mutter: "Looming disaster." Then I did obtain a feeling of recognition. What Elise was playing suddenly seemed to me to be a tentative response to my unfinished painting.

But the petals aren't finished, I thought. *And in any case, she's only glimpsed it.*

But I accused myself, promptly, of being silly. She wasn't responding to my painting at all. She was responding to something much further away, to which my paining was also a response. Perhaps, I thought, she had heard Hecate recite her reconstituted poem—almost certainly, in fact—but what she was doing wasn't simply a response to that, either. In fact, it couldn't be, precisely because it echoed my painting, which was a deliberate variation on what I could remember of the gist of Hecate's poem.

What is she doing? I asked myself. *And why?*

Had she been called upon to account for it, I suspect she might have said that it was the result of a sudden inspiration, which she wanted to follow immediately in case she lost it by virtue of setting it aside. Playing the cycinnis had suggested to her variations that she might make to its fundamental theme, so she had made them, experimentally. That exploration had led her mind to invent, or discover, further possibilities, which she had wanted to try out immediately: possibilities relevant to the music she had been trying to compose for two days, in collaboration with Hecate, specifically in order to accompany Ananke in the Pool of Mnemosyne...or, as Fion had dubbed it, with deliberate insult but not without a certain propriety, Looming Disaster.

It did not seem to me that it was the right time for Elise to be doing that, and it was certainly not the right place, but any true artist, especially an artist as naïve and inexperienced at Elise, would have felt fully entitled to reply to that sort of criticism that when inspiration occurs, one is not merely entitled but bound to follow it—that precisely because one has free will, one is compelled by conscience to obey the impulse, even if the circumstances seem inappropriate.

In all honesty, the piece wasn't very good. Elise wasn't at her best, by any means, and the composition obviously wasn't properly finished, any more than my painting was—the melodic petals, so to speak, were woefully incomplete, and she was barely doing more than indicate their position, without detail, or even clarity—but she wasn't playing the music in order to show off her virtuosity to an elite company of connoisseur dinner guests. She certainly wasn't playing it for the Marquise de Mesmay, or for me, or even for Hecate.

A rapid glance at Hecate told me that she understood what was happening, and understood that, even though the piece wasn't being played for her, she needed to pay the most scrupulous attention to it, in order to obtain whatever inspiration from it she could. Her concentration intensified, becoming almost tangible. Even though the others didn't understand, some of them realized that *something* significant was happening. Mariette certainly did, as time went by, and her stony expression gradually became anxious.

Vashti Savage knew too, if only by studying Hecate's reaction, and I could feel the resonance of waves of jealousy that she was emitting. That reaction was utterly ridiculous, of course—there was no possibility whatsoever of a sexual relationship between Hecate and Elise, now or in the future; the nexus they had wasn't that kind of nexus at all—but Vashti was possessive; in wanting Hecate, ultimately futile as her desire might be, she wanted *all* of her, body and soul. It was an impossible covetousness, but Vashti had never been the kind of person to be intimidated by the boundaries of the possible; and in the final analysis, she simply couldn't help feeling what she was feeling, even though she must have known herself that it was ludicrous, and unworthy of her.

I turned round again. The African twins were listening intently too. Their faces were no longer impassive and inexpressive. The music was finding some kind of echo in them too, and they were smiling. They liked it; something in their shared soul was responding to it, at a deeper level than mere hearing.

Fion still didn't like it. Neither did Alectryon.

Parenot still had tears in his eyes, and others trickling down his cheeks. I felt sorry for him. Stealing his mistress was one thing; he hadn't deserved her—but stealing his adoptive daughter was something else entirely. For that, I felt culpable. She didn't love him, but that wasn't his fault. He had done his best.

The Marquise appeared to be studying the piece intently, but as if from a distance, clinically, examining it without feeling it. That reaction worried me; I would far rather that she had yielded to it, allowing herself an emotional response. But that, I thought, was the entire problem with the Marquise's dreams of mastering the fragments of the Cult of Orpheus and becoming a power within the Empire. She considered the whole affair as a matter of strategy, devoid of empathy.

I realized that it might, in fact, have been preferable had she reacted to my return to the island as Tommaso Dellacrusca had imagined that she would react, viscerally, perhaps even violently, rather than in the calm, intricate fashion in which the ultra-methodical Lord Dellacrusca would have reacted, had he not had the fatal flaw of nursing deep-seated grudges, in the spirit of vendetta.

It wasn't the Marquise's reaction and its possible implications that held my attention, though. Unlike her, I did react emotionally to the music and the situation alike, and my concern, primarily, was for Mariette.

Mariette, I could see very clearly, was gradually becoming frightened by the music, increasingly anxious for an adoptive daughter who could create such things…or who could allow such things to possess her. Seated as she was, between Parenot and Alectryon, she did not feel that she could turn to either side in search of reassurance. She met my gaze, but I was distressed to see that there was uncertainty there too. She did not trust my affection. She felt alone. She felt estranged even from Elise.

Had I been seated next to her, able to take her hand, perhaps I could have eased her anxiety, but I was not. In retrospect, perhaps that was a good thing. Perhaps she needed that anxiety.

And who, in fact, could blame her for not trusting my affection? Who, in all the world, could have trusted the affection of Axel Rathenius? Even Hecate doubted it.

I, by contrast, felt increasingly frustrated as the piece went on. The music wasn't *right*. It might be Looming Disaster, but it wasn't Ananke in the Pool of Mnemosyne. Neither was my painting—not yet, at least—but it seemed to me that Elise's inspiration should have waited until it was. It had no right to seize her now, prematurely. It was untimely, inept, stupid and wrong.

But we do not work magic, no matter how hard we might try or hope. Magic works us. And we cannot choose the timing of disasters, or expect them to wait for us to complete our preparations and perorations.

Elise felt frustrated too; that was obvious. In the end, she stopped playing, and apologized for not feeling able to continue.

"I'm not at my best," she said, apologizing to the Marquise. "It's too soon, I fear. I thought that coming back here wouldn't affect me, but…"

"Of course," the Marquise was quick to say. "It's entirely my fault, my dear; my haste was undue. The responsibility is entirely mine, and I am the one who owes you the apology."

She was right, but it was only her politeness dictating the words. She didn't feel a thing. Perhaps, in fact, she was actually glad that Elise had been unable to measure up to the occasion, pleased that she had played poorly. Perhaps she had measured her, and had been glad to find her wanting.

If so, it was a mistake—but I didn't realize it at the time. At the time, I just thought that things weren't going to plan. That was vanity speaking. Had I been humbler, I would have realized that the fact that things weren't going to my plan didn't mean that they weren't going to Ananke's.

The Marquise, I thought, failed in her duty as a hostess then. She should, at the very least, have given me permission to take Elise home, or to ask Mariette to take her home—but that was the last thing that the Marquise wanted. She still had her own *pièce de resistance* in reserve, and I had already provoked her sufficiently to make her utterly determined to show it. She insisted that we all go to the small drawing room, in order that Vashti Savage could summon spirits to advise us. Politeness required us to go.

Before we had even left the dining-room in order to make our way along the corridor, however, Elise took urgent possession of my right hand, and murmured: "I'm sorry, Axel; I couldn't get it right. I couldn't help it. I'm not sure that I'll ever be able to get it right. It's too hard...and I think it's already too late."

"I know the feeling," I murmured back. "But hold on; there'll be time yet to do whatever we need to do. Trust me."

She did trust me. I felt that. Perhaps she was foolish; perhaps it was just naivety; but she did trust me. And she wasn't entirely wrong. At any rate, she had no intention whatsoever of surrendering the hand she had seized, although she didn't have to fight hard for its possession. If the Marquise had had a seating plan for the séance, nobody would have taken any notice of it. There was a keen but scrupulously polite competition for hands, some attempted seizures, and some determined evasions.

Elise having staked her claim, there was a tacit competition between Mariette and Hecate for my other hand, which both elected in the end to lose gracefully by mutual consent, surrendering my left hand to the Marquise, whose own left hand grasped Alectryon's while his grasped Vashti's. Parenot claimed Elise's other hand, avidly, and surrendered his own to Hecate, who placed Fion Commonal between herself and Mariette. That left Mariette's free hand with no alternative but to grasp Vashti's—thus sealing, purely by the accident of elimination, a bond between two mediums, one very conscious of her power and the other still unaware of it.

Was that a crucial factor in determining what happened? I don't know for sure, but I think so.

The two African women also came into the room, but they sat down on the floor again, only holding hands with one another, seemingly in a world of their own. Was their presence a crucial factor? Again I don't know for sure, but I suspect so. I suspect that we were all crucial, that we all formed a bizarre nexus of sorts, full of psychological tensions of every possible kind, and perhaps all the more powerful for it. None of us was ready yet to work his or her own magic, but the magic didn't care about our readiness at all.

The one thing of which I can be certain is that the phenomena manifest at the séance were not all due to trickery, nor to the conventional summoning of shades. That at least some of the shades that came were no mere figments of our collective imagination, I have no doubt at all—and that the climactic manifestation came from further afield than the Underworld of Hades, even if it channeled Eurydice in the process, I am absolutely certain.

I had no active part in it, however; my part was to become evident later, and to be perfectly trivial in itself, although it was fortunately magnified by circumstance to have a very considerable effect.

The room was furnished and arranged in much the same way that it had been the last time I had been seated in it, with one important exception. The wall on which Charles Parenot's portrait of Mariette as Eurydice had gone—a crime against art, if it really had been burned— and the other painting that had been carefully positioned on the same wall had also been removed. They had been replaced by a single image, so fresh that I strongly suspected that the paint was not yet dry: a flattering full-length portrait of the Marquise, in a pose normally characteristic of military men, although she had no sword.

I would have liked to be able to agree with the Marquise that it was unsatisfactory, even poor, but it was not. Charles Parenot might have his limitations, but he was a true artist, and a good one. When painting with passion, he was capable of greatness of a sort. The passion with which he had painted the Marquise was by no means purely erotic—although I knew from experience that the fact that he did not like her would not necessarily have undermined the intensity of his attraction to her—but it had been no less intense for being mixed, and no more perverse. The painting was good—but it was not Eurydice Redeemed. I was naturally reluctant to plagiarize Fion Commonal, but it was Looming Disaster—and definitely not Ananke in the Pool of Mnemosyne. It was not an image of triumph, but of vainglory, although I could understand why the Marquise, in spite of her tendency to lay hypocritical claim to that sin, had not been able to see herself accurately within it.

The Marquise and Parenot were both on the alert to catch my reaction to the sight of the painting, but I don't know what they saw in my reaction, or what their own response to that reaction might have been. Elise only squeezed my right hand more tightly.

The Orpheus triptych, of course, was still in the grand hall. I had not seen it, and had not wanted to see it.

The lights were dimmed, as convention demanded. Squeezing my left hand with a surprisingly strong grip, as if determined to demonstrate greater strength than Elise, the Marquise leaned toward my left ear and whispered: "Now we shall see, my dear Axel, who is a mere instrument and who is not. I truly hope that we can still be friends."

I had no doubt that she meant friends on her terms, not mine, Madame's or Tommaso Dellacrusca's. But she was out of her depth. It was her vanity talking, and her vanity alone.

Evidently, the Marquise had faith in Vashti's abilities—and equally evidently, she had provided her with a program of sorts, in order to assist her to use them fruitfully, from her point of view. I knew, though, that such programs often fall apart when there are more minds in a circle of summoners than a medium's sensitivity can easily encompass, especially when some clients are unknown to the medium and difficult to weigh. In my experience of séances, the spirits much prefer the comfort of the familiar—expectably, given that the Underworld from which they come to drink metaphorical black blood is located in the depths of the medium's unconscious rather than the bowels of the Earth.

First of all, Vashti summoned the shade of the Marquise's mother; who was, of course, also Sister Ursule's sister. She advised her favorite daughter—the Marquise, naturally—to be wary of wolves in sheep's clothing, who pretended to virtue, but were essentially unreliable, if not actively treacherous. She did not mention a name, but there was no one present who did not know to whom she was referring.

Then came Fion Commonal's father, who had nothing much to say of any interest, even to his son. Both spirits, naturally, spoke with Vashti's vocal cords, albeit with recognizable simulacra of the voices that they had presumably had, which I had no way of recognizing.

The next voice, however, I did recognize, although it was a long time since I had heard it. I suspected that Vashti had summoned it many times before, and had mastered its intonations very well. Vashti, of course, had known Roxane d'Alectryon while she was alive.

This time, she had not come from the other world to offer comfort to her father, but to admonish me.

"I can see you, Axel," she said. "I have always been able to see you. No one ever forgets the man who caused her death."

I had not caused Roxane d'Alectryon's death, by any stretch of the most malevolent imagination. Even Claudius Jaseph had not caused her death, although there was a sense in which he really had stolen her soul. She had committed suicide, for foolish reasons. I raised no objection to her slanders, however. I merely glanced at Mariette, sitting beside Vashti—but Mariette did not even seem to be listening. Her eyes were closed and she appeared to be descending into a deep trance herself. If the Marquise hoped to attack our nexus through her jealousy, the artillery fire went completely to waste.

Roxane accused me of being heartless individual, who discarded those who loved me heartlessly, leaving them wounded and vulnerable, putting their very souls in peril. It was puerile, and also inaccurate. I thought that Hecate was about to intervene at one point, but she looked at me first, seeking my authorization. I shook my head slightly, and she let the moment pass.

But Roxane was only the warm-up. Next came the Marquis de Mesmay, and after him Lord Dellacrusca. The latter worried me a great deal more than the former—not because of the expectable demands he made for vengeance, in ostentatious harmony with Mesmay, pointing the finger of accusation a trifle obliquely, but unmistakably, against the bacchantes of the Cult of Dionysus, but because I was worried about what he might say thereafter.

I was not mistaken. The Marquise was not a gentleman, and nor was Vashti Savage. The fake shade turned his attention to his granddaughter, and advised her to beware of deceptive and unworthy guardians. He did not name names, but a glance at Parenot informed me that he did not consider himself to be omitted from the judgment.

The shade did not go so far as to say that there is no such animal as a trustworthy man, but the fake Lord Dellacrusca was not about to put in a good word for his own sons. That was not implausible, in fact. In what Fion Commonal thought of as the good old days, Dellacrusca had often seemed as exasperated by his sons as everyone else. Nor was he about to exempt women from his judgment…and that was not implausible either, at least insofar as he and Elise might have Mariette in mind.

But Mariette still seemed to be utterly oblivious, incapable of hearing anything that Vashti was saying in her faux-baritone voice

I tried as hard as I could to remind Elise with the pressure of my hand that it was all imposture, not to be taken seriously. But that, I think, is the point at which the imposture became confused. Perhaps the next "apparition" had been planned, but perhaps not, for the next voice to materialize from Vashti' versatile vocal cords was one that nobody recognized, which had to be asked—by the Marquise, playing the role of prompter—to identify herself.

She named herself as Lord Dellacrusca's daughter: Elise's mother.

If Vashti had been fed cues as to how to improvise her monologue, however, she presumably went off at a tangent, because Elise's mother did not endorse what her grandfather had said.

"I am with you, my darling," the shade said, very obviously addressing Elise, and ignoring the rest of us completely. "I am always with you. I died, but I never left you. Do not hate your grandfather, even though he was the cause of my distress, and, indirectly, my death. Pity him. He was not incapable of love, but he lost his way. He died loving you, but had he taken you, that love would have killed you as it killed me. Love can be treacherous. Rather trust kindness. Kindness is never

267

perverted. But always remember that you are never without love, and never can be, while I am with you."

I felt the Marquise de Mesmay's grip on my left hand weaken. I sensed annoyance in her, because she had not expected that monologue, but it seemed to me that she was not annoyed with Vashti, because she did not regard Vashti, as Alectryon, Charles Parenot and Fion Commonal surely did, as a mere instrument who was supposed to do as instructed and nothing more. The Marquise believed sincerely in magic, and she believed in Vashti's power as she believed in her own. She believed that Vashti really was responding, if not to the crudely literal spirits of the dead, at least to something real within her unconscious mind, to resonances from elsewhere that were, in some sense, authentic.

And she was right to believe that.

Vashti tried to speak again, in a different voice, but only produced a few inarticulate grunts, as if the voice that was trying to make itself heard could not master her vocal apparatus.

She tried to organize the grunts into meaningful syllables, but she failed. She gasped and she coughed…and then she vomited—but it was not the food and wine that her stomach was patiently digesting that she vomited.

She vomited ectoplasm

I had seen Vashti produce ectoplasm before, but only in the form of thin wisps of vapor, no more substantial than the condensed vapor of breath in icy air, never anything coherent, even as a visual image. It has always seemed to me, in fact, that they really were the vapor of her exhalation, mysteriously chilled into fog. Perhaps, in the course of her experiments with the Marquise, Vashti had already done more than that, on occasion—I remembered that Fion Commonal had avoided the question when I has asked it—but I was certain that she had never been able to produce such quantities as she was producing now, which she was certainly not producing alone. The ectoplasm was still vaporous, but it was no exhalation of breath; it was a far denser fog than that.

Mariette seemed to have fallen unconscious; she was horribly pale, as if her constricted carotid arteries had cut off the blood supply to her face. In fact, she seemed as purely white as the ectoplasm itself: the color of ghosts and specters. Her blonde hair seemed almost silver. But Mariette was not the only contributor to the mysterious substance that was flowing through Vashti from somewhere beyond her material envelope.

I could not turn my head—I literally *could not*, my gaze being held, as if in a psychic vice, by the ectoplasmic cloud, but I could see from the corners of my eyes, and perhaps senses other than my mere sight, that the African twins were locked together in a tight embrace, writhing, perhaps with ecstasy and perhaps with terror, their eyes wide open and staring into their twin reflections, but surely not seeing anything that was of this world.

More directly, diagonally across the table, I could see Hecate Rain. She too was exceedingly pale, but she was fully conscious and staring. Her gaze could not meet mine—the angle was wrong—but I am certain that we were both aware of one another, and I believe she was aware, at that moment, of the entire pattern that she had come so close to piecing together, and understanding. She was caught, I think, between terror and joy—but there was just the faintest hint of a smile on her lips, and in that ghost of a smile, there was trust: trust in me.

Elise squeezed my hand, and there was trust in the gesture.

The Marquise was squeezing too, but convulsively; hers was the grip of someone at a loss, someone afflicted by panic. She had no trust in anything any longer, including herself. She knew that her plan had gone wrong—and she sensed, I think, the irrelevance of that fact. She sensed that something far worse than her petty machinations had gone wrong—had perhaps gone wrong, in fact, even before any of her guests had touched the silverware on her table, even before Mariette, Elise, Hecate and I had climbed into the sociable.

Hades and the forces of destruction had not waited to be summoned or appeased.

The nine of us gathered around the table were not writhing, and perhaps not moving at all save for minimal tremors and quivers, but a frisson was running through us all, and through the entire circle that we formed like an insubstantial serpent symbolically enveloping the entire cosmos. It bound us all together, but not as a conference of equals, nor as subjects of a tyranny. There was no empire, no throne, and hence no power behind a throne, but there was order, and there was expectation.

Perhaps the ectoplasm was attempting to form itself into the resemblance of a human being, or a being of similar species. Perhaps it had the intention of forming vocal cords of its own, which would be capable of spelling out what Vashti Savage could not. If so, it failed.

I think that whatever force was forming the cloud did have that initial intention, that it really did attempt to deliver its message verbally and explicitly. What form would it have taken had it succeeded? I don't know; perhaps that of Madame, but far more likely that of Eurydice: Eurydice in Mariette's image, not Aethne de Mesmay's, lamenting rather than anticipating a glorious return. On the other hand, perhaps it would have attempted to synthesize an avatar of Orpheus, or Dionysus Zagreus—more probably the latter, if it really wanted to seem something more than merely human, to be an object of divine authority, or worship, in order that there should be no question of anything but obedience to its edict.

Either way, it failed. It could not master sufficient coherency. It could not even maintain the whiteness of the ectoplasm, which began to turn black.

Even with the aid of the ectoplasm, the entity could not form a face, let alone an apparatus of speech. It could not speak to anyone in that room, except for me, and in addressing me, it could not make use of any language but the authentic suspiric language—which as I had observed before, was not merely the language of sighs but also the language of screams.

The ectoplasmic form dissolved into an apparent chaos and confusion, but its chaos and confusion were only apparent. There was still fusion, still order, still expectation. I could see what it was, and I could understand why. I had been trying to create it on canvas for three days, and even though I had not come anywhere near to finishing it, and the petals had not yet come close to acquiring the necessary detail in the painting, I knew what it was that the black ectoplasmic storm-cloud was becoming, and I knew what it was saying.

It was Ananke in the Pool of Mnemosyne, and her scream was very loud and very clear.

She did scream, literally and horribly. She could not speak, but she could make herself heard.

I had heard one such scream before, but not nearly as loudly, and not in such agony. I had heard it on the evening when Dellacrusca was murdered, played by

Elise's haunted viola, and perhaps I had understood it even then—but only unconsciously, if so. It had ordered me to grab Charles Parenot, and, with his help, to pick up Elise and Hecate Rain and remove them from harm's way, and I had done it, without knowing why.

This time, I heard the scream consciously, and I understood it consciously. I knew exactly what it was telling me, exactly what I had to do, and why.

But I could not move, for the moment; I could not even blink or turn my head.

The paralysis could only have lasted a few seconds, and those few seconds did not matter, in the context of what it as necessary to do. I had hours in hand to make my own message and my own voice heard, indirectly— no longer than the night, to be sure, but hours. Enough time to make a few seconds irrelevant.

Perhaps the seconds were irrelevant, and not merely in material terms—but they did not seem so at the time. They felt like the mass of time itself, bleak and irresistible. To say that my momentary immobility was frustrating would be a drastic understatement. While they lasted, the scream cut through me, and seemed to fill my inner world. It was not physically painful, but it hurt nevertheless, seeming to be the distilled essence of dolor, distress in its purest form. I don't believe that the semblance in question was purposive; it wasn't the entity itself urging me to action, driving home its point with unnecessary force; the distress was just an aspect of the phenomenon, an inevitable, inherent cost of the magic.

It didn't hurt anyone else physically either, but it certainly shook them up—considerably more than me, because I understood what was happening far better than any of them.

XVI. Spreading the Word

When the dark ectoplasm folded up upon itself, as if the snake sealing the circle of hands and minds had devoured its own tail gluttonously, or as if the whirlpool of souls had disappeared down its own funnel, and all the clutching hands—or almost all—let go of one another, I didn't hesitate. I knew what to do and in what order.

First of all, I grabbed Fion Commonal. "Mount your horse and ride as fast as possible to the port," I told him, speaking rapidly but precisely. "Go directly to the police station and tell Clovis that he has to evacuate the town, completely. Tell him that there's going to be a bigger flood than any seen before on Mnemosyne, and that it will hit at dawn, or a few moments thereafter. Tell him to get everyone with a horse to spread the news in all directions. The able-bodied have to get every single child, invalid and elderly person to high ground—half way up Snowspur won't be too far. Tell him to spread the news in my name. Then spread it yourself—start with the Sprite, and don't neglect the Convent of Shalimar; make sure it reaches every covert of the town."

Fion, still shaken up, hesitated.

"Trust me," I said.

He did. He turned and ran out of the room.

"And send Jean-Jacques in!" I called after him. "He should be waiting by my carriage."

Then I turned to the Marquise and Alectryon. After a single glance at the pair of them, I addressed Alectryon, "Milord, you have to mobilize all the men that you and the Marquise have, camped on the hill between the house and the bay," I said. "Tell them to scatter in all directions and spread the flood warning to every corner of the island, in your name as well as mine."

Neither of them moved a muscle. The Marquise opened her mouth to object.

"If you don't believe me, Milady," I said, curtly, "look to your seismograph. And consult your telegraph operator. I don't know when the trace of the stylus went mad, or why the telegraph has been stubbornly silent, but tell your man to start transmitting now to anyone capable of receiving."

I knew that Madame must have started sending messages to the Empire as soon as her own machines give her the warning, and that action might have prompted the overload that was preventing the messages from getting through to the island, but it didn't really matter. We had to handle things ourselves.

Alectryon finally reacted, but as soon as she saw that he was about to speak, the Marquise made the gesture I had seen before, with her forefinger, instructing him to shut up. This time, though, he was having none of it. He swatted her hand away as if it were a fly, and all the authority that the Marquise had had over him, whatever its nature had been, went with it. All her ambitions died with that gesture of casual contempt.

All Alectryon said to the Marquise was: "Do it!" Then he nodded to me and strode out of the room. He simply took it for granted that his command would be carried out. He was a Duc, after all, and the Marquise was only a minor aristocrat by marriage.

Her nexus had been smashed.

I was genuinely impressed by Alectryon. The man detested me. He probably believed every word of what Roxane's faked voice had repeated to him a few moments before, even though he knew that it was only Vashti Savage's imagination speaking, but he knew that it didn't matter. He detested me, but he trusted my word. He hadn't understood the vision of darkness and the scream, any more than Fion had, but he sensed that I had. He trusted that I knew what I was doing.

Jean-Jacques arrived, breathless, pistol in hand, ready to do battle with an army if necessary.

"You won't need that," I said. "Get a horse from the stables—unhitch one from the carriage if there isn't one there that's fit enough to ride all night. Gallop to the nearest hamlet, and rouse every house. Tell every man there who has a horse to mount up and spread the word in his turn. The island will be flooded at daybreak. Everyone needs to get to high ground—the higher the better. Tell the fishermen who don't want to abandon their boats to take them into open water, and when they see the big wave coming, to steer directly into it. No matter how steep it seems, they'll be able to climb over it, prow first—but if it hits them sideways on, they'll go down. Spread the message in my name. Go now."

I didn't both to add Alectryon's name. The people Jean-Jacques would be speaking to wouldn't pay any heed to his title.

Jean-Jacques didn't hesitate. Having been told to go, he went, without prevarication.

I turned to Parenot. "Can you ride?" I demanded. As a Lutecian, it couldn't be taken for granted.

"Yes," he said.

"Then go. You know what to do."

He looked at the Marquise. Perhaps, if she had made her hand gesture, he would have waited. She didn't.

"If you're wrong…," she began.

"Laugh at me then," I said. "For now, get your operator to your telegraph and start dictating messages to anyone he can reach. If you don't want to risk Alectryon's name, use mine—but try with all your might to get the word out. We have time in hand, but none to waste.

Without waiting to see whether she did as she was asked, I went to help Hecate and Elise, who were trying to bring Mariette and Vashti round. Their hands were still closed together, Mariette's right in Vashti's left. Both were unconscious, but obviously breathing. I went to check on the African twins. They were still conscious, seemingly terrified, but unharmed.

To Vashti, who had just recovered consciousness, I said: "There's going to be a big flood. This house is probably far enough above sea level, and sufficiently solidly built, to be safe, but yours isn't. You have time to get to Snowspur if you don't want to stay here."

"How do you know?" Vashti asked.

"You told me," I told her. "Or something using your voice."

She didn't question that. She didn't like me either, and might not have been as quick to trust me in spite of it as Alectryon had been, but she trusted her spirits. If the message had come through during one of her trances, that was good enough for her.

Then I picked Mariette up, as yet only barely conscious, and headed for the courtyard, swiftly followed by Hecate.

Before we got there, the Marquise reappeared. As I had suggested, she had checked her spectroscope. She knew, and she too was prepared to take my word for it that I had somehow been informed of what the crazed charcoal trace signified for Mnemosyne. She looked at me with muted hatred, but also with naked envy. She thought that she was the one who should have received the warning; she felt that she was the one who was *entitled* to have received the warning.

But she wasn't. I was.

I continued running toward the courtyard, carrying Mariette in my arms.

"Is our house safe?" Elise asked, trotting alongside me.

"I think so," I told her. "At any rate, we need to get to Helen and Luzon as fast as we can. Helen needs to send messages to anyone and everyone along the coasts of Gaul and the Cassiterides, if she can get anything out at all. The wave will flatten out as it overflows the coast, but the channel will have a funneling effect. When it hits us here, it'll be at its maximum height."

"What's happened?" she wanted to know.

"Exactly what Madame anticipated: there's been a massive upheaval of the sea-bed in the Great Archipelago. It's displaced a huge wave that has already traveled part way across the Ocean, and is heading directly for the entrance to the Channel."

"Is the Island of Dionysus safe?"

"The island, no…but the people, probably. Madame had contingency plans in place. We hadn't, but we have a few extra hours to prepare. The telegraph seems to have let us down thus far, but it might still give us a means to sound the alarm."

"We weren't in time," Elise said as Hecate and I lifted Mariette into the carriage and laid her down on the seat. "We didn't respond quickly enough."

"We couldn't" I reminded her. "We got here as soon as we could, and we're still in time to make a difference."

"I'll look after her," said Hecate, meaning Mariette.

I jumped down again.

"I *knew* we were too late," said Elise, still a trifle confused. "I told you so."

The Mesmay stables were evidently well-stocked, as one might expect. Jean-Jacques hadn't had to unhitch one of my horses, so all I had to do was climb up into the seat and pick up his whip, I took the time before doing so to reply more fully to Elise.

"We were *exactly* on time, Elise," I told her. "You did your part, Mariette did hers, and Hecate did hers. Mine was minimal by comparison—but let's thank the gods for the Marquise de Mesmay's vainglory and inclination to cunning. If she hadn't gathered us all together for her own purposes..."

I left it at that. Hecate was holding on to Mariette, making sure that she couldn't fall off the seat. I lifted Elise in, closed the door, climbed up and drove off.

The journey across the island seemed to take more than twice as long as usual. In fact, I'm certain, thinking back, that it did take more than twice as long—probably a full two hours—partly because it was dark and the sky was cloudy, leaving the road plunged in almost total gloom, and partly because I stopped in every village and alongside every house on the road to shout: "There's a big flood coming! Run to Snowspur! Word of Axel Rathenius!"

I wouldn't have believed, a few months earlier, or even a few days earlier, that my name could have any substantial effect, but that evening, I felt that it might, and hoped that it would.

I didn't feel that because I'd put around the rumor that I was the Hierophant of the Cult of Dionysus, or even because I was widely reputed to be a sorcerer, although a few of the people who reacted me to my warning probably quoted that as their reason for doing as they were bid afterwards. The reason I felt strangely certain that my name would galvanize people into action, without more than a few seconds or minutes of hesitation, was because I felt that over the years I'd been on Mnemosyne, without anyone really being conscious it, at least until the day I disappeared, I had somehow become symbolic of the island: not merely of the artist's colony, but of the island itself.

It was vanity speaking, of course, and perhaps it was absurd vanity, but I didn't think it was absurd. Even people who disliked me, thinking that I was a poseur or a rake, or both, had nevertheless come to identify me subconsciously with Mnemosyne, and think of me as a personification of it. Perhaps that was because I had never aged, but always remained the same; a few had suspected me of sorcery on that score, and deemed it one more reason for being suspicious of me—but even so, the fact remained that I had been an enduring, unchanging rock, an emblem of stability and solidity. People for whom I had done the occasional favor, or to whom I'd shown a little casual kindness, like Constable Clovis and Nicodemus Rham, were doubtless even more forcefully affected by that subliminal identification than people who looked at me askance, but even the people who detested me felt, deep down, that I was Mnemosyne personified, and that if I had an intuition that the island was in danger, then it was best to act rather than quibble.

That's what I thought at the time, at any rate, while I was shouting my warning, and I still think so.

I can claim no credit for it, of course. It was a mere accident of circumstance that I was a Macrobian who had come to settle on Mnemosyne, and felt so much at home there that he had lingered a little longer than I had thought wise. Even that was foolish of me, because times had changed without my noticing it, and I had not overstayed my welcome or outlived my usefulness at all. I didn't deserve any credit, therefore, for any strange status I had attained. Perhaps it had helped a little that I was a great artist, and a loudmouthed braggart, but in the final analysis, it must have be a matter of pure chance. I had merely been a pawn of Ananke and the Pool of Mnemosyne.

In any case, the effect that I believed that my name was having was subconscious, not conscious. The people who reacted to it had no idea why they were reacting— but they did react.

When I pulled the horses to a stop, Helen ran out of the house to meet me.

"Axel!" she shouted. "Thank the gods! The telegraph has gone silent, after one garbled message that I couldn't decode, and I can't get a response from the mainland. It might be just a mechanical breakdown, but I have a terrible feeling that something's wrong."

"There's been a massive submarine earthquake on the far side of the Ocean, in the borderlands of the Great Archipelago and the Weed Sea." I told her. "Don't worry about Madame. She'll already have moved the entire population of the island to higher ground. We still have a couple of hours in hand, but the wave will reach us at daybreak. Everything is in hand; the word is being spread. By the time the wave arrives, the slopes of Snowspur will be a vast gallery from which the people of the low-lying districts can watch their homes collapse from a safe vantage point. You have plenty of time join them if you wish, but I think we're safe enough here. Go back to the telegraph and keep trying to get a message through to the mainland."

She stopped, momentarily bewildered. Then her face cleared. "The Marquise has a telegraph too," she concluded.

"And a seismograph," I supplied. "But we didn't have time to try to make sense of what was coming through them. Mercifully, we had magic…a substantial accumulation and concentration of it, in fact. The voice of the resonant unconscious sometimes has difficulty making its messages heard and understood, but not this time. I read the message loud and clear. Get back to your tappers, though. Keep sending. It's a horribly awkward and unreliable technology, as yet, but we'll have to make the most of it, until something better comes along."

She did as she was asked. She didn't want to disappoint me.

I lifted Mariette out of the carriage, and carried her into the house. I took her into the studio, where a lamp had been lit, and laid her down on the divan.

Luzon fetched a bottle of brandy and a glass. I sent her back to the kitchen for three more glasses. She hesitated.

"And one for yourself, if you like," I added.

"No thank you, sir," she said, "But… are we going to drown?"

"I hope not. Go to Snowspur, if you like. There'll be quite a crowd there by the time you arrive. Half way up should be more than enough, but you'll get a better view from the top."

"I'll stay here," said Luzon, decisively, "and save my corns."

Mariette was conscious, but weak.

"I feel terrible," she said. "I'm so sorry."

"You have nothing for which to apologize," I said. "What Elise began with her exploratory music, you completed, with a little help from Vashti Savage, Eurydice and the African twins. They might not understand any language we speak, but they understood what happened in the manse tonight, and lent themselves to it."

"In fact," observed Hecate, mournfully, "the only person who was completely useless, among the entire company, was me. I should have ridden off with Fion Commonal, to spread the word."

"You were far from useless," I said. "It's thanks to you that we were all there, and you've provided more than one vital link in the chain along the way. Without you there, Vashti couldn't have played her part, nor I mine. Without you, I wouldn't even be who and what I am."

"Which is more than can be said for me," murmured Mariette, taking a substantial gulp of brandy."

"Not true," I said. "Hecate's work has taken far longer, and has been far more patient, but what happened tonight couldn't possibly have happened without you and Elise…or, for that matter, Aethne de Mesmay. You had to put your blood and your soul into it—all I had to offer was my name."

"And your artist's eye," Elise put in. She was standing a few paces away, in front of the huge canvas suspended from the wall. "Without that, you wouldn't have understood what Mariette's blood and soul were telling you. I suppose there'll be no need now to finish the painting."

"There'll be every need," I told her, emptying my glass with a convulsive gulp, "just as there's every need for you and Hecate to finish your composition. Those completions are esthetically necessary."

"But they can't change anything," Elise objected. "We can't use them in any kind of spell to inhibit the destruction caused by the earthquake."

"We never could, any more than the Marquise could really summon the destructive force of Hades with her spell, even if she'd found the musicians she thought she needed. That isn't the way that magic works. But the endeavor was part of the amelioration we did manage to being about—which *is* being brought about, at this very moment. And now I must go, at least to show myself and continue playing my part. Tomorrow, I'll continue with the painting, and you can continue with your work, but tonight...I have a lot more riding and shouting to do."

"I'll go with you," said Hecate.

"I'd far rather you didn't," I said. "It's not necessary, and I'd feel less anxious if I knew you were here, to look after Mariette and Elise."

"I don't need looking after," protested Elise.

"Nor do I," added Mariette, even more insulted.

"Of course you don't," I said, "But I do. I need to know that you're not riding around in the dark. I don't much care if Fion Commonal has a fall and breaks his neck, but if anything were to happen to one of you...well, please stay here. I have to go."

I ran out, not knowing whether they were going to take any notice of me or not. given that I had to right to give them orders and they didn't need my permission. There was, however, only one fresh horse in the stable, a bay mare. Leaving the other two hitched to the carriage, and hoping that no one would take it into her head to unhitch them, except to put them away for the night, I saddled the mare, mounted up, and rode northwards, in order to bring the succor of Dionysus to the remotest parts of the island.

I didn't manage to get back to the house before dawn. The mare didn't take a fall but she cast a shoe, picked up a stone in her hoof and went lame. I managed to get her to Snowspur, in good time to watch the first light of dawn appear in the east.

The sea was still calm. The sky was still direly dark to the west, but there was absolutely nothing beneath it to suggest that disaster was about to strike.

What if I'm wrong? I thought. *What if I've just made myself the biggest fool in creation? How the people who detest me will laugh! No one will ever trust me again.*

My vanity must have been terrified by that thought for at least fifteen seconds, perhaps twenty

Then the wave came, the faint light of dawn reflecting off its crest like a long row of frail sparks.

I had never imagined that it could be so high, or that it might be moving so rapidly. I was used to seeing ships at sea, yachts and steamers alike, and my notion of marine progress was based on that experience. Tidal waves are, however, another kind of animal entirely. No sooner had the monster become visible, it seemed, than it was upon us.

I couldn't believe, in that brief interval of horrified alarm, that the flotilla of little boats that was steering straight for it could ever climb that high—but they did, all but a handful. The wall advanced across the island to the right and left of Snowspur, but the upper half of the mountain remained majestically untouchable. I was afraid for a few moments that the seething surf might even reach my house, but the water poured into the coves to either side, almost as if the waves were actually dividing in order to spare the house the trouble of getting its feet wet. The water didn't touch the Toustain house

284

either, which would have been engulfed first if it had swept over the headland. The Mesmay Manse wasn't entirely untroubled, but all those still inside it would only have got their feet wet, if that. On the other hand, most of the tents of the camp on the hillside to the west were simply swept away. Had Alectryon's petty army been asleep in their bunks, many of them would have died there.

Lucifer's Light collapsed. Nicodemus Rham was standing beside me when it happened, sticking to my side assiduously. I wasn't sure whether he thought that I was his talisman or that he was mine.

"Good riddance," he muttered.

"It's taking a lot of your memories with it, Nicodemus," I observed. "Not to mention your ghosts."

"They left a while ago, Master Rathenius," he said. "Times have changed. Nothing ever lasts." Wisely, he didn't make an exception for me.

"Your house is gone too," I observed.

"But the Sprite's still standing, although the taproom will be full of mud—and the Convent of Shalimar too. There'll be a deal of cleaning up to do, but that's just work. This can't kill the island—not with the people safe"

""I hope you're right, Nicodemus," I said.

"And don't worry, sir," he said. "Whatever a few imbeciles and old women are muttering, no one with an ounce of common sense blames you."

"Blames me?" I said, utterly astonished. "I'm the one who gave the warning! How could anyone blame me?"

As soon as I'd said it, though, I realized exactly how they could. I had given the warning; I had known in advance what was going to happen. Only a short imaginative leap separates accurate prophecy from an implication of causation in the minds of the credulous...and even without that superstitious gymnastics, the well-known psychological tendency to blame the messenger who brings bad news was bound to have some effect.

As Nicodemus said, no one with an ounce of common sense would believe it—not consciously. But the feeling of triumph and self-satisfaction I'd had while riding around, spreading the word and believing myself to be a hero, disappeared in the wake of the fast-traveling wave, over the horizon.

Looking down at the wreckage of the port, it was difficult to share Nicodemus Rham's stubborn optimism. Hundreds of other people—probably several thousand, although they were too widely scattered over too vast an area to be counted—were doubtless thinking the same. Cleaning out the buildings made of good brick and sturdy stone that were still standing would, indeed, only be work—but there were a great many poorer edifices that had collapsed under the pressure of the racing water.

Needless to say, when the exodus from Snowspur began, I wasn't carried down the hill in triumph. Nobody called me a hero, or even thanked me for spreading the word. Later, I thought, the wiser heads might weigh things up and feel gratitude, but for the time being, the perceived loss was too great.

Anyway, I had only done what was expected of me. If fate appoints you as a personification of a place, in the unconscious minds of its inhabitants, that position carries responsibilities. It wasn't as if I'd worked any magic. All I'd done was lend my name to an alarm call.

When I finally got back to the house, I staggered up to bed, trying conscientiously not to wake Mariette, who was fast asleep, utterly exhausted herself.

When I woke up, after noon, I went back to work. Hecate and Elise were already busy.

XVII. The End

The Duc d'Alectryon didn't come to thank me for enabling him to save every last one of his men; instead, he immediately decamped to the mainland, taking his little private army with him, and headed for Lutèce. The Marquise de Mesmay didn't come to see me either, although she remained on the island, opening her house up to selected refugees from the devastated town, including Vashti Savage, Fion Commonal and—at least briefly— Sister Ursule and the Sisters of Shalimar. If anyone was being hailed as a hero it was Fion Commonal, the savior of the port, who had ridden his borrowed horse through the streets for hours, commanding the evacuation in the name of the Island Council.

The only man who did visit me, the following evening, was Constable Clovis, who probably had less time to spare than anyone, but felt that I deserved some recognition for sending Fion to him—and to him, at least Fion had quoted my name, and it had taken immediate effect. Clovis had trusted me, not Fion, and had acted on my assurance, not his.

He told me that the known death-toll was presently less than forty—which sounded too high to me, but he assured me that if I hadn't got the message to him so quickly, it would have been forty times higher.

"That would have destroyed the island," he said. "As things are, it's just a matter of rebuilding. A lot of faint hearts will scamper for the mainland, but the true islanders will stay. We have the arms and we have the will. By next summer, with luck and better weather, things will be back to normal."

"Insofar as anything here ever was normal," I said.

"It was and it will be, sir," he assured me, "as long as you're here."

"It's going to be a hard twelve months, even if you can make provision to house thousands of people temporarily while the port and the coastal villages are being rebuilt, and also find enough fertile land to plant crops before next year's tourist season," I said. "It's going to take time for the rain to wash the salt out of the fields, and importing food for the population will surely leave the entire island in debt for decades."

"Not so, sir," he assured me. "We can pull through. All but a few of the boats came through, thanks to your warning. There are always plenty of fish in the sea."

The following days suggested that he might be right about the will of the islanders to repair their fortunes. One way and another, accommodation was found for many of the island's dispossessed. Three families moved into the old Toustain house, and all the summer cottages owned by summer visitors that stood on high ground were commandeered. All of Alectryon's remaining tents were filled. Hecate's house and most of her personal property had been destroyed, but she had a home with me for as long as she needed one, indefinitely if that turned out to be the case.

Charles Parenot returned to Lutèce promptly, and a good many members of the artists' colony followed his example with alacrity, but the artisans and skilled laborers necessary to the island's reconstruction mostly stayed. Accurate assessment of the lowland fields suggested that they would, in fact, take a long time to recover their fecundity, but the higher ground offered a good many previously-unexploited opportunities for cultivation, while still leaving sufficient pastureland to support most of the island's livestock.

Jean-Jacques gave me regular reports on the situation on the island when he came back every day from foraging for food, and also gave me news of how the coastal towns were faring, but I hardly stepped outdoors myself. I was busy in the studio. Hecate and Elise were equally busy upstairs.

Tommaso Dellacrusca arrived five and a half days after the flood, in the early afternoon. I was in the studio, at something of a loose end because my sitter was late for her session. When Jean-Jacques came to ask whether he should send the visitor in, I had just turned away from idle contemplation of the incomplete painting on the easel in order to study the canvas on the wall, wondering whether it was really complete, or whether I ought to go back to it in order to add a few more final touches, while I had nothing better to do.

Tommaso made up for what was beginning to seem like a disappointing dearth of congratulation. "Well, Master Rathenius," he said, "you exceeded my expectations, and even my hopes. Binding your name to Alectryon's like that was a stroke of genius. In a matter of hours, you sealed a tacit pact that might have taken months to negotiate and years to cement. Alectryon's back in Lutèce, nominally in charge of the entire organization, but the Marquise is no longer the power behind his straw throne. I don't say that it's perfect, but it works, for now—and I kept my part of the bargain. I haven't struck a single name off the remainder of my list. Even the Marquise is alive and well."

"I didn't realize that we had an explicit bargain," I said.

"Well, perhaps I dreamed it—in fact, I'm sure that I did. But I kept it anyway. I'm sorry I couldn't get here any earlier, but I came as fast as I could. I have a boat in the harbor, ready to take you all to the mainland as soon as you're packed, where we can catch a train for Lutèce, as soon as you like. For the moment, Lory and I will put you up at home, but we'll find you all suitable accommodation as soon as we can."

I looked at him quizzically. "You seem to be laboring under a misapprehension," I said. "I have no intention of leaving Mnemosyne. Nor, I suspect, has anyone else in the house—although you're welcome to consult them all."

"But you can't stay here!" he objected. "That's absolutely crazy! The island's a wreck. You wouldn't starve, I dare say, but that's about all I can say. It doesn't have to be forever—three years, perhaps even two—but you really can't stay until the port is rebuilt and thriving. The summer visitors won't come back until then, or the artists."

"In fact," I said, "I can't go. Three months ago, I thought I had to, but I was wrong. Without realizing it, I'd become part of the island, part of its identity and personality. I had to go to paradise to find that out, but I know it now. This is where I belong."

"But what are you going to do?" he asked. There was still a good deal of naivety about him.

"Paint," I said succinctly.

After the initial salutation, he had already turned to face the easel, where the incomplete portrait of Elise was making good progress. This time, she was exactly was she wanted to see herself—for now. He turned to it again now, puzzled and disappointed, in order to take a longer look,

"It's a good likeness," he said, after a long pause. "Where is she?"

"She's gone with Hecate to visit Sister Ursule at the Convent—the sisters have just moved back in. She should be back very soon. In fact she's late for her sitting. She'll be pleased to see you."

"But you don't think she'll come back to Lutèce with me?

"That's up to her, obviously."

"She'd definitely come if you came."

"I can't. She'll understand that."

"Are you sure about that?"

I wasn't, obviously. All I could do was shrug my shoulders, and focus on the petals that might still need a few further amendments.

"Well," said Tommaso, uncertainly, "as you say, it's her decision. If she does want to stay, though, you're going to have to look after her. I hope you're not intending to entrust her education to the superior of the Convent of Shalimar. A religious vocation would be almost as bad as running off with an artist. Father would turn in his grave."

I didn't want to think about Lord Dellacrusca stirring in his grave. I still remembered all too clearly what he had said to me while ostensibly doing that on the night of the tidal wave.

"Shall we take a seat?" I said. We were still standing between the supposedly finished painting hanging on the wall and the unfinished one on the easel, looking at the painting that wasn't called Looming Disaster.

"In a moment," he said. He had turned his attention to the wall and he was scrutinizing the image carefully, squinting theatrically. Finally, he said: "What's it called?"

"Ananke in the Pool of Mnemosyne," I told him, easily resisting a whimsical temptation to cite Fion Commonal's title.

"The pool in Hecate Rain's letter?"

"Yes."

"It's symbolic, isn't it?"

"Yes, it is," I said

"What of?"

"Life," I said.

He nodded. "Not exactly like the letter, though," he said. "If these are the petals, they're not dark at all—mostly quite bright, in fact."

"That's true," I said. "I modified the idea slightly, because I needed to make the petals stand out against the background. Anyway, I wanted some brightness in there. There was far too much black for my liking—there is still is, but that's life, isn't it?"

"Life seems quite bright to me at present. Funny petals, though. Some of them look like people."

"True," I said. "That's what we people are, you see: just petals in the pool of Mnemosyne, briefly whirled in the vortex of time, obscuring the legacy of the past."

"Very poetic. I prefer this one, but I suppose I'm biased." He waved a neatly manicured hand at the portrait of Elise.

"So am I," I admitted.

"You'll sell it to us when it's finished, won't you? I know we didn't commission it, but..."

"I can't," I said. "It's promised to Elise."

"In that case, we'll commission another. And one of ourselves, although I don't know when we'll be able to sit for it, if you're really determined not to come to Lutèce. You wouldn't have to stay long. I'll talk to Myrica Mavor about it. She came over on the boat with me, by the way, but I asked her to let me see you first. She couldn't say no—if it weren't for me she'd have been here during the flood. The Marquise de Mesmay had sent her a telegraph message telling her that you were here and urging her to come at once. She would have, if I hadn't advised her against it. When she's in the capital, she always takes my advice."

"I imagine that almost everyone does—or will from now on. Your father would be proud."

"Would he? I'm not so sure. His murderers are still walking around, because we made a bargain with the Hierophant of the Cult of Dionysus. I suspect that he'd consider that a double abomination."

"I doubt it. Your father understood politics, and the dictates of diplomacy. I don't think he'd have any reason to be disappointed, if he could see you now. From what I hear, you and Lorenzo are doing an excellent job, and the absence of bloodstains on your daggers is a testament to that. With Madame's help, you might hold the Empire together for a long time yet, and your father would approve of that wholeheartedly."

"No one can run an Empire any more, Master Rathenius. With change accelerating under the pressure of technology, it isn't controllable. The locomotive has no brake. But as father always used to tell us, when he was ranting at us, a wise and judicious man, by means of a small action at the right time and in the right place, can set chains of causation in action that extend over continents, oceans and decades. The actions he meant often involved sticking a dagger in someone's back, but the principle holds even far more moderate actions. Eirene taught us that."

"She was a wise woman," I said, "who illustrated her own point very well. She went mad, alas, but that's a hazard for anyone with imagination, and it's a risk worth running."

"Not for you, it seems," said Tommaso. "But you've had time to develop and secure your sanity. If you want to change your mind about coming to Lutèce, you know, I can fix you up with a comfortable position—a chair at the university, for instance."

I laughed at the absurdity. "No," I said, "I'm here for good, no matter how long that turns out to be. Mnemosyne wouldn't be Mnemosyne without me, and I'd be nothing at all. I might be able to take a vacation one day, on the Island of Dionysus, if I can ever travel by steamer without being seasick, but even that might be difficult. There are people here who detest me, but they still need me, and their wives and daughters aren't in as much danger as they once were."

"You've no intention of casting Mariette aside just yet, then?"

"None at all. Elise would never forgive me, and I can't disappoint her."

"Not until the next grand passion comes along, at least."

I shrugged. "I'll have to cross that bridge when I come to it," I said.

"Unless, of course, you stick to your new style to painting," he said, nodding his head toward the not-quite-completed depiction of Ananke in the Pool of Mnemosyne, with every confusing petal in place, but not yet perfectly ornamented.

"I haven't given up portraiture, as you can see," I told him, nodding my head at the picture of Elise. "The Marquise de Mesmay seems to have forgotten the commission she offered me, and I have a strong suspicion that she might not be simply hesitating. In the meantime, though, I might offer to paint Sister Ursule."

It was Tommaso's turn to laugh, although there was nothing in the least absurd about my intention. "Not your lovely telegraph operator?" he said. "I got the impression on the ship that she'd really like you to paint her. You should, and soon—after all, she's not getting any younger."

"Elise would never forgive me," I repeated, "and I can't disappoint her."

"That's only a useful mantra as long as she doesn't disappoint you," Tommaso pointed out, perhaps with a wisdom beyond his years, or perhaps simply being glib.

Elise finally arrived then, cutting that topic of conversation abruptly short. I excused her from the afternoon sitting, so that she could take a walk with Tommaso, and I had actually picked up my palette and brushes in order to add some absolutely final touches to the painting on the wall when I was interrupted again, this time by Myrica. She looked long and hard at the picture.

"Unusual," she said, "but no matter. I can sell it. Will you be able to have it crated up and shipped, with the island in chaos?"

"It's not for sale," I told her,

"Why not?"

"It belongs in my studio."

She looked at me skeptically. "Where your sitters can see it? Bad move. Never mind. I'll take this one when it's done." She indicated the unfinished portrait of Elise."

"Already promised."

"Damn," she said. "I knew I shouldn't let Dellacrusca come in ahead of me, but he's not a man you can say no to nowadays."

"I just did," I told her. "He wanted the picture too. I told him the same thing. He also wanted to take us all back to the mainland, but I said no to that, too."

"Oddly enough," she said, "that doesn't surprise me as much as it probably surprised him. It's insane, of course, but it doesn't surprise me. I know you, you see— probably better than anyone else."

She was not only wrong about that but absurdly wrong—but it didn't surprise me.

"Tommaso wants to commission another picture of Elise, though," I said, mildly. "I'll let you handle the negotiations."

"Well, that's something," she said. "You left me in the lurch, you know, disappearing like that. You really ought come back to Lutèce with us—you're going to be direly short of sitters if you stay here, and it's not fair to Elise and Mariette to keep them her...if you can."

"I'll manage," I assured her.

"I was going to ask whether you could put me up tonight, with the Sprite still being uninhabitable, but your man Jean-Jacques says you haven't got a room to spare. Apparently, Hecate's moved in, and some chit who use to work in the Sprite. Don't you think living with three women is a bit excessive, even for you?"

"We all have to pitch in while there are so many people on the island homeless," I said.

"If that's the case, could you put me up here, or in your reception room, just for a couple of nights? It's you I came to see, after all."

"Really?" I said. "Not your good friend the Marquise de Mesmay?"

"I shouldn't even go to visit her—but Dellacrusca's warning probably doesn't apply any more, and I need to see Vashti. I suppose I can ask, although the Marquise has a houseful too. Don't you think you owe me one, for introducing you to Mariette?"

"That's not quite the way it happened, as I remember it," I said, "but if the Marquise can't find room for you, I suppose I can ask Jean-Jacques to improvise a bed for you in the reception room, if it's only for a couple of nights. I suppose the Hierophant of the Cult of Dionysus can't have too many Bacchantes."

"I heard about that. I wasn't surprised, even though I took your word for it when you assured me that you hadn't put a curse on Dellacrusca with your Orpheus painting. You really are over a hundred years old, though, aren't you? I always knew there was something weird about the way you never looked any older. But that's all by the by. What we have to discuss, seriously, is your future plans. Do you have anything else lined up after this." She waved a hand at the unfinished portrait.

"As I was just telling Tommaso, I'm thinking of painting Sister Ursule."

"The Marquise's aunt?"

"Yes. After that, well, it's been a while since I last painted Hecate, and since she's here..."

"And the chit from the Sprite too, no doubt?"

"Probably not—but the painting I did of Mariette on the Island of Dionysus is a long way away, now, and we don't know yet whether it survived the tidal wave. In any case, I think I owe it to her to paint her again. I have plenty to keep me busy, even without commissions."

"Maybe so, but without paying customers, what are you going to do for money? Or is Hierophant of the Cult of Dionysus a salaried position?"

"I have a little saved, and the Dellacrusca twins want me to paint them again, if we can find some arrangement that facilitates sittings. I won't starve."

"To judge by what I've seen today, the entire island is likely to starve."

"It won't," I assured her. "There are always plenty of fish in the sea."

She sighed. "You're incorrigible," she said, "But I know you, Axel. I'll go to see Vashti, since you're in a recalcitrant mood, but I'll probably be back—your reception room seems quite an attractive option, after what I've seen of the island so far."

She left, and I squeezed paint on to the palette, ready to wield one of my most delicate brushes—and then Hecate came in.

"Sorry," she said. "I didn't think I'd be interrupting, as your sitter has wandered off with her uncle. I thought you'd finished that one."

"So did I," I said, "but I'm beginning to suspect that it might never be finished…which wouldn't be entirely inapt, in a way, given that the petals keep falling into the pool of Mnemosyne, and Ananke keeps on rising from its murky depths."

"It's a brilliant painting, of course," she said, "but would it offend you terribly if I said that I didn't much like it? If it's any consolation, I never liked my poem either—that's probably whether I never finished it."

"And the new one? Is that finished?"

"No," she admitted. "Anyway, what I came to tell me is that I'm moving out tomorrow. The Convent of Shalimar isn't quite ready for habitation yet, but the Sisters are moving back in to finish the job. They saved most of the musical instruments, thanks to your timely warning, but Sister Ursule has lost her entire library.

She's heartbroken. There's not much I can do about that, obviously, but I can at least help with the clean-up, and I can stop being an embarrassing presence here."

"You're not," I told her. "Your presence could never embarrass me—or Elise."

"But you can't say the same about Mariette. It's better this way, Axel, trust me. You'll always know where I am and I'll always know where you are, and we'll both be on Mnemosyne, so nothing will change between us. We'll be back to normal—normal for us, that is."

"If it's what you want," I said.

"It is," she assured me. "I'd better leave you to your petals now, and save the adieux for tomorrow."

She left, and I tried to apply the dabs of paint that I'd been planning before she came in—but for some reason that I couldn't quite fathom, my heart didn't seem to be in it. I stared at the painting, hard, but I suddenly felt weak in the face of it. There was far too much black in it for my liking. There always had been.

Eventually, the door opened again and Elise came in.

"I'm sorry," she said. "I haven't come for my sitting, but I had to talk to you."

I turned to face her, and I knew what she was going to say. My heart sank further.

"Tommaso wants to take me back to Lutèce," she said. "He says that that's where my future is, and that's where I belong. He says that he knows that my name is Almeras, and that my father was an artist, like you, but he says that I'm also a Dellacrusca, and that that's what I need to be, or at least to try to be. You and Mariette don't need me here...not now...especially not now. It might not be forever. If it turns out that you're right, and this is where I need to be, I can come back...but for now, I'd like to explore the alternative. I'm sorry."

"There's no need to apologize," I told her, with the utmost courtesy. "It's entirely your decision. You're no longer a child—I can see that now—and you must do what you think is best for you. I respect that."

She looked strangely disappointed, although she surely hadn't expected me to fall to my knees and beg her to stay.

"Tommaso said that if I told you that I had decided to go to Lutèce, then you would change your mind and come too. I thought..."

"I'm sorry," I said. "I truly don't want to disappoint you, but...I do belong here. I can't go to Lutèce, even for you."

She shook her head, a trifle sadly—but even in that, she looked every inch a Dellacrusca.

"We'll give you time to finish my portrait," she said, "If you still want to."

"Of course I do," I said. "It's getting late now, but if you can manage a sitting in the morning. I'll do my best to bring it to a point where you'll be free to go, at any time that suits you, and I'll finish it in your absence. Myrica will be able to get it to you in Lutèce."

"Thank you, Axel," she said, and she simply left, knowing that there would be time for adieux later.

I was still staring at Ananke in the Pool of Mnemosyne when Helen knocked.

"I've had a telegraph message from Madame," she said. "It was sent the day before yesterday, but the system is only just up and running again. She wants me to go to Lutèce. She needs me there. She doesn't think that there's anything left for me to do here."

"She's probably right," I said, in a tone whose careful neutrality surprised me.

"I would have liked to stay," she said, "but I can't disappoint her...and I'm an embarrassment to you and Mariette here...and I don't suppose there's any chance now of your wanting to paint me..."

I almost laughed. I almost suggested that she stick around, in order to reappraise that judgment, but I didn't. I couldn't, even though I already knew, now, what Ananke had in mind...if Ananke could be said to have a mind, rather than just a blind, whimsical, deeply ironic impetus.

Helen left, without saying adieu, for the moment.

Mariette, of course, was the most difficult of all. It must have been very difficult for her, too.

"I'm not just going along with Elise," she told me, "and I'm certainly not going back to Charles. I'm not going because Tommaso Dellacrusca is bribing me, either. I'm going because it's what I feel I have to do. What you and I have can't last—we both knew that from the very beginning. I don't want to reach the stage where I'm just clinging on, desperately. I been there before, and it's not good for anyone. You know that I've loved you, so I don't have to tell you that, and I know that you've loved me, in your own fashion, but I need to find a life of my own...a life befitting a common mortal, which can't involve gradually getting older while you stay the same. I don't know whether I can find that in Lutèce, but...well, if I can't find it there, with the help of the Dellacrusca twins, where can I find it?"

"I understand," I said, and wished with all my heart that I didn't mean it.

She looked slightly disappointed too, even though she hadn't expected me to fall to me knees and beg her to stay, any more that I had expected her to fall to her knees and beg me to come with her.

Nobody I realized, was going to do that.

She didn't have to say adieu there and then either. None of them did. Tommaso's boat wouldn't be leaving for at least another twenty-four hours. They were all just giving me advance notice, because they thought it was only fair and polite to do so.

And yet, in the only sense that mattered, they had all said adieu already, without shedding a single tear.

When Mariette had gone, I turned back to the wall again, and continued staring at the picture.

"And then there were none," I said, aloud. "But life goes on…and on...and on...and there are always plenty of fish in the sea."

I didn't shed a single tear either, but not because I was beginning to cultivate the kind of Macrobian indifference to mere human sentiment that Madame seemed to have developed over the centuries. I was hurting, more than I would have expected, had I not been taken completely by surprise, but I knew that it wasn't an occasion or tears. I knew that tears were futile…but more than that, I *understood*.

I really did. I had only been a mere instrument of the magic that had saved Mnemosyne, but that didn't mean that I didn't have to pay the cost.

I looked at Ananke in the Pool of Mnemosyne, with my artist's eye, and I saw it looking back at me. It was as if I were looking into a magical mirror, symbolic not merely of life in general, but of my own soul.

There was far too much black in it for my liking, but what could I do about it?

As an honest artist, I had to paint what I saw.